WHERE DID EVERYBODY GO?

WHERE DID EVERYBODY GO? SERIES • BOOK 1

Thomas L. Madden

PROLOGUE

This story is about actual future events. Actual and future? How can that be? Ray Ferrari, our main character, is set to embark on a fictional journey placed within a backdrop of real future events. He is about to enter a world where extraordinary experiences will transform his life in unimaginable ways.

Where Did Everybody Go? is the first in a series. Ray's company, Mimtrin Technologies, has developed three significant programs: Mimstruct Pro, used for large construction management software projects; MimHealth, designed for leading healthcare facilities; and MimBank, a facilitator of international banking transactions.

The Bible-based prophetic events that Ray will experience are bound to happen at some point. For those who might want to close this book after reading the words "Bible" or "prophetic," please stick around a bit longer. The good news is that you don't need prior knowledge of the Bible to follow Ray's adventure. Even if you don't subscribe to Biblical principles, you can still follow the unexpected developments, corporate espionage, and product sabotage in Ray's story. Ray would likely have found himself in the "close this book" category.

There are references to various books that make up the Bible, but Ray's experiences are mainly based on the Book of Revelation. Appropriately, the last book of the Bible describes the end of the world as we know it. That may not sound like a happy ending, but it truly is. At the end of Revelation, there is a teaser about the beginning of a new, beautiful world.

Unfortunately, not every soul will have a place in this next ideal universe. When God created man and woman, He gave us a remarkably functioning body and a moral will - the ability to make decisions of right or wrong. Ray upholds strong ethical standards that are rooted in logic and factual evidence. According to Ray, all religions are based on faith in some intangible being or multiple beings.

Hopefully, you will read this before the Pre-Tribulation Rapture. For those new to all of this, the Rapture is a time when all believers in Jesus are taken from this Earth to be with the Lord "in the twinkling of an eye". Essentially, in the time it takes to blink, every believer in Jesus disappears from the Earth at the same time. According to Mark 13:32, *only God knows that day and hour* when this will take place.

The Tribulation Period is seven years of judgments on the evil in this world. Many intelligent individuals hold differing views on whether the rapture occurs before, during, or after the tribulation period. Some think the events described in the Book of Revelation may never happen. Despite these opposing opinions, everyone can find common ground in the lessons Ray learns along the way. Ray's story assumes that the Rapture occurs before the tribulation judgments begin.

As a man of science, Ray finds himself asking about some irrational phenomenon that caused millions to disappear: **Where did everybody go?** He is a mid-level manager at a tech company and describes himself as a realist. He can write code in his sleep and is a perpetual student of all technology-related things. As an avid reader and a skilled problem solver, Ray prefers definable ideas. Religion does not fit in that category. He has not studied the Bible, knows little about it, and sees no compelling reason to learn.

Unfortunately for Ray, he will be forced out of his comfort zone and must learn about the Bible. Mimtrin Technology has developed highly sophisticated construction management software and is bidding to become the software of choice for the Temple III project, which involves rebuilding the third Jewish Temple in Jerusalem. Many people in the company disappeared. As a result, Ray finds himself thrust into this project as a leader.

Ray must understand the Bible from Jewish and Christian perspectives to establish credibility and communicate effectively with the potential new client. His challenges include learning how the Bible is structured, interpreting symbols of strange creatures, making sense of confusing passages, and recognizing the underlying simplicity of this complex text.

In addition to these intellectual challenges, Ray needs to outsmart spies inside the company and unscrupulous people on the outside. Despite being an atheist, Ray possesses a strong sense of right and wrong and a clear understanding of good and evil. Ultimately, he will strive to outsmart the forces of evil that threaten the project.

Where Did Everybody Go? On the day of the Rapture, Ray begins his search for answers. Ray confronts choices he never thought he would face. If he chooses to accept that the Bible is the word of God and that Jesus is the Messiah who came to take on the sins of the world, he must make a critical decision.

John 3:16 states, *"For God so loved the world that He gave His one and only Son, that whoever believes in Him shall not perish but have eternal life."*

Conversely, John 3:18 warns, *"Whoever believes in Him (Jesus) is not condemned, but whoever does not believe stands condemned because* he has not believed in the name of God's one and only Son."

If you are wondering where people around you suddenly went, this series of books is written for you. Ray may have missed the first train to Heaven, but he, like everyone else, will have a chance to catch the next train. The only thing left to do is to get on board with the prepaid ticket.

CHAPTER ONE

It was a day like any other. It just didn't feel like it. This uneasy feeling caused Ray to think back to his interview with Mimtrin Technologies five years ago on this very date. Question: Do you consider yourself an optimist or a pessimist? Without hesitation, Ray said, "Realist," and saw no need to elaborate. Today, "pessimist" might have been the answer. Even the perfect April 15th Spring weather in Southern California on a Friday afternoon could not swat away that pesky feeling.

Ray is not obsessive, but he is a creature of habit. He orchestrated his morning sequence with precision. There was one glitch in Ray's morning routine today. A new neighbor was moving in across the hall from Ray's eighth-floor apartment. The man was directing the movers from the hallway close to the large utility elevator at the end of the hall. At first glance, he thought it was a business associate, Enrique Martin. The similarities were beyond remarkable. He even called to the man, "Enrique, I didn't know you were moving into this building."

When the man turned, Ray realized he had spoken too soon. The neighbor introduced himself. "Elias Martinez. Nice to meet you." Ray apologized and explained that the resemblance to a colleague was uncanny. The two had a great conversation. Ray informed the new neighbor of the ins and outs of the building. Elias gave the condensed version of being transferred from Mexico City to Los Angeles as VP of Marketing for a publisher of Christian materials.

Elias sheepishly said, "Can I ask you a favor? I know we just met and I don't want to impose." Ray was more than happy to help. "After the movers leave, I need to go to the office and it may be too late before I can return. Some boxes are coming later today. They won't be heavy but they will be bulky. I would ask you to put them in your place, but that would be a big inconvenience. If I give you the extra key, could you just move them into the apartment?"

Ray thought it was strange that Elias would trust him with the key, but then again, they did connect. It was as if they had known one another for a long time. Ray agreed, took the key, and left for work. He now had to mentally reset his customary sequence. This morning's disruption in his routine was nothing major, but the events reinforced his uneasy feeling.

Ray Ferrari is a successful mid-level manager at Mimtrin Technologies' headquarters, a leading tech firm in the Los Angeles area. Even though each day poses unique challenges, Ray's job is straightforward and at times tedious. The last line in his most recent performance review said, "Ray is the most under-employed person in the company. Even though it is not in his job description, he has pointed out flaws in our security. He has advised the cybersecurity personnel on the fixes."

His seventh-floor office had a nice view of the marina and Pacific Ocean when you look past the parking lot full of delivery trucks and vans. The office is pristine. Ten different tech magazines, delivered each month, are organized alphabetically and by month in special holders on his credenza. He keeps only magazines from the past six months because, according to Ray, information older than that is worthless.

Ray enjoys his lunchtime routine. He has a favorite deli and knows most of the people who work there. Every day, Ray orders a club sandwich with extra bacon. There are very few exceptions to that rule. He enjoys spending solitary time away from the office on his favorite bench in the park. As a creature of habit, Ray strolls calmly down the same path to his refuge. The two guards outside the exclusive Kensington Department Store he passed would always smile when they saw Ray coming. "I feel safe just seeing you two on duty," was Ray's daily mantra.

Three short years ago, the casual stroll was uneventful, at least for the most part. Now he needs to walk around ever-growing encampments to avoid unconscious people lying next to used needles or empty bottles of cheap alcohol. Today, he is taking a slight detour because three teens are on his usual path. Ray thought they were looking for trouble. A street preacher had his usual spot. Many people were listening to his rousing sermon. Ray thought, "Good crowd for the Bible Thumper today."

The park bench for lunch is in the perfect spot. He can see the cityscape on his right and the unending Pacific Ocean on his left. Ray maneuvered to the center of the bench. With his drink perched beside him and the sandwich bag spread to make a tablecloth, Ray began enjoying his club sandwich, which he imagined was a gourmet meal.

Once he finished lunch, Ray liked to read the old-fashioned way – with a book. As he opened the book at the marked page, he heard a scream for help. He looked up to see the three teens mugging an older man while the wife begged for help. Most people just walked quickly away, while others recorded the event. He mumbled to himself, "Glad I didn't go that way."

He opened the book again. Just as he started the first sentence, he heard cars honking and the sounds of crumpling metal as crash after crash gridlocked the street. Then the sound of shattering glass. He looked down the street to see that a bus had powered through Kensington's display window.

Ray did a quick scan. He spotted the three teens looking confused. There was no elderly couple. On the other side, the street preacher was gone. The crowd had dwindled to five people, all looking around, trying to figure out the same thing Ray was thinking: **Where did everybody go?**

Then Ray heard a woman crying for help. That is not the sound of a mugging, he thought. Someone was seriously injured. Typically, Ray's avoidance behavior kept him at a distance, but this was somehow different. He felt an unusual sense of urgency.

There were too many crashes to count. Ray ran to the street and spotted the driver, who was calling out for help. The woman was trapped after a delivery van sideswiped her car, pushing it into the back of a truck. The van continued past the car and appeared to adhere to the side of the truck. Ray was laser-focused as he headed to help. He passed by other accidents while attempting to reach the cries.

Ray passed the van that caused the accident. With a glance inside, he saw that the airbags had deployed, but no one was in the vehicle. Ray struggled to get to the woman. Her calls seemed more desperate. Other accidents were only part of the problem restricting Ray's quest. He was being pushed and shoved by the crowd headed for the bus that had crashed into the department store. They were not going to help the people injured on the bus; they were going in to loot the store. Where are the two security guards that he always greeted?

A myriad of runaway vehicles left pedestrians dead and injured. Ray spotted the teens from the park rummaging through the pockets and purses of the lifeless victims. He held himself but wanted to scream, "Has the world gone completely mad?"

Ray didn't understand why he felt compelled to reach the woman trapped in the car. As he finally approached, he saw her injuries. The look on her face projected severe pain. His instinct was to try to stop the bleeding from her head injury. Ray pushed the deflated airbag away as best he could.

"Please, help Jenny," the woman pleaded. She opened her eyes but quickly shut them, hoping the darkness would ease some pain.

"Who is Jenny? Where is she?" Ray was looking frantically around.

"She's right next to me!" The woman struggled to get the words out, but Ray could hear the panic in her voice.

"There is no one there!" Ray ran to the other side, thinking Jenny might have gotten out. Ray was always one who could control his emotions, but this time his voice stuttered, "Th- the-there is no one here."

The woman struggled but looked over to see an empty seat with the seatbelt still fastened. Ray just stared at the woman. The woman's hands trembled. She groaned as she turned to see Jenny's Bible in the empty passenger seat. "My daughter tried to tell me this day would come, but I didn't listen." The long sigh that followed pierced Ray's heart. That abnormal feeling baffled him even more. The woman saw Ray's confusion.

"The day that Jesus lifts all that believe in Him to Heaven. Today is that day. Now I believe…" She grimaced as she inhaled slowly. "No! Now I know she was right. I know my Jenny is with Jesus. I hope she will forgive me for doubting her. I pray it is not too late for Jesus to forgive me."

Her eyes met Ray's. "Please, take Jenny's Bible." To appease the woman, Ray leaned in and slowly lifted the Bible from the seat. He raised the book to acknowledge that he had done as requested. Ray was then awestruck as he watched the agony leave her face. She suddenly showed no signs of pain. She seemed at peace. She smiled warmly at Ray, closed her eyes, and then stopped breathing.

Ray thought aloud, "What is going on?" He stared at the Bible in his hand. There was a bookmark. Being an avid reader, he was curious. Even after all that just happened, even with all the confusion around, he opened the Bible to that bookmark. At the top of the page, he saw the name *"Thessalonians,"* which was meaningless to him since he knew little to nothing about the Bible. His eyes moved to the highlighted words:

For the Lord himself will come down from Heaven, with a loud command, with the voice of the archangel and with the trumpet call of God, and the dead in Christ will rise first. After that, we who are still alive and are left will be caught up together with them in the clouds to meet the Lord in the air. And so, we will be with the Lord forever.

Ray had read the verse as he would have read one of his novels. He was about to close the book when he thought out loud, "What? What did that say?" He reread it. He said to the Bible as if it were a person, "No. Can't be." Ray closed the Bible with the bookmark still in place.

The last twenty minutes of Ray's life had been a mental and emotional earthquake. Instead of books falling from shelves, dishes coming out of cabinets, and pictures flying off the walls, Ray's beliefs and paradigms had all come crashing down. People who have been through a significant quake know that they cannot put everything back the way it was. Ray's world just got rearranged. Little did he know that it would never be the same.

Talking things out was one of Ray's problem-solving techniques. Mostly, other people did not hear or, if they did, just ignored those self-talks. "I must get back to the office. Cars are on fire over there. Use the shore route." He saw an opening in the crowd and headed that way. His plan started going wrong right away. People were running in all directions, colliding with one another and tripping over those who had fallen. Ray could not tell if they were running toward someplace or trying to escape.

A man across the street was on one knee while holding his chest. His wife was crying frantically for help. No one stopped. A mother was standing over a baby carriage that must have been the Rolls-Royce of baby carriages. With all the commotion, she checked on her child. With a look of terror in her face, she screamed, "Where is my baby?! I just put him in the stroller. Where is he? Somebody, please help!"

Ray did not feel the same sense of urgency he had for the woman in the car. "Stay focused." He kept true to his quest to reach the office. The noise from planes landing at LAX was a normal, irritating fact of life since the airport was only a few miles away. The sound Ray heard was far from normal. As he blocked the sun with his hand, Ray spotted the culprit. "That jet is way too low," he called out as though someone would hear and do something about it.

After the plane disappeared from view, Ray refocused on his goal. That focus was short-lived when an explosion in the direction of the airport seemed to shake the ground he was on. A volcanic plume of smoke and fire catapulted upwards. Within minutes, there was another.

Ray picked up the pace. His destination and, hopefully, his safety were only minutes away. As Ray was turning the corner on Pacific Street, the sound of metal scraping caught his attention. A cargo ship was grinding against the pillar of the Pelican Island draw bridge. Then the bridge started moaning as though it was in pain. The vessel could not get out of the way as the bridge unfolded in slow motion, taking the vessel's aft with it. Cars and trucks tumbled into the water.

Ray shouted again as though someone would hear, "Where is the tugboat?" Then he caught a glimpse of the usually reliable navigating vessel. It was just drifting. There was no one on board.

Ray finally reached his destination. The courtyard at the side of the building was typically full at this time of the day. People would get their meals from gourmet food trucks and gather in small groups to catch up on the latest gossip. Today was eerily different. The crowd had thinned. The courtyard was almost empty. The people remaining were virtually paralyzed, not knowing what to do.

Freddie's Famous Franks was always a popular mobile venue. Beef, pork, veggie, and soy dogs were truly famous, at least in a three-block radius. Smoke was billowing from the side of the truck. The smell of burning grease and food permeated the air. Then a flash. Flames engulfed the food truck. "Where is Freddie?"

"Get in the office," Ray mumbled. Ray was going against the flow of people flooding out. The building's lobby was comparatively empty. Marianne, the receptionist behind the expansive, speckled granite counter, was on the phone in panic mode. Where is her trusted sidekick, Carmen? Where is Derik? The massive security guard never leaves his post behind the wall of monitoring equipment.

The elevator's numbers were moving in slow motion. Ray took the option. After winding his way up seven floors of grey, steel steps, Ray's heavy breathing slowed as he walked through the stairwell door into a large room of cubicles surrounded by offices on the outside walls. Several workspaces were empty. Phones were ringing, but no one was answering.

Debbie was the department commander according to the organization flow chart. Her office faces north. Ray always thought that was the best office. No morning or afternoon sun to force in lumens beyond pleasant. Ray approached her office, hoping Debbie might know what was happening. Debbie was one of the few people Ray liked. She always took the time to listen to his ideas on improving systems.

Ray started tapping on the door to signal to Debbie that he was coming in, but Debbie was not there. Ray noticed something highly unusual. Debbie's computer was on, and her mobile phone was ringing to the music of 'God Bless America.' The reflection from the window showed open files on her screen. Debbie was a pro and would never abandon an open screen like that.

Stressed and confused, Ray made it to his office. He reclined in his office chair trying to make sense of the madness. Then he realized that Jenny's Bible was still clutched in his hand. As he tossed the book on his desk, a piece of paper inched out of the pages. Curiosity again got the best of him. The paper acted as a bookmark with several notes. "Daniel 12:1-3." More Bible stuff that again meant nothing to him. Ray fixated on the bullet points.

- Written around 600 B.C.
- Clear Vision God gave Daniel.
- Time of distress – tribulation, severe judgments – used to open eyes and hearts.
- Written in the Book of Life are those to be saved – believers in God and Jesus.
- Everlasting life – eternity in Heaven.
- Disgrace, contempt – for non-believers, haters, evil – eternity in the lake of fire.

Then Ray read the highlighted words in Daniel: *Now at that time Michael, the great prince who stands guard over the sons of your people, will arise. And there will be a time of distress such as never occurred since there was a nation until that time; and at that time your people, everyone who is found written in the book, will be rescued.*

Many of those who sleep in the dust of the ground will awaken, these to everlasting life, but the others to disgrace and everlasting contempt. Those who have insight will shine brightly like the brightness of the expanse of Heaven, and those who lead many to righteousness, like the stars forever and ever.

Dumbfounded, Ray questioned his atheist beliefs, but only for a brief moment. Religion had never been part of his lifestyle. Ray had nothing against those who believe in religion. He could not grasp why so many people were attracted to this abstract system. He reread the bookmarked passage, which did nothing to clear some of the mind fog. Arguing with himself as he regularly did, he muttered, "This is just a coincidence, right? God just snatched people? No. How is that possible? But Jenny was nowhere to be found! All the others disappeared."

Still confused, he tried to reason why pilots, drivers, and tugboat operators disappeared. No one had control, and that led to all the disasters. "I don't know how or why," Ray said as though there was someone in the room who would be interested. "I understand what I read, but logic tells me this is impossible. Hopefully, someone will figure out where everyone went."

Ray was abruptly jolted out of his deep thoughts when Duggie and Karen, two members of the analyst team, burst into his office as if being chased by rabid rottweilers. The verbal machine gun started firing before Ray could look up.

In panic mode, Karen asked, "Ray, what are we going to do? Leticia is at a conference in Denver. Debbie just disappeared. Ray, she just disappeared! I was headed for her office. I could see she was in her office. I glanced down at my notes. I looked back up and she was gone!" Duggie had to sit down. His mouth opened as if there was more to say, but no words came out.

Duggie finally spoke. "I was on a video conference call with marketing in New York, Chicago, and Omaha. I was updating Marcie in Omaha on her client's project. While she adjusted her camera, I opened a file folder. I am talking like for two seconds. I looked back at the screen. She was gone. Her headset was on the desk."

Ray gazed at Duggie. "Ray, I am not crazy. New York

and Chicago participants had the same experience. I called Omaha. Marcie is not there. Lila's workstation is on but Lila's not there. Where did everybody go?"

Ray pictured the org chart in his head. Debbie was a VP reporting directly to Chas Jenkins, CIO. Leticia Jefferson had a director title reporting to Debbie. Numbers one and two were out. Ray reported to Chen Huang. He should be the go-to guy at this point.

"I know you're not crazy. It happened to me." Ray's default setting was logic over emotion. He spoke softly to calm the storm. "Karen, I believe your story as well. We don't know what happened, but I am sure we will get some explanation. In the meantime, we still need to focus on several projects." Ray's expression changed. "Where is Chen?" Duggie told Ray he had seen Chen heading out, but was unsure where he went. "So, at least we know he didn't disappear."

Completely out of character, directives started coming from Ray. "You two gather everyone still here for a meeting at the Big Board for a strategy session." The high-tech whiteboard takes handwritten notes, converts them to typed text, and emails them to stakeholders. Flow charts and diagrams are cleaned up, saved as PDFs, and sent as attachments.

Ray was already writing as people were gathering. He had never taken charge like this, but it looked as though he needed to step up. Ray looked around the office and could find no stragglers. So, he began. "Nobody can explain at this point what just happened. Speculation and rumors will do us no good. Answers will come." After an extended pause, he added, "Eventually." Because no one on the floor had ever seen Ray in a leadership position, they were all astonished as he took charge.

His awareness of the anxiety level in the room caught people off guard as well. Not known for his tact, Ray's empathy came as a surprise. "When we break, our priority is to make some calls. First, call your family. If they do not answer, leave a message that you are fine and move on. If you do connect, everyone will have a story. We do not have time to chat.

"Second, we need to call people who are not here. I want you to give Duggie the names of the people that you know are out today. If you have their mobile number, go ahead and call and then update Duggie. If they answer, tell them to get here ASAP. If their mobile phone rings at their desk, assume they are not returning to work and let Duggie know. If you know they are on vacation or out for a reason, let Duggie know."

Ray continued to give directives. He handled questions and concerns quickly and with ease. Ray wrapped up the meeting with, "We know there is some, well okay, a lot of confusion with what just happened. But we don't know the facts and we don't know what we don't know about what is going on. Assumptions and speculations will just make things worse. What we do know are the tasks at hand for immediate action. Let's stay focused and work on our plan." Everyone headed for their stations. Even though the unease remained high, Ray's unexpected leadership lowered the tension.

Chas Jenkins, CIO, had been monitoring the meeting in the background. He made a beeline for the whiteboard. "It's Ray, right?" Ray nodded. Chas surveyed the action items listed. "I caught most of your meeting. I have already been to the other departments and did not see or hear anything like this." Chas looked around. "Where is Debbie?"

Ray answered: vanished. "Where is Leticia?"

"She is at some conference. I don't know where." Chas was astonished by Ray's apparent lack of concern. Ray caught the attention of Leticia's Administrative Assistant and waved her over. "Maria, could you update Mr. Jenkins on what is happening with Leticia? And make a note to give Nancy, his secretary, updates as things change." Ray excused himself and rushed toward Debbie's office.

Chas told Maria, "We don't know where Nancy is. Just send me an internal email." Maria began to think that Ray and Mr. Jenkins were aliens with no emotions. They were way too calm, she thought.

"The problem is, Mr. Jenkins, that all flights have been grounded due to the terrible plane crashes. Leticia sent a short email saying she was trying to rent a car in Denver to drive back. Of course, everybody stranded is trying to rent a car." Maria hesitated with a sigh of contrition. "The truth is that I have no idea where she is right now."

"Denver? I don't know about any conference in Denver." He saw that Maria was at a complete loss. "Alright. Just update me when you hear from her." Chas looked around the office. "Where's Ray?" Two people pointed towards Debbie's office. "This Ray is an interesting character," he whispered. The two gave a wry smile, looked at each other, and nodded in agreement.

CHAPTER TWO

Chas worked his way through the maze of cubicles to see Ray securing Debbie's office. "I thought Chen Huang was next in line to manage things." Ray was concentrating on the screen. He did not look up, but he held his index finger in the air. The hand didn't stay there long since he needed all fingers to set a new speed-typing record. When Ray looked up, he realized that Chas was not used to being told to hold his thoughts, especially with a one-finger wait-a-minute gesture.

"Sorry. I just had to… It doesn't matter. Chen, yeah, he had something urgent. He normally asks me to get things organized when he is out."

Chas knew Ray was hiding something, but at this point did not care. He saw the leadership and appreciated Ray's loyalty. "Can you email me the whiteboard info?" Ray nodded. "Good. We have a meeting in the large conference room in fifteen minutes. Don't be late." Before the word 'but' came out of Ray's mouth, he heard, for the second time, "Don't be late."

Ray could hear the whispers as he walked into the vast conference room. "What is Ray doing here?" Some asked, "Who is that?" Others had a hard time keeping their mouths from gaping open. Ray found an open chair and plopped his computer notebook on the massive conference table. Ray hated 'waste-of-time meetings.' Almost everybody knew about his attitude, so he was usually not invited.

Before Ray could sit down, Chas held one finger in the air. Ah, revenge, Ray thought. "Ray, could you join me up front?" Ray froze just long enough to gather his senses. He had to hold his tongue to keep from saying the derogatory word that popped into his head. Chas waved him to the front. As he approached, he saw Moshe Abrams, CEO, Paul Smiley, President, and three other "suits" as he like to call executives. He guessed they were on the Board of Directors but had no idea.

After the obligatory comments by the CEO, Chas took control of the meeting. He began with, "I made the rounds to each department. The analysts' team was my last inspection. In each department, I saw confusion and, in some cases, complete chaos. When I heard Ray's final pitch to the team on my last visit, I saw calm and focus. The far-left screen shows the outline he used in a meeting with analysts and programmers. The far-right screen shows the outline he used for a team leader meeting. The middle screen is open for Ray to add anything."

Chas handed Ray what looked like a TV remote control. "Start with the outline on the right screen. I was not there for that."

Ray took a deep breath and smiled at Chas. "Okay," Ray said with some trepidation. "Just remember, you asked." Ray started down the outline.

Everyone, especially those who knew Ray, was stunned by his command of the issues, his logical solutions, and his overall performance. They had no idea Ray could masterfully take charge. Ray always played along to get along. One manager who observed Ray's demeanor whispered, "This guy must have ice water running through his veins. He acts like nothing has happened."

Ray ran through the outline while occasionally pausing for questions and suggestions. Then the surprise. "Some people are not going to like these next two recommendations. Job titles are meaningless." There were several chuckles from the audience. "Matching the goals to our talent is vital right now. For example, I currently have Enrique Martin from our maintenance company working on codes for our non-classified upgrade projects." Ray saw Chas spring out of his chair. "Not to worry. Enrique was a programmer in the Mexican military for 6 years. He knows what he is doing but I still check his work." Chas just shook his head.

"I am also setting up a coding crash course for three clerical people. Okay, I know I shouldn't use coding and crash in the same sentence." Someone from the back of the room said, "I thought everyone disappearing was a miracle, but Ray telling a joke beats that." The people in the room who knew Ray burst out laughing.

Ray ignored that reaction and continued, with full knowledge, that the Marketing and Product Development team would not be fans of his next idea. He wrote on the board, **Pause the two new projects**. "We are susceptible to mistakes right now. We do not need or want a replay of the Dolphin Project. I knew that project was doomed to miss at the end of phase 2."

Chas was still standing. "You knew? What did you know?" Ray did not hesitate to inform Chas and the rest of the room about the mistakes made in Phases 1 and 2. He ended with "The flow was going to, actually had to, hit a wall, which it did. If we had paused for about three weeks to make some fixes, we would have made the deadline. As it was, we were six weeks late." A hush of expectation settled over the room.

A department manager abruptly broke the silence . "Ray is right. I saw the same thing and was told it was under control. I let it go because I was not put on the phase 3 team. I don't know what happened, but I was not surprised when the beta failed."

Although he could have asked the manager, Chas directed his question to Ray. "If you knew this, why didn't you say something?"

"I did, in detail, on three occasions. I emailed Leticia and copied three others."

"Who did you copy?"

Ray hesitated.

"Who?" Chas insisted.

"Debbie, Paul Smiley, along with his office of the President general box, and you. The first was the official date phase two ended. The second was two weeks later. That was the official start date of phase 3. The third email was the date that confirmed the project team had been split up, shuffled to other projects. I was taken off the project as well."

Chas was a bit indignant when he asserted, "I never got any emails from you." Chas saw Paul's secretary move to where Paul was sitting. She turned her back to the people in the room. Paul waved Chas over to join them. He discovered that his email, along with those to Debbie and Paul, had been deleted. Paul showed Chas the President's general box with the email. Whoever erased the others missed that box. Even though he was trying to control his anger, everyone in the room could see it when he turned around.

Chas returned to his chair and sat down. As calmly as he could, he said, "Keep going." Ray turned his back to the audience and looked at Chas. Ray's eyes closed as he mouthed the words, "They were deleted." When he opened his eyes, there was a very slight confirmation nod in response.

Ray did not miss a beat as he wrote **Customer Service** on the board. "When speaking with customers, reassure them that we're committed to providing the highest levels of service and security. At least that is what the brochure says." Most people laughed again. Some of the ice in the room melted. When Ray realized what was funny, he said, "Maybe I shouldn't have said that out loud." The room warmed just a little bit more. Ray laid out several more ideas. Hiring contractors who had lost too many people to stay in business was at the top of his list. He finished his presentation. The questions ended.

Paul was moving to center stage for the next agenda item. Chas stood as Ray handed back the controller. Ray's voice was barely audible when he said, "I don't know what is going on in the room next door. The door was open enough so that I could see the work on the whiteboard. I walked in and looked at the code on the board. In the little time I had, I found two distinct problems. I secured the room when I left." Chas was completely surprised and genuinely worried. This piece of the confidential algorithm should have been secured. His mind raced with questions. One he could not set aside: How did Ray manage to spot two errors with only a quick look?

Ray looked around, making sure no one was within earshot. "The strange thing is that what I saw was similar to the Dolphin project. But it gets worse. There were very slight smudge marks on the board where the problems occurred.

I think somebody might be trying to sabotage your project. You should have someone compare the previously saved backup to the current board. There may be other changes I did not see."

Chas put on a poker face, but the tension in his body told a different story. "I assume you are coming in tomorrow." As soon as the words came out, Chas knew he was stating the obvious. "You will get a call letting you know when and where to meet me. By the way, good job today." Ray held on to that last statement for a few moments. 'At-ta-boys' did not come his way often. Ray took his seat and prepared to absorb the anticipated flood of information.

Now in control, Paul took the meeting to the next level. He emphasized that each department should develop a structure similar to the one Ray presented. Paul ended with an encouraging note, but everyone saw the stress on his face and heard concern in his voice. "We have no idea what just happened. We need to work through this together."

Ray headed back to his office. He thought this day could not get any stranger. As he approached his destination, an impeccably dressed, distinguished-looking man was waiting in the hallway just outside the department entrance. Ray figured he would have to spend a month's salary to buy a suit like the man was wearing. The man's hair was pure white. Even his eyebrows were a distinctive white. When he got closer, Ray was mesmerized by the man's bright blue eyes.

"Are you the man they call 'Crazy Ray'?"

Ray smiled. "That is the latest trending name for me. Yes. Why do you ask?"

"I apologize for what might have been an insulting question, but I needed to make sure I had the correct Ray. I understand there is more than one Ray working here."

"I don't insult easily. I decided long ago not to take things personally. The other employee goes by Raymond."

The man returned the smile. "Got it. Is it true you subscribe to ten tech magazines?" Ray typically would have interjected a myriad of questions before continuing the conversation, but he decided to let the game play out. In anticipation of the next question, Ray nodded once. "Why ten?" The man asked.

"Because I want to stay up with all the latest technology and techniques. I cross-reference the different magazines to look for consistent ideas and discount inconsistencies. Fringe ideas go onto my research to-do list."

The man continued, "I understand you were gifted a Bible recently." Ray thought, "Okay, the day just got stranger." He gave the man a curious look and hesitantly nodded.

"I have a message for you. Study that Bible in the same way you research your tech magazines. We would like your help. Being prepared will be vital to your success. When you hear or see information that is inconsistent with your Bible research, know it is false. If information is partially true and partially false be aware that it is propaganda. Reject that information and stay committed to the directions the Bible gives you."

Ray's patience ended. "Who are you, who is 'WE', how do you know about the magazines and Bible, and why are you telling me stuff that makes no sense?"

"I am somebody trying to help you. I cannot tell you everything right now, but it will become clear. You will meet others who will have had a similar experience to the one you are having right now. You will meet people who will fill in your knowledge gaps. When you notice something resembling a coincidence, recognize that parallel and concurrent events are part of a larger plan. A coincidence is not necessarily a coincidence." He paused, then added, "As a side note, remember… fourth line on the middle section of the whiteboard."

"But why me?" The man turned and walked toward the elevator. Ray followed. The up-button light came on.

The man entered the elevator, turned around, pushed a button on the panel, smiled, and said, "That answer is above my pay grade. But today is Good Friday. Whatever the plan, it must be good." With that, the doors closed.

Ray tried to process what had just happened as he walked to his office. He glanced at the bookshelf where he had placed the Bible. It was not there. He scanned the room. Someone had moved the Bible next to his stack of newly received magazines.

Saturday Morning, a knocking sound stirred Ray out of a deep sleep. He looked around and realized he wasn't in his four-thousand-dollar bed with the special memory foam mattress, temperature control, a five-speed vibrator, and mechanics that turned the bed into a recliner so he could watch his 80-inch, high-resolution TV with surround sound. He suddenly realized he was reclining in his office chair.

Ray had been working through the night reviewing the notes and checking the computers of the people he suspected would not be returning. When he was able to focus, he saw Chas standing in the doorway. "It's obvious you have been here all night." Ray looked at his computer screen - 6:42 AM.

"Time flies when you are having fun," Ray said while still in recovery mode. "I had to know where we are with projects and workflow. There will be an organizational meeting on Monday once everyone alive and well shows up. At this point, I am half expecting to see ghosts sitting at a desk or two."

Chas shook his head. "Ghosts. That's all we need. Go home and unwind for about two seconds. When you are back, turn your findings over to Chen. Then get ready for a meeting that will start at eleven. We set this meeting up three weeks ago. Unfortunately, we may have several empty seats.

"It will be in the room with the formula you saw. We will have security at the door. When they scan your badge, your name verifies a top security clearance. You were right about the changes to the code. This level of security is probably overkill, but whoever made the change will know we are watching. You will be sitting in for Leticia. Bring your 'A' game."

Before Ray could utter a word, Chas abruptly turned and left. Ray began talking to himself as though Chas had just knocked on the door. "Good morning, Ray. How are you this morning? Oh, great. How about you? Good. Anything on your agenda today?" Ray ended the fantasy conversation and finished organizing his notes for Chen.

When he returned after rejuvenating at home, Ray stopped by Chen's office to drop off his ideas. Chen working on the weekend was rare, but these weren't just rare times; they were 'never-before' times. Chen was putting together his own plan. There was a slightly empathetic tone to Ray's voice when he asked, "How are you doing?" Ray wanted to ask: "Will you hold it together today?"

"Yeah, I'm good. Hey, thanks for covering for me. Duggie told me what you said to Mr. Jenkins. I don't know what happened. I was with two people getting a project update. There was a flash of light outside. I remember blinking. When I opened my eyes, they were gone. Just disappeared! I couldn't breathe. I had to get some fresh air." Ray thought four hours of fresh air before going home might have been a bit much, but he let that one go.

Ray felt that Chen was about to lose it again by the look on his face. He quickly transitioned to a different topic. "Were you able to call your family in China?" There was no time for chatting, so he hoped the answer would be short. Any good news at this point would be a welcome change.

"Yeah, actually I did. They are fine. Confused, but fine. There is minimal chaos in China compared to here for some reason. The good news is that my sister may have escaped the prison camp in all the confusion. No one knows where she is. I think I told you she was arrested on some bogus charge because she became a Christian and refused to bow to the People's Republic."

Ray became acutely aware of the pattern. Only Christians seemed to have vanished. Maybe Chen's sister just escaped, but that was unlikely. "Sounds like good news for you." He handed Chen a folder before he could say another word. "This is a project update. There is also my best guess at who will be here on Monday. You will need to reassign people to focus on our priorities." After a quick review, Ray headed to the conference room.

Security was as advertised. The wand scan was a bonus. Ray was also required to sign a confidentiality agreement. Lawyers earning their pay, he thought. He inspected the room as he entered. He had worked with several of the people there, had crossed paths with some, and did not recognize two. Those two must have been from another location because Ray knew just about everyone working at the LA office. He was hoping to find out why the three "suits" were there. Mr. White Hair, the name Ray assigned to the stranger in the hall, was not present today.

Ray found his seat. It was hard to miss his name on the bright green tent card. There were also yellow, blue, and white name cards. He placed a computer notebook on his little plot of land but did not sit. Focus turned to the code as he slowly moved to the three whiteboards that essentially covered entire back wall. The code was continuous but broken into parts like it was written on three pieces of paper. He read it line by line. He decided that this had something to do with a highly sophisticated project management program.

The first thing that caught his eye was the corrections he and Chas had talked about. As a result of those changes, adjustments were made downstream. Ray focused on the third section of the formula. He stopped, went back to the middle grouping, then to the third, then back to the middle.

Unknown to Ray, Chas and one of the suits were watching Ray's laser-focused exam. Again, second board, third board, second board. He knew something was not right. He was frustrated that he couldn't find it.

He walked to the back of the room, pictured the boards, and closed his eyes. All the movement of people trying to find their seats, all the testing of equipment, and all the juggling of visual aids just disappeared. Then Ray remembered Mr. White Hair saying, "Fourth line."

Ray looked up and focused on that line on the middle board. He picked up the notepad provided at every location on the way back to the front. Chas and his sidekick just looked at one another and shrugged. They would be very disappointed if this turned out to be pointless. Ray started writing on his pad like a man possessed. Before he knew it, the page was full of notes. He flipped to the next page and finally stopped halfway down. Chas came over to Ray. "You should sit down. The meeting is about to begin."

Ray asked Chas for a quick, private conversation. Ray deliberately moved away from the others mingling around. In a low voice, he informed Chas, "I have seen this. The code is not new or unique. Well, maybe five percent is new. It could be great, but right now it's not." Ray looked back at the board and pointed to the two glitches he had mentioned. "I see someone fixed those two lines, but they were incorrectly adjusted based on the downline changes." Chas was speechless as he glared at Ray.

"You were talking to that guy in the blue shirt. Who is he?" With a slightly condescending tone, Chas told Ray to have a seat. A full explanation was about to be presented. Ray understood but was not patient, "Who is he? His first name is Byron, I think."

"It's Bryan, Bryan Thorton." Ray needed more than that. Chas added, "He and his team are the lead consultants for our current, highly confidential project." The emphasis was on "highly confidential". "They have already saved us several months of development."

"You hired a competitor as a consultant?" Ray snorted a laugh. "That is a new one on me."

"What do you mean competitor? He is the owner of a highly respected consulting firm, Aliton Consultants."

Ray moved Chas further away from the audience. When they were isolated, Ray lowered his head and took a deep breath, then exhaled quickly. "The first three letters of Bryan's mother's name, Alicia, and the last three letters of Thorton equal Aliton." Ray rhetorically said, "You know CPS Metrix Technology in Colorado is one of our biggest competitors." Chas wanted to know where Ray was going with this.

"There is an LLC. I forget the name right now, but I can find it. That LLC owns 55% of CPSM. Warren Thorton, Bryan's father, owns the LLC. He formed the LLC to keep his name directly out of the ownership of CPSM. He had settled an SEC violation with a previous company he ran. He did not want, nor could he have, his name as a majority shareholder in another company."

Chas was amazed, baffled. "How do you know all of this?"

Ray quickly responded, "By reading ten different tech magazines monthly for the past seven years." Ray pointed his finger to the sky, but this time waved it back and forth like a metronome. "It is coming back to me. This happened about five years ago. Ninety percent of what I read is boring, or I already know what is in the article. There may be a gem or two. But, for some reason, I got fixated on this one."

Ray's hand went up this time. "One correction. When I read about this, I thought it was brilliant. Warren does not have any ownership in the LLC, but he is the Managing Director in his role as an employee. Five family members are the owners but have signed their proxy over to him. Brilliant.

"Simply put, Bryan's father is your biggest competitor." Ray noticed a slight panic. "Don't do anything right now. There may be a reasonable explanation. I doubt it, but there may be. Let me do some more research. Go ahead with the meeting as planned. Once I know more from this session today, I will have some ideas for the next steps."

As an afterthought, Ray added, "Don't ask him directly, but you should check to see if Bryan disclosed any of this in his original proposal. Also, check whether Aliton was involved in the Dolphin project. Looks like I will be busy again tonight." Ray looked intently at Chas, grinned and nodded. That translated to 'I've got this.' "I hope for everyone's sake I am wrong, but if this turns out to be true." Ray stopped his train of thought. "Before I say anything, let's see what I can find out."

The meeting was starting, and Chas needed to be up front. "Wait, quick question, who is the suit with the white hair and eyebrows that I met in the hall last night?" Chas shrugged, then hustled to the front of the room.

The meeting had started as Ray worked his way back to his territory at the table. He knew he had not missed anything important because Moshe Abrams, CEO, was still talking about people disappearing and the need to focus on the new normal. Ray despised all those little catchphrases. 'New normal', what is that supposed to mean? Fortunately, things got down to business quickly. The CEO wrapped up with, "Paul Smiley, your esteemed President, will now introduce the next major project."

Paul eased onto the stage. For dramatic effect, three large screens lowered to cover the whiteboard. The right and left screens revealed the words: **MIMSTRUCT PRO**. The subtitle that scrolled below the title read, "state-of-the-art construction management platform." Ray instinctively, in his glass-half-empty, cynical way, thought this was going to be doomed. Millions of people likely disappeared. Buildings are going to be empty. Houses and apartments will be vacant. Commercial construction projects already in place will not change platforms. He had to have one of his internal debates. 'Come on Ray, refocus. Stay open-minded.'

"Good morning! Today is a great day for Mimtrin Technologies despite all the chaos around us." Without turning around, Paul extended his arms like a giant bird stretching its wings. "Mimstruct Pro! Everyone here has been working on the upgrades of Mimstruct, our current construction management product designed for small builders and trade businesses. Some of you have been working on new modules to be added. Until now, each new component has been developed as a stand-alone add-on product.

"You are here today because each of your departments has been selected to help merge the new modules. We are going to supercharge Mimstruct into our new Mimstruct Pro. This will be the Tesla of construction project management."

The screen changed, but the title MIMSTRUCT PRO remained. Words swirled onto the screen one at a time: Artificial Intelligence, Security, Instant Language Translation, User Intuitive, Video Instruction, Finance, Distribution, Transportation, Engineering, Upgradable, Customizable, and 24/7 Helpline. Paul's pitch was high-level with attention-grabbing features and benefits. He accomplished his goal, and everyone seemed enthusiastic. Ray remained cynical and had no idea why he was there.

"To go deeper, Chas will take over to give the next steps and answer your questions." Chas popped out of his chair like a boxer when the bell rang for the next round.

"Thanks, Paul. That was a perfect intro for the merger plan we will be discussing." Chas introduced the three guests: Legal, Government Liaison, and Board Member. All three have been involved since the inception of this project. Ray's mind became a pinball machine, careening ideas from one corner to another. Ray wanted answers to the who, what, when, where, why and how questions.

Chas continued, "Everyone here is now part of the big picture. The core components are in place thanks to everyone's hard work and dedication. This project will start moving at lightning speed. This meeting has been scheduled for a while. In light of yesterday's..." Chas paused to collect his thoughts. "I don't even know what to call it. Phenomenon is probably the word to use. We thought it was vital to keep the scheduled meeting. As you know, some people previously on the project are missing. There are some new faces to the project. Today is our first chance to show everyone the big picture.

"Your job, as leaders, will be to analyze your department's strengths and weaknesses. Call Sophie with personnel needs. Call vendors and contractors. Debbie's crew." He stopped himself from finishing his comment. A brief sidebar was necessary. "As many may know, Debbie vanished, but it is still Debbie's crew for now." There were several nods of agreement. "Her team has already set up two interviews with our outside contractors. I need to give Ray credit for that idea."

Chas introduced Bryan and his company, Aliton, who were contracted as the Project Manager to oversee the merger of all components. He highlighted Aliton's reputation as one of the top firms in the nation. Due to the unexpected disappearance of the Mimtrin employee originally assigned to this project, Chas stated that he would be personally take the lead and coordinate this upgrade until further notice.

"Bryan, could I ask you to come up front? I know this is not exactly what we had planned, but since you have been working on the nuts and bolts of this project, I thought it might be better for you to give us an overview of each module. You can discuss how we plan to put all these pieces together."

As Bryan headed up front, Chas added, "For those who have not yet worked with Bryan, his company, Aliton, helped design several of the Mimstruct Pro modules. His company will be merging all modules as Project Manager. Our team on this innovative software is doing a phenomenal job, and with Aliton's help, we are six months ahead of schedule. Bryan, it is all yours."

Bryan took the microphone, thanked Chas, and then started with the slides he helped to prepare for today's meeting. Chas walked by his seat and discreetly exited through the back door. Ray questioned why Chas would do that but quickly refocused on the project. To his surprise, Ray was impressed by the explanation of how the modules would merge to expand the Mimstruct software. Suddenly, a red flag started waving in his head. CPSM has already perfected four of these modules. That is why Aliton has been so helpful. Pushing the beta forward by six months now made sense. But why would CPSM give up its proprietary software? Mimstruct Pro will be a significant competitor in the large project arena.

Then a whole runway of lights came on. They do not have advanced Artificial Intelligence or sophisticated language translation capabilities. They would need both for a significant international project. Ray looked at his notes again. And, characteristically for Ray, he started a full-blown discussion with himself. "The formula on the board was incomplete. How do I know this? Why would I know this?" Then it hit him. There was a lawsuit. A consultant working for CPSM brought these formulas to them. The developer was from a one-man operation. CPSM modified the formulas. They filed for the copyright, squeezing the little guy out.

During the lawsuit, the consultant knew he would lose. He did not have the money, leverage, or influential lawyers to win. To exact some revenge, he made sure that his codes and their changes were made transparent as part of the case in the public record. As a result, the algorithms were made available to any developer with no restrictions. By the time CPSM had the court documents sealed, the consultant had posted his and CPSM's versions on his website as open-source code.

When he read about it, Ray was so enthralled with this code that he downloaded both formulas before CPSM could have their version taken down. Saving design tactics and techniques to study was more than a hobby; it was Ray's passion. He had not opened the files since the download. There was no reason to, until now. "Wow," Ray thought, "what a series of coincidences?" Then he remembered what Mr. White Hair said about coincidences not being coincidences.

CHAPTER THREE

Ray was in his office on Monday morning still trying to figure out why he had been in the meeting. He thought, 'They may want me to be the interim manager until Leticia returns. But when would that be? Chen is available, so why would they bother putting a lower-level person in?' He convinced himself that he didn't want the job anyway. 'Stay focused,' Ray whispered.

Maria passed by his office. He called out, "Maria!" She retreated three steps.

"Yes." She refrained from saying, 'What do you want? I am busy.'

"Have you heard from Leticia?"

Maria's facial expression turned to that 'oops, I made a mistake's look. "I'm sorry. I thought you knew. Letecia was in an accident just outside of Napa. She was on her way back from Denver when her car was sideswiped. Her car veered off the road into a signpost. The hospital called us. They got the number from her business card." Ray asked about her status. "They said she is in a coma. I have already updated Mr. Jenkins."

Ray was trying to ignore the ringing phone. "Keep me updated as soon as you know any more." The phone stopped.

"Does Chen know?" Maria nodded her head as the phone rang again. Typically, the screen would announce the caller. The screen displayed, 'Unknown.' He answered the call. "This is Ray," he said, thinking, 'I don't want to talk to you.' His tone immediately changed. Maria only heard one side of the conversation. She became more anxious with each pause.

"Chas, I just heard… Brain swelling so forced coma… Yes, somebody should go up there. The person I would recommend disappeared… Well, I am thinking that Maria is going to need to stay here to cover Leticia's desk." Ray held up the one-finger wait-a-minute for Maria to see. "Sure. I can give her remote access. You will need to call security to let them know what I am doing. She's here now. I will ask and call you back."

Maria did not hesitate. "You don't need to ask. I will be glad to go." Ray knew she was familiar with travel expenses, so that discussion was short.

"I will have a remote access password texted to you so you can do whatever it is you do while there. It is only good for three days but that should be sufficient. Chen will be your contact, but please keep me informed." She gave Ray a confirming nod. "Chen and I will need your help today and tomorrow trying to regroup. Plan to leave Wednesday morning. If she is not out of the coma by Friday, come back because it will more than likely be a long haul.

"Two more items. Leticia's company cell phone and laptop, you need to bring them back. I am sure the hospital is not going to let you just walk out with them. Have their security call me and I will get them whatever authorization they need. Technically those are company property."

Then Ray gave a slight, quick grin. "Second, and before I say it, I am not prying into your personal life, so if you want to tell me to mind my own business, that's fine. I do have my reasons for asking." He paused for a reaction. "Are you and Enrique an item?"

Her eyes opened wide, her head tilted slightly, and she tensed up. Ray knew he had struck a nerve. Her response was curt: "First, you are right; it is none of your business. Second, the answer is that we met at my cousin's wedding. We are just friends. Now it's your turn. How could you possibly know Enrique? He is a maintenance guy working for a contractor."

Ray's facial expression reminded Maria that he knew almost everyone at Mimtrin. "Come over to the window. Leticia's view from her office has spoiled you. You can see that I have a great view of the parking lot. It's amazing how you happen to be there almost every day to greet Enrique when he gets off the maintenance company's shuttle bus. It's also coincidental that, on multiple occasions, when you come to work, a fresh flower is placed on a notecard in the center of your desk. I am willing to bet it does not come from the flower fairy."

Clearly irritated, Maria retorted, "If you must know, I am helping Enrique earn some extra cash." Maria decided to cut this short. "An acquaintance of mine in San Diego owns a delivery business. Before you ask, Delivery Especial is the name. Her sister's friend works for a law firm. The firm needs documents and whatever to be delivered. Marta's fees are less so they use her company when they can." Maria could see the skepticism on Ray's face. "Marta gets a gig in LA. She calls me. I give the information to Enrique. Since he works at night, he delivers during the day. Enrique lets me know the job is done by giving me a note with a flower. I inform Marta. She pays me. I pay Enrique in cash."

Maria thought she had finished this conversation, but Ray's critical thinking kicked in. "Okay. I think there is more to this than I may want to know. But why doesn't Marta pay Enrique?"

Ray could see that Maria was pondering whether to answer. Almost under her breath, she said, "Because he is not technically legal. The maintenance company pays him and many other workers in cash." Ray thought the word 'technically' could have been left out of that legal comment.

"Well, now I have more questions, but I am not going to ask, at least right now." Ray paused to think through what he needed to say next. "When I work late, he and I discuss economics, world events, or whatever pops up. He is wasting his talents." What Ray did not say is that Enrique has extensive computer experience. Unfortunately, his experience had nothing to do with any Mimtrin projects.

Ray decided to make lemonade with two lemons. The first was his lemon. Ray was assigned mundane programming tasks. What would take the average programmer an hour or more, Ray could finish in twenty minutes. Those irritating tasks took him away from researching solutions to more significant issues. The second lemon was Enrique's lack of industry experience. Training Enrique to complete those jobs gives him new, qualified skills, allowing Ray to use his talents elsewhere—Voila, lemonade.

Ray put an idea on the table for Maria. "Enrique seems like a good guy. Maybe we can get him a job here. He needs to get some form of federal ID to get on the payroll. Can some relative's friend's cousin help?"

A laugh popped out of Maria before she realized it had happened. "It is already in the works. Enrique just needs to find $10,000 to get it done. That is why he works all the time. He's trying to raise money."

Ray needed to know, "And this ID won't come back to bite him down the road?"

"Not a chance." The absoluteness of that response took Ray back. "The law firm makes it happen for those who are in the same boat as Enrique, especially now."

"Why especially now?" This scheme had Ray's full attention.

Maria's wry smile was her first reaction. She finally knew something Ray didn't. "The floodgates opened Friday afternoon. After people went missing, lawyers started adapting to the situation Friday night. Most of the people who were blocking questionable applications are gone—disappeared. There is no one to stop the process now. Lawyers, government officials, and politicians spent zero time realizing they had just struck gold.

"Thousands of those here illegally will soon be legal. It is a matter of the almighty dollar. Enrique can get a green card in a matter of days, once he has the money of course. After the green card is issued, for $30,000 he could get citizenship within a matter of weeks. Thousands more are heading this way from around the world."

"Update me. Who is coming in?" Maria recognized that was not a question but a command.

"With mass citizenship approvals on the horizon, the Chinese will take over San Francisco, Portland, and Seattle. The northwest will be theirs politically and economically within a year. The Chinese already own vast plots of land in Idaho, North Dakota and South Dakota. Even though those states will stay primarily white, they will be under economic control by the Chinese.

"The Latinos will have political control of Southern

California, Nevada, Arizona and West Texas in the same way. Even though the cartels have already started preparing an invasion, a physical war will not be needed. Billions of cartel dollars will be coming in to buy businesses at a huge discount. Many businesses are failing for lack of employees or lack of customers. Many of the owners disappeared in whatever just happened a few days ago."

Ray had not considered any of this. Maria continued as if she were briefing a news conference. "BLM groups and their multi-cultural sympathizers will gain majority control of Minneapolis, Chicago, Detroit, Boston, New York City, Newark, Philadelphia, Pittsburgh, and surrounding areas.

The 'Bible Belt' states have lost tens of millions of people. The BLMers are using Atlanta as the hub to take control of Georgia, Mississippi, Louisiana, and Alabama. I am not sure about the Carolinas. The Midwest lost millions as well but will still be mostly white. The agricultural belt will struggle since family farms, either owned or leased, are mostly deserted."

Ray combined a statement with a question. "You didn't mention Florida."

"Florida is a problem that could start a Civil War. The Latinos, through the cartels, will shortly control Miami and the southern tip of Florida. They should also control most of all the agricultural counties. The Florida Panhandle will be controlled by the BLMers. As long as both groups accept that division, a territorial war might not happen."

Without hesitation, she added, "That is just the US. Percentagewise, the US is estimated to have the largest loss of people. South, Central America, and Mexico are next. The EU and UK combined are estimated to be third. Europe has similar issues with the influx of migrants from the Middle

East and Africa."

Maria took a short breath before continuing. "I would not have thought this, but there was a substantial number of Jews missing. I guess they were in the Jews for Jesus camp. The Muslim countries had negligible loss as a percent of the population. Russia lost most of its people from the rural areas. China was at the bottom percentagewise. With a weakened US and Europe, the countries of Taiwan, Korea, Japan, Singapore, and Mongolia will all be fair game for China."

Ray had a difficult time keeping his mouth from gaping open. "How do you know all of this? I don't even know how numbers could be calculated that fast."

Maria looked down briefly, closed her eyes, and shook her head. "You need to get a life beyond Mimtrin. I subscribe to Worldly Chat and talk to people all over the world. The site has a great translation software. It is not as fast and accurate as our new program, but it is great for chatting." Ray cocked his head like a dog that had just heard a strange noise. Maria qualified her comment. "Leticia is on our translation module team. She speaks four languages.

"Now, for your second question about the numbers. I will send you a link to the results by religion. You can see the details and methods used to capture the information. As inept as the United Nations is, these stats came out amazingly fast. It was almost like they were prepared for this day. About ninety-five percent of the UN offices worldwide reported estimated numbers by late Sunday." The amazed tone in Maria's voice added, "The most shocking part is that the people claiming to be Christians on the latest United Nations census were 90% of the total that disappeared.

"Categories under a heading of Christians, such as Evangelical, Catholic, Morman, Jehovah Witness, and so on were analyzed. According to the online report, Evangelicals and Protestants represented 55% of the 90% that vanished. The percentage of Catholics that vanished was also high, but Morman and Jehovah Witness numbers were extremely low. I don't remember the exact numbers." She looked at Ray and nodded, "Are you still with me?"

Ray admitted, "I have only read two passages in the Bible. Both described what just happened." Then Ray's analytical mind kicked in. "So, if all believers in Jesus were taken off this earth, why isn't the number 100%?"

Maria's expression told Ray she had the same question. "You have read two more passages than me. I had the exact same question. I posted it on World Chat. The consensus answer was: Just because you say you are a Christian doesn't mean you are a true believer in Jesus. Many go to church as an obligation to the family or their social group. Some become leaders or even ministers or priests for power. Some go for greedy reasons using their association with the church to promote their own business. In other words, they do not go to church for Jesus but for their own selfish desires."

Ray's bobblehead moved back and forth, indicating that the answer made some logical sense. As much as Ray wanted to reject the idea that Jesus had taken Christians from the Earth, he couldn't deny the facts surrounding their sudden disappearance. He recalled those first minutes when he asked, "Where did everybody go?" There must be more to this, he thought.

"Thanks for sharing but that was way more than I wanted to know. We will just have to see if your Worldly Chat guesstimates are right. As far as Enrique's quest to become a legal citizen with a cash payment, I know nothing, I see nothing." The smiles were short-lived. "I'll get an update from him the next time we talk. Let me know if you need anything for the trip."

On Wednesday morning, Maria's desk was clean, and her chair was stored neatly under the desk. Ray was never one to waste an opportunity. Leticia's office and, more importantly, her computer were no longer guarded. He would wait until almost everyone had left for the day before putting on his forensic hat. Ray had already checked which conferences were running in Denver last week. Other than a few small local conferences, there was no reason she should have been in Denver. Could it be she is colluding with CPSM?

Leticia had a slight paranoia streak. Her door would be locked when she left for the day. Maria has Leticia's key. Now, Ray has Maria's key. Ray did not think that Leticia would be dumb enough to leave any clues related to her trip on the Mimtrin computer. But then again, even the most intelligent criminal makes mistakes. If she did, he would find it. He was looking forward to opening her laptop as well when it arrived.

Ray knew the security cameras would capture him entering Leticia's office. He had reasons for being there. For everyone not returning, his job was to determine where each project was in the workflow. Even though Leticia would be returning, assuming she emerged from the coma, her workflow would also be subject to review and status updates. Due diligence would be his rationalization if questioned about being in her office.

Once Ray started, he figured it might be a long night, but he struck paydirt early. He opened a folder at the top of the list labeled 'Archive.' Twenty alphabetized folders rang-ing from 'budget' to 'projects retired' were inside. Starting at the top and working down made sense, but that last file piqued his curiosity. He decided to go from bottom to top. Ray recognized every project in that folder except one. Ray identified a series of files right away. They were all related to the CPSM lawsuit he had discussed with Chas. Leticia's files were far more extensive than Ray's.

The file he opened next was going to save him significant research time. The code written on the conference room whiteboard was there. The missing pieces were highlighted in red. Ray's mind went on full alert. What was she doing with this information? If she knew what was missing, why didn't she tell someone? If she were the mole, why would she keep it on the company server? Was this the criminal's mistake? He copied the folder to a flash drive. Then he covered his electronic tracks.

Back in his office, Ray opened the flash drive on his computer. He methodically followed the subfiles. A folder labeled 'PWS' was opened. It contained a complete list of passwords for Leticia's downline employees. At the bottom of that list was another folder. That included a list of passwords way beyond Leticia's authority, including his. Ray changed his passwords regularly. Leticia had Ray's latest. His first reaction was anger, but it quickly turned into admiration. Leticia was a force to be reckoned with.

It was not surprising to find Chas Jenkins and Paul Smiley in the password list file. Could this have been how the emails on the Dolphin project got deleted? The Office of the President's email was missed. She would have known about that one. Criminals do make mistakes, but these errors were not consistent. As he went down the list, a pattern became blatantly obvious. All names were directly related to the Mimstruct Pro project. Leticia had access to every piece of the puzzle.

The rest of the search was quick and generally a waste of time. Ray was sure the laptop would provide information to fill the gaps. He resisted the urge to make Leticia the mole despite evidence building in that direction. Now, he needed to wait for Maria to return with the phone and laptop.

Ray was startled by a knock on his door. Enrique was making his rounds, and Ray's office was next to be cleaned. "Hey boss. Are you ready for me?"

"Not right now if you don't mind. I have hit a wall and need to figure out what is going on."

Enrique could see that Ray was unusually stumped. "Well, like you taught me, talk through the problem. Even if it is with someone who has no idea what you are saying, your brain gets focused when you try to explain the problem. The person you are talking to might ask a simple question that causes you to rethink the problem. Those are your words."

Ray gave Enrique a big smile. "Wow, I must be pretty smart. That is good advice. I should take it. Have a seat. Let's talk." Ray wanted to be careful not to expose Leticia or let Enrique know the how and why of his discovery. "I changed my login password last Friday. I just discovered that someone has that login. I just scanned my computer and nothing unusual popped up. There is nothing to indicate anyone used the password or that I have been hacked."

Enrique started, "Knowing your skills, some of these questions I am going to ask may seem rhetorical but just play along. Also, if you don't mind, can you sit in this chair?" Enrique invited Ray to the second chair on his side of the desk. Ray's face clearly showed doubt, but he shrugged and played along. "Sometimes you need to look at a problem from a different angle. Do you have confidential meetings in here?" Ray indicated no. "Do you have a pattern to your password?" Again no. "Do you lock your office when you leave for meetings?" Once more, no. "So, anyone could walk into your office when you leave." That was a yes.

For clarification, Ray said, "Anything high-level or confidential is in somebody's office way more important than mine. Second, when I leave my office, I log off. Third, someone would be way overconfident to just walk into my office with security cameras watching. Even if someone did come in, how would they get my login?"

Enrique needed one more piece of information. "Have you had any maintenance work done recently? Problems with the lights? Loose ceiling tiles? Anything?"

Ray scanned his memory bank. "About five or six months ago there was a light flickering, but over that first set of cubicles, not in my office. It was not the bulbs, so they figured it was some wiring issue. The crew came in that night. The next morning when I came in there was no flickering. Problem solved."

"Ah yes. Now I remember. It was our maintenance company that did the work. They checked the wiring in your office and two others that I saw. They said something about the ninth floor. Another crew came back about two months later to check those same offices. I just thought it was some follow up procedure."

Enrique looked at the ceiling lights. "I'll be right back." Enrique was out of the office before Ray could even ask him where he was going. When he returned, Ray's look was saying, "Well?" Enrique pulled a device from his pocket. It looked like a new flip phone. He tapped the screen several times. He shook his head like he was agreeing with the phone. Then he said, "Okay, we can talk."

Ray was baffled. Why would he say that? Enrique prompted Ray, "Look at the ceiling light above your desk. Then look at the surrounding tiles. What do you see?" Ray circled the tiles around the light, then looked at Enrique and shrugged. "Look again. I need you to see it." Ray was confused, but he had played along so far.

Then Ray spotted a tiny hole next to the light's frame. If he hadn't been attentive, a minor defect in the tile would have gone unnoticed. This defect, however, was a perfectly round hole. Enrique was watching and knew that Ray had made the discovery. "That same hole is in three other offices. I just checked." He continued, "Part of my job is dusting the ceiling tiles once a month. I spotted the hole in Leticia's office but didn't think it was a big deal. I had no reason to check."

He went to his maintenance cart to retrieve the duster extension pole. His anticipation was high as he slowly inched the tile from the frame to expose the back side. Ray could see the disappointment. There was no camera. As Enrique attempted to reposition the tile, wires fell on Ray's desk. Enrique automatically said, "These wires would have been used on surveillance equipment."

Amazed by that comment, Ray sat back in his chair. Before he could ask, Enrique told him that he had worked with the Mexican government. His job involved creating software to clean up surveillance stills, audio, and videos. He received the same extensive training used by top international security firms. How and where surveillance equipment could be installed was part of the program.

Still curious, Ray asked, "Why did you say we can talk

now? Why now?"

"This particular phone has an app that can jam low frequency listening devices. I have a different app that recognizes those devices. There is one in this room, but I am not sure where. It will be easy to find." Enrique wished he could have taken a picture of Ray's face. "Hey, you have your hobbies, I have mine."

"Enrique, if I believed in God, I would say you are a Godsend."

Ray kept staring at the tiny hole. "Someone is spying on me and at least three others. This project just took a major turn." Ray could see that Enrique was puzzled by the last comment. "Okay let's keep talking this out. Assume someone saw me type in my new password. It would only be good until the next change. So why not leave the camera equipment to continue spying? Why would they even want to spy on me? I learned the details of a major project Saturday but I am not in the loop, at least for now." Ray could see that Enrique knew something. "Well, spit it out."

Enrique went into consultant mode. "Remote access. If someone knew your password, they could login and install a remote access program. Then they would allow your computer to give access to theirs. There is now a sophisticated software that could see anything on your computer when your computer is on."

Ray immediately questioned that idea. "But I would need to invite and accept," then a light came on. "Unless, of course, someone was logged on and either sent or accepted." He continued the argument with himself. Enrique was fascinated by the process going on in Ray's head. "But that access would end once I logged off." Ray looked at Enrique, letting him know he could jump in at any time.

"That would be true if you had a standard retail product. But there is software that can be imbedded in your start-up menu. When your computer boots, the receiving computer is alerted. They can decide if they want to see what you are doing or not. The software can track every one of your keystrokes. While your computer is on, they can look without you knowing." Ray squinted at Enrique. It was an 'I don't believe you' look.

His expression changed as an ah-ha moment struck. "Maybe I do believe you." Ray went to his bookshelf. He ran his finger across the perfectly stacked magazines. He stopped, pulled a magazine from the shelf, fanned through the pages, and stopped again. "Here. This article talks about the software that can record every stroke. Is this what you worked on?"

After a quick scan, Enrique said, "Not that exactly, but yeah, that's the concept." Enrique examined the article in more detail. Ray watched Enrique read the same section multiple times. He returned to the beginning and quickly turned to the end. "I know who wrote this! The person is not the name that is in the article. It has been modified, but this is from a classified Military Intelligence document. Captain Arturo Guitierrez presented this report to get funding for one of his pet projects."

Ray sighed. "Congratulations. Now I have two problems." Enrique's expression asked for clarification. "Why would Leticia spy on herself? I think we are dealing with two separate issues. I think spies might be spying on each other."

Enrique shrugged and stood up. He pulled his phone out and tapped it a couple of times. He then started walking around the room. He pointed the phone to the sky as if he were trying to get a signal. He stopped and motioned for Ray to follow. 'Play along,' Ray thought.

They walked to the large, walk-in storage closet that held maintenance supplies. When they were inside, Enrique closed the door. "You have an audio bug in the smoke detector. I have different apps on my phone; the best ones on the retail market." He texted Ray the names and told him to buy and download the apps. "The jamming app I used in your office is limited to retail-quality listening devices. Whoever is behind this may have more sophisticated equipment."

"Normally, a combination camera-audio device is stored in the smoke detector so it could be hard wired. The smoke detector was not in an ideal location to be able to see your keyboard. They split the two devices. The listening device is powered from the smoke detector, but they needed to hardwire the camera. They would have used wires just like those that fell on your desk."

Enrique's demeanor dramatically changed. "Ray, I consider you a friend. You have gone above and beyond to help me, and I appreciate it. I think I can tell you something. Before I do, you need to know that if it leaves this room you will put both of us at extreme risk. More precisely, dead. So do you want to hear it or not?"

Ray put on a droll smile. "Dead has already been tried on me, but that's another story for another time. If you have broken any major laws like murder or grand theft, then don't tell me because I will need to turn you in. Anything else is up to you. Now the ball is in your court."

CHAPTER FOUR

Enrique began his story as a First Lieutenant in the Mexican military. Military Intelligence was working with the Mexican DNI, their version of the CIA. The objective was to gather information on various criminal activities. Cartels were the main target. Other focus areas included minority party politicians, business leaders, and multiple organizations.

Enrique was on one of the projects. He had hacked a politician under investigation for accepting construction bribes to secure a lucrative highway extension deal. The road would provide greater access to a military base that needed to expand. The assignment was routine for Enrique. He would gather information by hacking into the construction company's computers. As he tracked the shell companies used to facilitate various financial transactions, he opened Pandora's Box.

Following the links between shell companies, he discovered an active LLC set up as a photography studio. Enrique was able to see the photo and video files. None were images of weddings or birthday parties. File folder names included executives, lawyers, press, and community leaders recorded in lewd compromising positions. Most resided in

Mexico, but there were some in the USA.

The Sinaloa Cartel was connected to every shell company, including the LLC. The cartel's extortion was not for money but for favors, protection from prosecution, and intel on any cartel investigation. One of the files had incriminating photographs of Colonel Torres, the Mexican Military Commander. Enrique also found files on high-ranking police officers, and the Municipal President of the town where the army base was located. Although the trail was not as evident in the USA, border state congressmen found in the file cache coincidently had voting records opposing funding for the border wall. Post-Rapture, those same officials are pushing to defund the Immigration and Customs Enforcement Department.

Enrique advised his Commanding Officer, Captain Ricardo. Enrique described the documents, bank statements, and evidence of collusion without showing the hard evidence. He recommended a strategy to expose this massive corruption.

Following protocol, Ricardo advised Captain Arturo Gutierrez who served as a Combat Engineer overseeing the road extension to the army base. The project was loaded with corruption across nearly all areas of its execution. Unexpectedly, a significant shift in plans occurred when Colonel Torres ordered Captain Gutierrez to a meeting. Enrique was to arrive an hour later than the Captain.

Once Enrique arrived at the headquarters, he was escorted by two Military Police Officers to the meeting. Captain Gutierrez, a clerk, and one other high-ranking officer were already walking away from the conference room when Enrique arrived. The Colonel had dismissed everyone but Captain Ricardo. Enrique knew he was being tested when the Colonel asked what physical proof existed. Enrique laid out about half of what he had found. But that was enough. Even though the Colonel's name was not mentioned, Enrique figured Torres knew his transgressions had been discovered.

The Colonel dismissed Captain Ricardo. He thanked Enrique for his investigative skills. Then Enrique was told about his promotion and reassignment to a remote base in southern Mexico. Enrique had anticipated what might happen in this meeting. He narrated the conversation as if it had just happened. "With all due respect, sir, I know that is my death sentence. I know what the cartel can do. My mother and father worked through a Christian church that helped children get away from sex traffickers. They were brutally murdered and put on display as a warning to others.

"My brother and I escaped. He is the only family I have. And just so you know, I have no idea where he is now. Basically, you cannot get to me through anyone; I am not afraid to die. Before you sign that order, there is something you need to know. I made four copies of every file I found. All four have been strategically placed. If I die of anything but natural causes, the files will be released to three cartels opposing Sinaloa. The others will be released in three different countries out of the immediate reach of the DNI or cartels. Even if you find who has the files, they each have a backup plan to release everything to their sources in the event they are killed."

Ray listened in awe, focused on every word as the story unfolded. "The cold, stern expression on the Colonel's face did not change, but I could see his unusually light-colored skin turning red. We reached a compromise. I would cross the border as an army officer assigned to the Mexican Consulate in San Diego. Once there, and all of the papers were in order, I would be given an honorable discharge that would take effect immediately. The orders for my return to Mexico would never be entered in the system. I lost all benefits but cashed out what little I had in the bank."

Enrique paused, reflecting on the potential dangers this plan had. "Torres knew that I had thought this through. The few flaws he could see were insignificant. Torres wanted assurances that nothing would be released. I told the Colonel I knew I could not stop the massive corruption. We both knew if this information did get out, there would be a significant disruption between the government and cartels, resulting in substantial bloodshed."

Enrique finished the story as if he were speaking to Torres. "I couldn't care less about the lowlifes I uncovered that control this evil. I am only concerned for people who would die or be injured in the crossfire. I have witnessed what these animals can do. I would not release anything for the sake of the innocent people. If I am safe, you are safe."

Enrique looked at Ray. "So here I am. Safe for now, but still at risk. If anyone discovers where I am, they may or may not act. If you let anything slip, they may assume you know more than you do or that you may have one set of the files." He paused to let Ray respond but suddenly resumed. "This is why I need a green card at a minimum. The ideal would be US citizenship under a new, legal surname."

Ray asked, "No one else knows, correct?" Correct was the simple response. "How about Maria?"

"No, but why would you ask that?"

"She knows you are saving money to buy a green card and she might have known the reason."

Ray dropped the subject, but Enrique wanted to assure Ray that everything would be legal but expedited. "Maria gave me the name of a lawyer at the law office Mimtrin uses,

Samson Englebright. So that should be legit, right? She called in a favor to get me a good fee. I didn't completely understand, but he is using a law firm that just does immigration law. He used to work there. She may have told me the firm's name, but I forget what it is."

Ray quipped, "I am going to guess that this lawyer is somebody's uncle's cousin's friend."

Enrique laughed and said, "Something like that."

"I hope it works out for you. Let me know if you need a letter of reference or something along those lines. I will be glad to help." Without allowing a response, Ray went back to business. "Why the storage room?"

"The short answer is, I don't have the device to jam a sophisticated audio bug." Enrique added, "I can find out whose offices might be bugged, at least on this floor. When I left Mexico, I helped myself to some small but sophisticated equipment. It is way better than the phone app. I can also probably find out if a sharing program was loaded."

Ray abruptly changed the subject. "Before we get to that, there is something I need to say. I'm sorry to hear about your family. My parents and sister died, I say were murdered, in a car accident by a drunk driver. They were coming home from a church retreat. I should have been with them, but I wasn't feeling well and had a slight fever, so I stayed home. My mother used to make me go to church with the family. To me, the science fiction books I would take to read made more sense. I think she thought I would become a believer through osmosis or some life-changing revelation. I know what happened to them is not the same, but the feelings are probably similar."

Enrique nodded with empathetic agreement. He was sincere when he thanked Ray for his thoughtful comment.

Then, he felt the need to tell Ray more. Since joining the army, he had not told anyone what he was about to tell Ray.

"My mother came to our town as a missionary from a church in Texas. She was a teacher who could teach any subject. As a leader in our town, the church selected my father to host and coordinate the community projects. The mission was for one year, but my mother stayed. Two weeks after the other missionaries left, my parents got married. The two of them carried on the missionary work." Ray had observed that Enrique's English was better than that of many people born in the United States. Now, it made sense.

The next part of Enrique's journey was difficult, but he marched on. "I was born about ten months after they got married. My brother was born one year and two days later. We hated that because both birthdays were celebrated on that middle day. It shouldn't have mattered, but the day was not as special to either of us for some reason."

Ray usually would have found a way to shorten discussions of a personal nature, but Enrique seemed to want to get this out. Enrique continued thoughtfully. "Every student loved my mom and looked forward to attending school. They knew she cared about each of them." Enrique paused to gather himself.

"She was running late one day and walked in just as the bell was ringing for classes to start. Some of the younger students were crying and being consoled by the older kids. She noticed that five seats were empty and asked where those students were. One of the cartels had taken them. This was her first exposure to human trafficking. She was having no part of that evil."

Ray could feel pride in Enrique's voice. "I, to this day, do not know how she did it. She put a plan in place that would rival the greatest military strategist. She had a large network in the communities through her outreach missions. With my father leading the team, four of the five children came home as planned. The fifth died, but none of the other children knew how." Enrique was struggling but continued the saga. "Both my mother and father were strong, smart, determined, and all in for Jesus. They prayed every day for Jesus to help them and the community.

"For the next five years, they helped protect the community. The men and women, primarily mothers and fathers, fought off cartels on several fronts with ingenious tactics. Phone chains warned people when the cartel was coming. Secret shelters were close to the school. Local hunters and fishermen had more aggressive defense mechanisms in place if needed. After each thwarted attempt by the cartel, the people involved swore there was an army of angels fighting with them against the evil.

"An increased demand for 'inventory' as the traffickers called it, prompted the cartels to get more aggressive. A new cartel leader came in with vengeance. They murdered the men and kidnapped the women and children. They knew my parents were the leaders. They murdered them and dragged their bodies through the streets as a warning to anyone thinking about resisting."

Ray was empathetic but this had wandered way out of his comfort zone. He protected his emotions with logic: "It sounds like your parents were devout Christians. How about you?"

Enrique did not see that question coming. He had to stop to get his head around the subject. "To be honest, I don't think I ever was. I knew about God, Jesus and the Holy Spirit, but I never had that burning desire to commit to any of that. My brother and I were supposed to be baptized on the same day. I will never forget the pained and disappointed look on my mother's face when I told her I was not ready. But in her gracious way, she told me that Jesus will be waiting for me. He would be there when I am ready.

"After that, I helped at the church but never attended the services. I worked in the kitchen, made repairs, and performed other tasks as needed. I *absolutely* did not get out of the home Bible studies. I am not exaggerating when I say that I could easily debate any Bible scholar. I remember watching my mother destroy the credibility of missionaries teaching false doctrine. They would come in with all of their grandeur, take donations, then leave. By the time she was done exposing their con, they left with nothing. I don't know how she did it, but she always debunked their teaching in a calm and caring way.

In college, I debated Christian students and even some professors. I learned more with each discussion. But I did not want to win people over, my ego just wanted to win the argument. All of those Bible studies provided a strong academic and historical foundation, but nothing ever really translated into a heartfelt belief in God or Jesus. But after the Rapture, I am an unquestionable believer."

Ray did not mask his skepticism. "An unquestionable believer? Okay, you need to tell me how that works."

Enrique asserted, "Faith." He paused to think through the rest of the answer. "When my parents were killed, I blamed God. Why would He allow this to happen? They were devoted to Jesus, they prayed for His protection, but instead, He let evil men murder my parents. The Rapture, when Jesus removed believers from the earth, forced me to rethink things. The Rapture made me realize that God is working His divine plan."

An extended pause preceded Enrique's next thoughts. Ray could see sadness. "I was 16 and my brother 15 when my parents were killed. A family from the church took us in, but they could barely support one, let alone two of us. My uncle lived month to month but would have gladly opened his home to us. My brother and I knew that would not be fair to anyone. It was decided that my brother would live with my uncle and I would stay with the family from church. We would now be separated by 200 miles.

"In less than a month, I moved to live with a different family from the church. I had met them once or twice because they worked with my parents, helping abused women, children, and sometimes abused men. The couple was older and financially better off. They had no children and were happy to take me in. I later found out they could not have children. I was treated warmly as their son."

Ray sat down on a big box of paper towels as Enrique continued. "He happened to own a store that sold and repaired computer equipment. I worked in the shop and learned everything I could about hardware and software. Pops, as he wanted to be called, joked that I had been possessed by a computer. I finished in the top five percentile on the entrance exam for a technical university. That landed me a full scholarship. Otherwise, I probably would not have gone to college."

"While at the university, I met a Christian who became a friend. He told me the story of Ruth. The death of her husband put her in a bad way but her faith in God led her to great things. He told me the story of Joseph who was going to be killed by his brothers but instead was sold into slavery. Had he not been put into those dire circumstances he would not have become a great leader that saved thousands of Jews from slavery and death."

Enrique was about to tell another story but saw that Ray was a bit overwhelmed. "Job, Esther, Daniel, and others described in the Bible endured suffering that God used for greater purposes. Every death, every hardship of one person led others to salvation. 'Others' could mean one person or the entire Jewish nation."

Enrique shook his head ever so slightly. "But I was so angry and disillusioned that I decided there is no God, or at least, no God that I would want to follow. Then, a few days ago, millions of people disappeared. I knew it was the Rapture.

"I could do nothing at that point but sit down and pour out my heart to God. All the anger I felt towards God and hate I had toward the men who killed my parents; it all came out. I finally grasped the extent of my pride and arrogance. I felt a deep sadness. Frustration overwhelmed me when I realized all of the missed opportunities to help others find salvation. I told God about it all and asked Him to forgive me. I pleaded for Him to take it all away. I don't even know how long I sat there. Before I got up, I asked Jesus to please help me help others find their way to Him."

Enrique closed his eyes. That was followed by an extended sigh. He opened his eyes, smiled, and looked directly at Ray. "I know He forgave me for every sin. It is hard to describe what I felt. Calm? Peace? I am not sure. What I can say with certainty is that I am determined. In the short time we have left on the current version of this earth, I am going to introduce Jesus to as many people as I can. You, by the way, are on that list."

Ray could feel Enrique's genuine and heartfelt belief. He could see that Enrique needed the Rapture to reach this level of deep commitment to Jesus. Then, again, Ray had to put on his skeptic hat. "For every up there is a down. For every in there is an out. What does God get out of this? I read about sacrificing. I will warn you right now, don't get me started on all of the non-sensical rituals I have seen or read about."

Enrique's smile widened. "God forgives as a gracious, loving parent would. God only asks that I believe in Him with all my heart, my soul, and my mind. If I can do that, nothing is a sacrifice. I gain wisdom. I get the satisfaction for helping others. If I need to give up anything, it would be the sin that needed to be forgiven." Ray was uncharacteristically silent. That was not what he expected.

Ray noticed tears forming as Enrique shifted back to his past. "There is one more thing about my parents' story. When everyone disappeared, I knew what had happened. I put myself at risk to call the Pastor of their church to see if he had any information about my brother. The Pastor, of course, was not there. One of the Elders answered. I learned something for the first time." Ray's anticipation level heightened. "The names of my parents are on a foundation that helps children who have been trafficked or abused. What happened to them, their brutal death, finally got the church to take a stance. Their murder led to the formation of this community-funded organization.

"Now there are, or were until recently, hundreds of people volunteering. Thousands of dollars of donations came in each month from a wide range of resources. My parent's death led to saving and helping hundreds of children per year. Using this model, organizations were established in different communities. Each one of those groups grew as well."

Ray seldom allows his emotions to influence his actions. Discussing his personal life with anyone was unusual, but he decided to inch out of his comfort zone. "You and I have more in common than you can imagine. My parents and sister were Christians. A drunk driver killed my family. Right then, I decided that I could not worship any God that would do that to two people devoted to His every word. I appreciate your story, your parents, the church, and the foundation. That is your parents' legacy. All I have is a dead sister and two dead parents with no legacy."

Enrique wanted to hug Ray, but he figured that might not be the best move. He put his hand on Ray's shoulder. "Ray. You are their legacy. You can fight it all you want, but I have this incredible feeling that Jesus wants you on His team. Jesus loves you. He has a plan for you. He just wants you to trust Him. Just trust Jesus and the plan will be revealed."

Ray's tone was somewhat sincere but mostly patronizing. "I'll think about it." For Ray, thinking about it was significant. The thought of considering Jesus never entered his mind. Then he remembered Mr. White Hair saying, 'We need you on our team.' Ray's logical world was starting to have cracks that needed filling. "I am a logical person. Faith, to me, competes with logic. But I really will think about it."

"Ray, when you look out your window and you see the leaves and branches on the trees moving, what causes that?" Wind was the answer. "When you see the ocean go from a gentle roll to whitecaps on the waves, what causes that?" Again, wind. "When you see a gull suspended in the sky with wings spread but not moving, what causes that?" One more time, the wind.

"Ray, all your answers were logical, but can you see the wind?" Silence was his response. "You can see the result of the wind, but you cannot see the wind. You know it is there. You have an invisible force behind everything that makes our planet work. God is the invisible force that made the wind. Just because you cannot see God does not mean He is not there."

Ray took a minute to let that sink in. Enrique did not interrupt Ray's contemplation because he was silently praying for Ray to believe the truth of who God is and of God's love for him." Ray suddenly found his defense mechanism and shifted back to his sleuth mode. "In the meantime, we need to figure out who is behind this sabotage attempt." They headed back to Ray's office.

Enrique asked. "Who is in that office with the plant that is dying?" That office had been empty since Debbie disappeared. It was also one of the offices with a manufactured ceiling tile defect. "Are you able to log in to her computer?"

Ray responded, "I have the login information for everyone in the department."

"Good, I would rather work at her station than yours. I want to see if the surveillance software has been loaded."

Ray knew the security cameras would see Enrique enter Debbie's office. He needed a story. He figured the training program for Enrique would be the best option. Since he had already told Chas about the coding and training, there would be a witness to justify Enrique's time in the office.

The scanning app was already on when they entered the office. Enrique found two devices he assumed to be audio and video transmitters. He would need the professional-grade detection equipment and jamming device from his bag.

Ray blocked the camera angle during Enrique's login. He gave Enrique a file folder and told him, for the benefit of the listening device, "You can pick up the coding from the last time you worked on this. Just some easy cleanup." Ray left Enrique to find what he could. Enrique turned on a jamming device.

Before Ray started work in his office, he decided to eliminate the audio device in the smoke detector. He retrieved the ladder from the storage room, disassembled the device, wrapped it in a tissue, and shoved it in his pocket. The device stimulated Ray to consider options from a different perspective. Enrique's search was about thirty minutes into the process. Ray thought he'd better check on the progress. As he swiveled his chair to get up, he heard. "Got it!"

Ray picked up the pace. "What did you find?" As Ray dragged the guest chair around to the other side of the desk, he thought Debbie must have ordered the heaviest chairs she could buy. Her screen was full of letters, numbers, and symbols. Ray was seeing code he did not recognize.

Enrique explained, "I was right. This program was installed on the start menu but hidden behind this icon." The circular icon was almost invisible on the taskbar because it matched the background color. Ray wanted to know why they would embed the software but leave an icon. Enrique could think of only two answers: the installer was not properly trained or made a mistake. Ray speculated that an unskilled person might use the icon to delete the program after it was no longer helpful.

Ray went to his office, looked at his screen, and immediately returned. There was no icon. That was either good news or bad news. His computer may or may not have the bug. Ray decided not to take any chances and assumed that the software was already installed. "Should I assume that whoever is watching online could see what you did to find the bug?" Enrique was impressed by Ray's question, considering his recent exposure..

"Maybe. But remember I was part of the development team. I changed two lines that blocked everything I was doing. An observer might have seen everything up to that point, but they are probably not watching this computer since it has been turned off for several days. I am hoping they took this computer offline figuring Debbie vanished."

Ray injected a thought. "I did take a look at Debbie's projects and where she was on her plan."

Enrique asked, "Did you do anything new?" Ray shook his head. "Then they probably figured it was not her."

Ray locked his fingers on top of his head. "Could someone delete an email?"

Enrique said, "I did that that once in my previous career. Saved emails could be edited before being sent. It is not unusual that the cc: and bcc: would be removed. The hackers will always want to cover their tracks. The email would have disappeared when the sender checked the sent folder. Most people would think it was a glitch."

Ray thought he was a genius, not just 'Crazy Ray.' "So, a bcc to my private email on my home computer is not so crazy after all."

Enrique didn't want to burst his balloon but did let some air out. "Unless there is an attachment." Ray's arms dropped to his sides. "Only a pro with the system could do this, but a virus could be embedded with the attachment. If you wanted to review that attachment it would activate the virus to do whatever it was programmed to do. That was a lot of work and the DNI only ordered that move for a very specific investigation. I would seriously doubt that is going on here. The person doing this is good, but not that good."

"Can you tell when this bug was loaded?"

Enrique responded, "Six months ago to the day. And this may be nothing to do with nothing, but today is my 7th month anniversary. I was hired the day my company got the maintenance gig here." Ray had so many what-ifs. Where to start?

Ray said, "Leave it as is." Enrique was confused. "We are going to send a special code through Debbie's station. It must be perfectly executed. If it is done right, we might find out if someone in the office is watching. You think of what you would do, and I will do the same. We can talk through the options. We will need an escape route in case it is not as perfect as we thought."

Enrique sat back in his chair. "You know that this is a big door to open. If the people doing this have gone this far to get inside, they will not hesitate to permanently remove any obstacles, like us."

"Then it absolutely needs to be perfect. I will give you the same option you gave me. In or out?"

There was no hesitation. "I am in all the way. Let's do this."

Both wanted time to think through their options, so they agreed not to dismiss any ideas. They would write down everything, no matter how ridiculous it might sound. These are exceptional times that need exceptional thinking. Saturday at 7 AM at the employee parking lot entrance to the building was the designated time and location to meet.

It will be time to go to war.

CHAPTER FIVE

Thursday morning, Ray stepped into his office at approximately 6:00 a.m. He was so focused on scanning the news headlines on his phone that he failed to notice Chas, who had already made himself at home. "Sorry, I did not see you there. Have you seen some of the news?" Chas turned his iPad to show Ray the news he had been reading.

"It is strange that Fox only has three or four veterans reporting. Newsmax and OAN are showing documentaries, and their online sites have not been updated. It's as if they have no reporters or staff to run the station. 'Scary' does not even begin to describe what is happening. Here are a couple of headlines from the CNN site." Ray read off:

- Gold rush to claim empty houses.
- Shoppers mugged in parking lots for groceries.
- Police ranks down. Gang control up.
- Over 100 dead in gang war crossfire.

"It's insane out there. I just quit reading."

Chas noticed the rare sound of excitement in Ray's voice when he continued. "There is a video on YouTube that you will want to see when, or if, you get a chance. Search 'Lady on Corner.' I don't know who was recording, but it has gone viral. A lady was shouting, 'Jesus has saved me. He can save you, too. Pray with me. Let me help you.'"

As he continued, Chas noticed that skepticism had begun to override Ray's enthusiasm. "Three gang bangers told her to get off their corner because she was bad for business. Defiantly, she said, 'This corner belongs to Jesus!' A backhand caught the side of her face, knocking her to the ground. She got up and repeated, 'He can save you.'

"The apparent leader took that as a threat. He said something like, 'When Jesus finds you dead in the alley, he will learn to respect my corner.' The sound of a switchblade caused the other two to burst out laughing. The lady just smiled at them. 'Why are you smiling, lady? If you don't leave, you are going to die!'"

Ray played the answer. "It's because I know where I am going when I die. It will be in a joyful place for eternity. I also know where you are going if you don't follow Jesus. I forgive you in advance if you decide to kill me, but Jesus will not forgive you and will pass judgment on you when you die. You will experience darkness. You will experience the same pain you have inflicted on others. Every stab wound, every bullet, every beating will be felt day and night for eternity." The three of them surrounded her. The video shook and then stopped.

Ray was more confused than stunned. "She could have just walked away. I'm not afraid to take calculated risks or take a hard line on what's right and wrong, but I can't think of anything worth dying for. I am not a religious person, but something has that woman completely committed to Jesus. I don't know. Maybe one day I will understand."

There was no more time for the outside world. Chas got right to it. "I also discovered news you are going to want to hear." Chas had Ray's full attention as he sank into a desk chair that was custom-designed by AI for his body shape. "There seems to be an up-and-coming star at the United Nations. World leaders are already arriving today at Bolling Air Force Base. All are coming in on private or military planes. The security is unbelievable."

Chas scratched his head. "I forget the guy's name, maybe Amir Acee, but I am not sure. Until Monday, he was a total unknown. There is a UN subcommittee that has been attempting to devise a framework for establishing a global commerce system. With so many people gone, the subcommittee had spots to fill. He must have impressed the powers that be because he is now the chair of that subcommittee.

"Negotiations are to begin next week between North and South Korea, China and Taiwan, Russia and Ukraine, and India and Pakistan. These things usually take years, but he is doing everything in a matter of weeks. I know these times are unusual, but he has assembled a team of highly persuasive negotiators for each treaty.

"My State Department contact said that within three weeks, every member of the Abraham Accords that President Trump brought together will be at the table. The Saudis have also agreed. There is even talk that Jordon, Syria, Lebanon, and Egypt would like to be part of the discussions. Right now, those countries have already agreed to meet with Acee. Israel is holding things up, but there is some optimism that the meeting will eventually take place."

Chas's phone beeped. He stopped to read the message. The pointing wait-a-minute finger became a connection of sorts for Chas and Ray. He tapped his phone. Ray could hear the ringing and then one side of the conversation. "Mo, Good morning. We're in his office. Perfect." Chas looked away from his phone and straight at Ray. "Mo is on his way here. He's about 5 minutes away."

"Mo?" Ray asked to make sure he understood, "Should I assume that is Moshe Abrams, CEO?" Chas nodded as he focused back on his phone. "Do you have any updates for me before he gets here?"

Ray had to shake off the fact that the CEO was coming. It was time to focus. "Yes. I did more research on Bryan. More importantly, on the code Bryan's company supposedly developed for us." Ray emphasized the word 'developed' with the two-finger quote gesture.

Ray walked through the code story. "I am going to give you this flash drive for your eyes only, at least for now. Do not, I repeat, do not download it. View it from the flash drive only on your personal computer. I have my reasons." Ray handed Chas some pages in a file folder. "This is the missing piece from Bryan's code. Page 2 is the added code. Page 3 is what I think should be modified. There are a few lines that don't make sense, but I will figure it out."

Chas glanced at the pages as he let Ray's evidence sink in. He knew Mo would be walking in at any time and wanted to absorb as much as possible. When Chas looked up, Ray could see the same anger Chas had seen when he discovered that someone had blocked the Dolphin Project emails to him.

Chas inhaled half of the air in the room. "I do not need this now!"

"Need what?" Chas turned to see Mo walking into the office.

After a quick introduction, Ray updated Mo on the theory that Bryan was only giving up proprietary code to access the AI and language modules CPSM needed.

To think about the next moves, Mo stood perfectly still with his eyes closed. He opened them to look at Chas briefly and closed them again. When his eyes next opened, they focused on Ray. "I have my thoughts, but I want to hear yours first." Contemplation and getting input first were standard operating procedures for Mo.

Ray jumped in without hesitation. "My first reaction was to get rid of Aliton. However, firing, suing, or any other similar action would not resolve the problem. We have a mole and maybe more than one. If we knee-jerk react, whoever is doing this will go to 'plan B'. We need to find out who is on the inside."

Mo abruptly interrupted. "Wait. You know for sure there is a mole?"

"It is worse than that. See the tiny, perfectly round hole in the ceiling tile next to the light?" They both scanned the edge of the light frame. Mo spotted it first, but Chas was only seconds behind. "Enrique from the maintenance company pointed it out. He said the last time he saw something like that, there was a camera on the other side. He moved the tile for me. There was no camera, but these wires fell out. The same hole is in Debbie's and Leticia's offices."

Both were surprised when Mo immediately said, "Wiring for micro camera power. This would have been a long-term surveillance." Based on Enrique's information, Ray confirmed that four and possibly six months is an accurate time frame.

Ray kept things moving. "I removed the listening device from the smoke detector." Mo and Chas looked at each other with a slight degree of panic. "So here is my immediate plan. On Saturday, several people will be working overtime. If anyone asks, Enrique will be checking for some electrical issues in the building. You will have assigned me to be with Enrique for security purposes. It would be suspicious if I were doing this alone."

Mo and Chas exchanged a look. They were curious about where this situation was going. In the short time Chas had been working with Ray, he would be surprised if he was not surprised by something Ray knew or did. "We will conduct a comprehensive scan or each floor. More importantly, we will need to check every office of key players on the Mimstruct Pro project. I will need the list." Ray saw the red flags waving in Mo's eyes, but he kept going. "I am going to need access to both of your offices as well as Paul's."

"I'll need the security cameras disabled while I'm investigating. We don't know if the cameras have been hacked. This will be for the seventh and ninth floors. Eight houses marketing, finance, and administration. Six is more logistical and would not have access to classified information. Unless, of course, there is something I don't know." Both indicated that there should be nothing of concern on the other floors.

"Security should shut down those two floors at 7 a.m. We should be three hours, depending on what we find. Chas, can you authorize that?" Ray did not wait for an answer because it was not really a question. It was an action item. "We will scan the offices for any type of recording devices."

"We? Enrique?" Mo asked. Ray's finger pointed to the sky once again. "Yes, but before I forget I may need access to the roof. Any cameras of ours would need to be turned off. Also, the parking lot cameras should be off at 6:30. As soon as we are finished, I will let security know to reactivate the system." The wait-a-minute finger retracted. Chas nodded in agreement.

"Enrique Martin from the maintenance company agreed to come in. It is his day off." Chas realized that Mo was not familiar with Ray's win-win arrangement with Enrique. He gave Mo the condensed version of the situation. Ray added, "Enrique knows these offices as well as anyone. He also has access to ladders and tools we may need to check things out. He has not been to the ninth floor. That is a different crew at the maintenance company, but the structure is the same."

"Scanning equipment?" was Mo's next question.

Ray confirmed, "Top of the line, and yes, I know how to use it." Ray did not want to expose all of Enrique's talents just yet. Perhaps Mo or Chas was involved in the sabotage. He did not believe his suspicions, but taking chances was not one of his options. "Our goal is to find out who is listening. It would be ideal if the person came from within the organization. That would make the exposure easier. I suspect it's a combination of inside and outside. Roof access is needed to determine if there is any unusual equipment up there."

"And how do you propose to find this person?" Chas asked, uncertain about this plan. Mo echoed the question.

"I think I know one person who is either the mole or knows who the mole is. I will need two or three days to verify that. Whatever you are about to ask next, don't. My process will be… creative. You could be culpable if anything goes wrong. I don't think anything will, but you will have complete deniability if it does. Worst case, you can throw me under the bus. That seems to be my pattern anyway."

The alarm bells went off for Chas when he heard that

last statement. He glanced at Mo but saw no concern. He thought it must be some department issue. Ray continued. "If this turns south, you can fire, sue, or whatever. If it goes right, we clean our house. If it goes perfectly, we throw the bad guys under the bus." Ray projected confidence about his strategy even though he had no real plan at this point.

Chas looked at Mo. "I have only worked with Ray closely for a short time, but he is the one who discovered the formula problem. I just found out that he had the answer to fix the Dolphin project, but his input was somehow shut down. He alerted us to Aliton. He is right; we need to confirm if there is a traitor among us. If true, we need to weed them out."

Mo stared at the floor, looking for an answer that might be there. He looked up as if he might have spotted something. "Chas, we have been friends for many years and have fought several battles together. If this goes wrong, you as the CIO will also be thrown under the bus."

"If this goes wrong," Chas responded, "the board will throw all of us under the bus, the train and will bury us at sea."

After weighing his limited options and with some reservations, Mo said, "Okay, we move forward." He checked Ray's reaction as he spoke the words, looking for any hint of regret. He saw nothing that would make him change his mind. "I had my suspicions but was still unsure when I walked in. You don't need to tell us the How, but we will need constant updates on What and Who." All nodded in agreement. Mo started looking at the next steps. "You are going to need more information before moving forward. I don't want you screwing something up while trying to unscrew something else."

Mo handed Ray a folder. The top form was a two-page nondisclosure agreement. Ray read so much that he had become a prolific speed reader. He finished the entire legalese text in record time. He asked three clarification questions. Mo was amazed at Ray's ability to absorb and comprehend the document that fast. Ray signed, and they moved on.

Next was a document titled "Temple III."

Mo started with some background. "About a year ago, a friend of mine advised me that the possibility of rebuilding the third Temple in Jerusalem was gaining momentum. So many Christians vanishing has thrown a wrench in the works since Israel was getting strong Christian support from around the world. The recent attacks from Iran have given Israel leverage at the negotiating table. Israel has put two bargaining chips are on the table. Iran must sign a peace treaty that allows Israel to rebuild the Temple with no interference from them or their proxies. If they do not agree to these stipulations, Isreal, in retaliation for the recent attacks, will destroy every nuclear site and oil refinery."

Ray took a deep breath and slowly exhaled as if blowing out a candle. Looking at Mo, Ray said, "Before you go on, full disclosure on my part is needed. I did some research on you. Your bio shows a PhD in Engineering. An article about you praised your dedication to getting the degree while working full-time and part-time jobs. The Computer Science PhD is also impressive, especially when you consider it only took two years while enlisted as a General in the Israeli Army Corps of Engineers."

Mo smiled. "It definitely was challenging." He was not sure where this was going but listening and discernment were among his many skills. So far, a novice could have found this to be the case.

"I also thought it was courageous of you to lead the Syrian road restoration project. In a gesture of goodwill, as I understand it, the Israeli government rebuilt a road between Israel and Syria that had been previously blown up for security purposes. You could have easily been put in harm's way on that project."

Mo was no longer smiling. Ray's initiative was moving beyond a standard background check. Mo's justification was, "The entire nation of Israel is relentlessly in harm's way every day."

"When I read about the road project," Ray continued in a calm, matter-of-fact tone, "I could see how your computer science skills were needed to place and network the highway safety markers strategically and accurately. I imagine that it took a lot of cooperation from several departments. Your picture with the Transportation Minister, the Foreign Affairs Minister, and the Mossad Director had to have been quite an honor."

Mo became a statue, his penetrating eyes fixed on Ray. Ray could hear Mo's silence shouting, "You should stop now." Ray had concluded that the security monitoring devices were likely embedded in the highway. He also suspected that explosives were buried in the concrete structure. Ray concluded that Mo has contacts beyond 'I have a friend.'

Ray could have continued but shifted the focus instead. The nerve had already been struck. "I also know you have already checked me out. Otherwise, you would not have accepted my offer to help find the mole so quickly. I assume you are aware that my resignations from two previous employers were not genuine. I stepped on too many toes, exposing, let's say, wrongdoing. If you want me to help, all I ask is to see the entire picture. My skill set is solving problems, but I can't solve what I don't know." Chas only knew about Ray from the HR files. The earlier comment about being thrown under the bus now became clear.

Mo decided to hit the ball back into Ray's court. "Yes, I am fully aware of your background, including the tragic loss of your parents and sister in the car accident. I was sorry to read about that." Mo paused before shifting to another sobering point. "The last company where you worked had, and still has, a contract with the Colorado Attorney General's office. It appears you took it on yourself to investigate the prosecutors that were hacking into the various policing authority's systems."

Ray jumped in. "The culprits were providing information to the defense lawyers for people that should have been taken to the desert, shot, and left for vultures to feed on. A drug-related organized crime group was ultimately responsible for the cash payments and, in some cases, blackmail."

"By the way," Mo interjected, "Did they ever catch the vandals that set your car on fire just as you were getting in?" Ray's veiled dialogue signaled to Mo that Ray had skills beyond his position. Mo realized that the conversation would have been straightforward had Chas not been in the room. Mo took that same approach indicating that he knew the fire was not vandalism. Someone tried to kill Ray or at least send a powerful message. He knew Ray needed special skills to find that level of corruption.

Ray's calm response was, "No. Kids these days. What are you going to do?"

Even though Chas thought the two were talking in some unknown code, Ray and Mo were now on the same page. That brief encounter created a valuable connection and added a layer of mutual respect. Chas, on the other hand, did not know either background to that degree. And he had no idea why that conversation had taken place, but he accepted it at face value.

The eye contact confirmed the new partnership. "To answer the question you did not ask, yes, I do want you working on this." Mo flipped to the first page in his binder. He paused for about five seconds, then closed the binder. He looked at Ray with a slight grin. "You are a speed reader with exceptional comprehension ability. I suspect that you can read faster than I can speak. You and Chas can get into the details.

"Here is where we are. My friend in Israel told me that the Abraham Accords are expanding to include just about every Muslim country that has wanted to annihilate Israel. Iran and Israel are the two key roadblocks. The Temple will be the elephant in the room, but Amir Acee has already met with key, high-level Israeli officials. The Temple was on the table.

"Everyone understands that if the issue of the Temple can be resolved, everything the nations seek will fall into place. Tariffs, restricted travel, immigration, and weapons of mass destruction will become unnecessary. Technology, Israel's ace card, will be shared. Mineral deposits are a close second. It is going to take some time to finalize a treaty, but progress has already been made."

Ray was on the edge of his seat. He was hoping that what came next would not disappoint. "I can see your question is, so what?" Ray thought Mo missed that one. It was more like, 'What is next?' "Starting about three years ago, Israel became optimistic that something could be worked out. Israel has been to this dance many times before. The difference is that tangible negotiation progress has been made. This time seems different. Amir Acee, UN's lead negotiator, is using that progress to solidify some other Middle East treaties."

Mo sat back in his chair. "So WIIFM, the famous FM radio station 'What's In It For Me,' comes into play. The answer is: Mimstruct Pro. My friend told me that the field of bidders has narrowed. There are only three pre-qualified companies that will be bidding on the Temple project if and when it launches. One is, and it pains me to say this, a token Israeli company. The company with the winning bid, I was emphatically told, will need to work with this company in some capacity."

The other company bidding, that I am not supposed to know about since bids are closely guarded, is – wait for it – CPS Metrix Technology." Mo looked at Chas, then he turned to Ray. "This conversation is to be kept strictly between us. I will inform Paul that we are investigating a possible problem, but I don't want him involved until we have more information. He needs to stay focused on the Temple project. When I found out CPSM was involved, I put someone from our team to research what we know will be unethical tactics. The information you provided this morning is proof of that."

Ray agreed that only essential information should be shared with Enrique. He added, "You just saved me a great deal of time and energy. I would have eventually figured out that CPSM was behind all the surveillance. My determination to destroy them before they destroy us has just reached a level I cannot explain."

Mo cut Ray off. "I would not necessarily rule CPSM out, but I would also look at who else may benefit from them getting the contract. I know Warren Thorton. He is as crooked as Lombard Street in San Francisco, but not smart enough to pull off sophisticated corporate espionage. He is smart enough to get someone else to intervene.

"Because of the risk factor to pull this off, I have to believe that whoever is behind this is desperate and dangerous." It seemed the room's temperature dropped by 20 degrees as a chill shot through Ray. There was no room for misunderstanding the seriousness of the situation.

Chas jumped in. "It's time to work your magic, Ray. Your challenge is to have something by Monday at 10:00. We will meet the Temple committee at 11:00 a.m. You will need to update us then." Chas handed Ray a business card for the office of Mimtrin's corporate lawyers, Martinelli, Sakowitz, and Martinelli. "Just let the receptionist know you are there for the Mimtrin meeting. One of us will come out to get you."

"One other thing," Mo inserted out of nowhere. "I see you have a Bible on your bookshelf. It is the only non-technical book you have. Can I assume you are a Christian now?"

"Putting it in that context, I can see how easy it is to draw that conclusion. The answer is no. I consider myself a realist." Ray told his story about the Bible. He included the marked passages that he had now memorized, as well as the experience he had in finding Jenny's notes. "That is the extent of my Bible knowledge."

Mo started talking to Chas about Ray as if he were not there. "With Debbie gone and Leticia out, do you think Ray could fill in if needed?" Ray sat quietly while they discussed Ray's strengths and weaknesses. He played along and clarified a few items on the list, even though he had no idea what he would need to do. In the end, Mo concluded, "Looks like you will be the backup for the injured backup. We will be making a presentation to three members of the Temple III selection committee. This meeting will be the last in a series of presentations. We have time to get you ready for whatever role Paul and Chas decide will work best.

"There is one issue that could be a stumbling block. Sounds like your baseline knowledge of the Bible is less than one percent." Mo turned to face Ray directly. "You must understand that the Temple is not just a building for the Jews. It is the embodiment of Jewish spiritual and social life. God's presence is there. It is a place where we mere mortals can connect with the glory of God.

"Even faithful Christians understand the significance of the Temple. Non-believers and some Jews are rapidly becoming believers in Jesus. Others are turning to pseudo-gods. The Jews want their place of worship for the one true God. Prophetically, once the Temple is built, the rightful Messianic Era can begin.

"I am not sure how this Amir character plans to put this treaty together, but we need to be ready if he does. If we get the contract, we will be dealing with Christians and Jews dedicated to what the Temple means. You need to understand their commitment and religious language. You will need to be informed of where both agree and disagree. The most obvious disagreement is about the Messiah. The Jews believe that the Messiah is coming but do not believe that Jesus is the Messiah that was prophesied. The most obvious agreement is that God is the Creator of the universe and all that is in it. The debate about who God is starts in the first sentence in the Bible."

Mo could see that Ray was trying to connect but was

not following. "The very first sentence in the Bible says, *In the beginning, God created the heavens and the Earth.* Both Christians and Jews believe that. In Hebrew, the name for God is Elohim. The 'im' on the end indicates a plural word, but there is no singular version. The plurality specifies that this one God is omnipresent and over any other god.

"Christian scholars interpret Elohim as plural. God, to the Christians, now becomes God the Father, God the Son, and God the Holy Spirit. Research Second Corinthians 13, verse 14, which says, '*May the grace of the Lord Jesus Christ, and the love of God, and the fellowship of the Holy Spirit be with you all.*' That one sentence will get you started. You will need to cross-reference that verse to get a bigger picture. There is so much more to this, but you get the idea."

He noticed that Ray's eyes were starting to glaze over. Mo decided to make a connection to Ray's world. "Let me ask you a question. When you are explaining some technical information to someone who has no clue, how much patience do you have with a person who should at least know the basics?"

Ray said, "Little to none. We are in the 21st Century. They should know something through osmosis alone. Something should sink in by just looking around."

Mo retorted, "Exactly. But your tech world began to evolve when research in the late 1960s led to an early version of the personal computer and workstations in the 70's. Sixty-plus years, and that technology changes daily. Information about the Jewish evolution started in the 9th and possibly the 13th Century BC. Christianity starts in the 1st Century. Neither Christians nor Jews will understand why you have no clue. The New Testament has been written for more than 2,000 years, and the Old Testament more than 4,000 years. None of what was written has changed in all of that time. Even though there is nothing new in the Bible, there is still much to learn."

As Mo was leaving the office, he added, "Just know this: Study that Bible as though you would your tech magazines. We would like your help. Being prepared with biblical knowledge will be vital to your success. When you hear or see information that is inconsistent with your Bible research, know it is false. If information is partially true and partially false, be aware that it is propaganda. Reject non-biblical information and stay committed to the directions the Bible gives you." Mo looked at Ray, nodded, then turned and walked away.

Ray leaned back in his chair, pondering what Mo said. He thought to himself, 'Those were almost the exact words Mr. White Hair told me.'

CHAPTER SIX

Chas stood, disrupting the connection. "Ray, I am not sure what exactly happened here. I have never heard Mo talk about the Bible like that. I also have never seen Mo decide something of this magnitude without sleeping on it. Asking you to attend the meeting on Monday is… unprecedented. So, I guess I'll see you on Monday. Call with any updates before then." They both nodded. Ray watched Chas disappear through the maze of cubicles.

Ray replayed his talk with Enrique and the unexpected meeting with the company's top executives. The realization that he couldn't afford anything less than a perfect plan weighed heavily on his thoughts. Ray had little time to focus on any of these issues. Within minutes of Chas leaving, Ray's phone started ringing. People began lining up outside his office door. He needed to help people work through the chaos and stay focused on their projects.

Ray had just wrapped up his analyst duties for the day. A group of three workers, calling it a day, waved goodbye as they walked by his office. That was another first for Ray. He set the timer on his phone for 10 minutes, giving him time to unwind at the end of the day. The well-deserved minutes of quiet relaxation were customary after those rare days he found himself under some work-related stress. Last Friday seems like an eternity ago when his life was generally uneventful. The toughest decisions included choosing meals, visiting museums, or deciding what to read.

Ray had many acquaintances but no real friends. He would occasionally go on a date if a colleague set him up. A second date would rarely happen. On more than one occasion, he was told by the matchmaker, "Your date liked you. You were the perfect gentleman, but she does not want to date an encyclopedia." Ray realized, with a hint of irony, that he wouldn't want to date himself.

Ray was about 10 minutes into his version of paradise. A gentle knock on the door broke through his trance and dragged him back to reality. Enrique was now the vision when he opened his eyes. "Sorry to bother you, sir. I can come back later if you like." Ray thought an alien had possessed Enrique until he saw the man with a perfectly pressed uniform who probably never emptied his trash at home. Mr. Clean, Ray's assigned name for this guy, was making a concerted effort to be invisible, but it wasn't working.

Playing along with Enrique would be tedious, but it was obvious that Enrique's performance was under review. "I am sorry, what is your name again?" Ray waited for the answer. "Enrique, yes. Do you know what I like? You are always courteous. I have never heard anything negative about the job you do here."

Mr. Clean stepped into the frame. "Good evening, sir." Ray could hardly wait for this play to begin. "My name is Eduardo. At Excellence Maintenance, we take pride in the quality of our work. My job is to make sure our service goals are being met." Ray realized that this play was turning into a tragedy.

"Well, Eduardo ..." Ray hesitated for dramatic effect and gave a backhanded wave toward Enrique as though he had already forgotten his name. He figured taking part in this play wouldn't hurt. "If everyone is like Enrique, you have surpassed your goals. Thanks for checking in." That told Eduardo he could move on.

Ray continued the charade. "Enrique, I will be here a while. If you want to dump this trash that will be all I will need for now." Enrique went to Ray's side of the desk and bent over to retrieve the plastic bag full of papers. "I have news," he whispered. "I will be in touch later."

Ray did not have time to dwell on Enrique's message. The perfect plan was now his focus. Ray went to his library and pulled out five magazines. A windstorm could not have turned the pages any faster. After about four hours of intense research, Ray was looking forward to getting home.

His apartment was on the eighth floor of a twelve-story apartment building. The corner unit was a few hundred more per month, but the view justified the expense. Money was not a significant concern for him. The trucking company involved in the accident that killed his family paid out several million dollars in compensation. The court found the company grossly negligent. They knew the driver was drunk when he left the docks.

Guido Bardolino, a lawyer and longtime family friend from their church, influenced the court's substantial monetary decision. Guido recommended that Ray set up a charitable trust in his parents' name. The church would manage the trust. Guido also happened to chair the finance committee.

Even after setting aside over ten percent for the trust, Ray still had more than enough to live comfortably. No one in Ray's circle of acquaintances would ever guess that was the case. Ray was always frugal except for his little luxuries. He never had to work, but what else was he going to do? His life was good until people vanished.

Where he lives is about a twenty-minute walk from work. At this time of night, the lack of rush-hour traffic would save him about 4 minutes. Ray had tried several routes before finding the most efficient one. The leisurely walk home mentally allowed Ray to wrap up all the tasks and projects from work.

When he arrived home, his routine included time at the workout facility in the building, a quick swim in the lap pool, and then back to his apartment. There, he had a combination steam room and shower installed in the apartment at his expense. He would then have a culinary delight for dinner. He enjoyed cooking dishes from magazines with gourmet recipes. After cleaning up and putting everything in its place, Ray would select one of his technical magazines or head to his computer to research the topic of the week.

The moment everyone vanished, Ray knew that life as he knew it was over. Tonight, he needed to focus on identifying and exposing spies, traitors, moles, or any individuals who could pose a threat. Before embarking on his anti-spy campaign, he thought he would begin researching some information about the Bible. Site after site was down. Ray tried a different search engine. Although he was not completely certain, the last site he found had no evidence of blatant censorship.

He tried using words from the passages that he had memorized. Every time he told the story of how he came into possession of the Bible, it reminded him of each verse. The key search words he used made no direct reference to the Bible. That was a major red flag for this site.

Finally, a search engine came up that would work. Now, where to start? Ray focused on the screen, waiting for divine intervention. After a few clicks here and there, he thought, "This is crazy. How am I ever going to learn all of these rules?" He searched for the keywords 'bible knowledge.' A screen opened titled Luke 11:52. *"Woe to you, experts in the law because you have taken away the key to knowledge. You yourselves have not entered, and you have hindered those who were entering."*

A commentary followed. "Jesus took the blasphemous stance to rebuke the lawyers. Even though the legal experts were familiar with the over 600 laws in the Old Testament, they were blinded by their knowledge. They would interpret the laws for their own gain. In doing so, they missed the realization that Jesus was indeed the Messiah, King of the Jews, fulfiller of prophecy. Their legalistic approach yielded the opposite of what they intended. They were keeping themselves from entering the Kingdom of Heaven. Equally as bad, they were keeping people from accepting the love, hope, and grace that Jesus was teaching."

Then Ray spotted a link to Acts 4:13. *"When they saw the courage of Peter and John and realized that they were unschooled, ordinary men, they were astonished, and they took note that these men had been with Jesus."*

Another commentary followed. "Peter and John were ordinary men. They had no formal education, but they had acquired knowledge from the teachings of Jesus. They learned how to apply and expand the principles of grace to the laws that had been handed down from the days of Moses. Peter and John trusted that the Holy Spirit would give them the wisdom to open people's hearts to the love of Jesus. In turn, the gates of Heaven would be opened for those who came to believe Jesus was indeed their savior. Knowledge and faith were integrated."

Ray saw another link after the word savior. He hovered over the link but stopped. He was beginning to glaze over again, but this time seemed different. Instead of closing his eyes and sticking fingers in his ears while singing "Na-na-na-na-na" to block the sounds in his head, he discovered an interest he never thought he would have.

He would ask himself at the end of each tech magazine article, "What is the takeaway?" Ray set up a new folder on the computer titled Bible. He opened a blank page on his laptop and began typing.

- You don't need to know everything to be a bible scholar.
- Organized religion is like the corporate world. Leaders at the top want money and power. Religious leaders who do not fit that description are no longer present.

To do

- Ask Enrique for help with this project.
- Understand the Bible from a Jewish perspective.
- Understand the Bible from a Christian perspective.
- How can faith and knowledge be integrated?
- Need a plan or outline to learn more.
- Need to prioritize.

Ray's list was more of a memory tool. By reading one line, he would have at least ten action items rise to the surface. He had no patience or time for this list at the moment. He refocused on catching the culprits.

Friday was spent researching the Temple. His logical mind attempted to understand the first and second buildings. By Cross-referencing Bible text, historical documents, and limited online resources, he developed a deep interest in the history of the Temple. Engineering and logistics had to overwhelm the project. Even though Ray understood what Mo explained regarding the relevance of the Temple, he still could not comprehend how one building could trigger a Middle East war.

Saturday morning, Ray arrived two minutes early. Enrique was waiting by the employee entrance. At his feet were two bags. One was about the size of a carry-on bag for an airplane's overhead compartment. The other was a tool bag. He was holding a leather notebook with a hand-stitched custom trim. Enrique was ready.

Ray only had his laptop secured in his computer bag. From a distance, he almost did not recognize Enrique. No uniform was on today. As Ray approached, he noticed Enrique's shirt with the logo 'Industrial Electric Services.' Ray wanted to laugh out loud as he thought, Enrique is in character today.

"Looks like you are ready," Ray quipped.

"Yes, sir, ready to go." Ray could feel a contagious motivation in Enrique. "So, my update. Due to the disappearance, several new hires have been made at the maintenance company. I recognized one of the new employees from the Mexican Army, Captain Arturo Guitierez. I was introduced to him by my commanding officer after I reported the fraudulent activity related to the road extension project at the army base. This guy would sell his mother for the right price."

"What was his job?" Ray asked.

"That is the interesting part. Guitierez was in the Mexican Army Corps of Engineers. Typically, this division builds roads, bridges, and buildings to support strategic and logistical ground operations. They also had their own tech group. Gutierrez oversaw the tech company contracted by the army that designed electronics under the guise of safety and security. Metal detectors in various forms enhanced security. Handheld wands the size of a cell phone and discreetly integrated detectors in doorway frames could detect a metal object as small as a dime. Undetectable security cameras, night vision equipment, and other advanced technologies were being designed or enhanced.

"Gutierrez pushed to establish a subgroup of micro cameras and listening devices. The company would send the hardware to the division I was in. We would write the software that enabled transmissions between different pieces of equipment.

"As we developed the software, he personally oversaw testing. He would bribe someone on our team to feed him the code once he was satisfied. Gutierrez got caught selling technology developed by this specialized team to a security company that just happened to be owned by his brother. His brother, in turn, would sell the technology in the U.S. and Europe, where he could get the best price. Ironically, he got caught by the Intelligence Division using the equipment he had created.

Gutierrez, his brother, and their families had an exit strategy. They fled the country before the DNI could use their interrogation techniques to extract information. The rumors were that they had bank accounts in multiple countries. I am sure the DNI would love to know he is here."

Ray was a bit anxious. "Did he see you?"

"Yes. That's the good news. He walked right by without seeming to recognize me. But then again, I had no direct contact with him during any of the tests. I only met him twice. Both meetings with him were brief."

Skeptical thinking cut off Ray's abbreviated sigh of relief. "Let's assume that he did recognize you and just did not show it. Let's avoid him for now. It would, however, be nice to know what he is doing here. He's obviously not a maintenance worker."

Security cameras were off as planned. Ray and Enrique went to work. They started on the ninth floor. They found four holes. The sensing equipment detected three cameras tracking Mo, CEO, and Chas, CIO, as well as the executive conference room. Paul, the President, had the hole, but the equipment did not register any signals. They removed the tile in Paul's office and found the camera. Some insulation had fallen from the HVAC duct immediately above the camera. The wires had come loose, so there was no signal to detect. Enrique noted that camera placement would have been an amateur's mistake.

That camera was a significant break. The two now had a manufacturer and model of the equipment. The fact that no one had come to retrieve or repair the failed equipment was another piece of good news. Although they could not rule anything out, the assumption was that the equipment installation worked as intended. Then again, Captain Gutierrez might be here as the fixer.

Ray typically thought out loud, and this was no exception. "It is unusual that the only chunk of foam insulation that fell was right above the camera. A lucky coincidence?" Mr. White Hair's words kept haunting him about coincidences, not always being just coincidences.

Enrique's audio microphone scanner had a unique feature. Before the scan started, a jamming signal would create static. The phone app was iffy, but this equipment was failsafe. If anyone were listening, they would not be able to pick up any clear conversation or sounds. Three offices and the main conference room had listening devices installed in the smoke detectors.

"These guys are good, but they are not real pros. A real pro would have replaced the entire smoke detector with a prewired listening device and camera." The jammer was on, so he knew no one would hear anything. "Ray, I have an idea. I am going to the middle of the room over by the cubicle where that red thing is sticking out. I want you to close this door and hit the test button on the smoke alarm." Enrique took the sensing equipment, calibrated it, and gave Ray the signal to go. Ray was getting used to this play-along concept.

The alarm screeched on for about five seconds. When the office door opened, Enrique waved Ray over. "I thought I picked up something from the coat closet. Go try it again from a different office." Ray moved to the conference room. This time, Enrique was standing next to the closet. He had completely opened the sliding door. He signaled for the test button again. There it was.

By the time Ray reached the closet, Enrique had a coat in his hand. It was still on the hanger. Enrique patted the coat down slowly and carefully. "Come to me, my little friend," Enrique quipped. He found the piece of equipment that relayed the conversations.

Ray was glad that security had turned off the roof cameras. Exploring that location was next on the list. They began the search at the nearest proximity to the closet. "Ray, over there. See that cone. It's a V-O-R." Ray thought he knew every technical term in the book. Enrique could see Ray searching his memory bank. "It stands for Very High Frequency Omnidirectional Range. It is used in aviation for guidance. The technology has been adapted as an alternative to small satellite dishes. This cone can transmit to someone who has a receiver tuned to the exact frequency. Basically, it is a mini-Wi-Fi dish with private access."

Ray jumped in. "I read something about this, but I don't remember it being called a V-O-R. The problem, if I recall, was that any amateur audiophile could accidentally hit the same frequency and listen in. The advantage was that someone knowing the right frequency could connect within a two-mile radius. One day they listen from location A and the following day from B, protecting their identity."

Enrique just laughed. "How do you just know stuff? I am starting to think you are an AI Bot."

"Busted." Ray joked. "But if you tell anyone, laser beams will come out of my eyes and kill you." The smile on Enrique's face quickly disappeared when Ray said, "This is too dangerous to leave open." Ray refocused on the cone.

Enrique responded instantly. "I have an idea. We only disconnect the unit. Since one of the cameras stopped inside, whoever is behind this might think it is another equipment failure. This one, they will not want to let go. You will alert security to remain vigilant to any activity on the roof. They need to keep one camera pointed at the cone. When someone shows up to fix it, we will have them."

"Can you describe this captain for me? I will have security watch for anyone poking around the equipment and let them know to be on high alert if they spot Gutierrez."

Enrique responded with a smile. "This is a first. I am

one step ahead of you. I just texted you the picture taken when Guitierrez got the promotion to captain. It is a few years old, but it's close enough to identify him." Ray's expression of curiosity was on full display. "I have saved several just-in-case files."

The two scanned the seventh floor. Leticia, Debbie, Chen, and the conference room had audio equipment. Besides Ray, only Debbie and Leticia had both audio and video equipment. Debbie was not a concern because she had disappeared. Ray thought that someone would eventually come back to move or remove that equipment.

They repeated the smoke alarm test. Ray was thinking that whoever was doing this would not be stupid enough to put a transmitter in a coat as they did on the ninth floor. But after the first alarm test, Ray knew that they were indeed that stupid. There was a receiver/transmitter in the lining of a coat in the closet on the seventh floor. Brilliant planning and terrible execution, Ray thought.

Ray returned to security to let them know to restart operations. Jolie Lange, the head of security, arrived on Saturday to oversee this project. She also wanted to thank Ray personally for the heads-up about a potential bug. Protocols related to vendors were now being reviewed and tightened.

Jolie was a retired, high-ranking Secret Service Officer. Her assignment was to protect the U.S. ambassadors to the United Nations. Knowing her counterparts working for the other country's UN delegates was essential. She was well respected inside the Secret Service. Internationally, she had a reputation for learning about an attack before the attackers knew the plans. No one knew how she did it, and no one asked.

Jolie took her job seriously. When Chas asked Jolie to

shut down the security system, she bluntly told him that he did not have the authority to turn off surveillance. Chas was amazed to see that Jolie had Mo's private number on the speed dial. After a minute's conversation, she confirmed that she would implement the plan. With a most indignant tone, she said, "No one hacks my system. Remember that for future reference."

When Ray advised the Security team to resume the standard surveillance, the guard asked Ray to wait in Jolie's office until she arrived. She was on her way. The change in plans was unexpected, but Ray wanted to thank Jolie for her cooperation. As Ray waited, he scanned every picture, award, degree, and certification. Ray was impressed.

Ray had forwarded the picture of Guiterrez to his contact in security and cc'd Chief Lange. Once he knew security received the pictures, Ray filled in the missing details as best he could. He was confident that Jolie's team had a backup plan and probably already had what they needed, but he briefed the guard as best he could.

When Jolie arrived, she quietly watched as Ray mentally photographed everything on the walls and shelves. "Find anything interesting?" Ray turned to see a woman standing just inside the door. Ray could tell she was an absolute professional by her attire and direct approach.

"Interesting is a relative term, but I do see evidence of a true professional. Ray was his unfiltered self. Jolie could tell Ray was sincere and not just sucking up.

"What exactly do you see that makes you think that?" Jolie would use that type of question to expose people who were making things up.

Without hesitation, Ray replied, "You are here on Saturday in a uniform that is not meant to look like a uniform."

She controlled her expressions, but Ray noticed she blinked. "The small bump in your slacks at the ankle tells me there is a weapon there." No reaction. "There are no pictures of your family or any other personal items. The few certifications on the wall are not ego driven. They are strategically placed so anyone sitting across from you will see them. It's a statement. Your awards for heroism and achievements are grouped. I am sure there are more, but these are meaningful in some way."

By now, Jolie was sitting behind her desk. She made the mistake of asking if there was anything else. She was intrigued. Ray seamlessly picked up where he had left off. "You are direct, blunt, and to the point. You are solutions-oriented but not without considering options. You have a perfectionistic side. You may not be a great orator, but you can persuade effectively through logic and facts. You are an intellect, but very few people would know that because you effectively protect what you know."

Ray was watching Jolie with every word. He was looking for any reaction. "Five quick things. One, you know I am right, but you are not going to acknowledge that. Two, that abstract piece of art is one of two non-business-related items. Three, there is a camera and probably a microphone behind that picture. Four, the Bible on your shelf is tucked in the corner, which is another discussion all together. It is the only non-legal related book. Five, the answer to how I know is that I have no personal life and read a lot. Learning to read people was one of my obsessions for a while."

Jolie knew to stop asking questions, but she could not help smiling. Both Mo and Chas had told her that Ray had unique skill sets. Ray was correct, but she would not confirm or deny anything he said. She just directed Ray to update her on what was going on. Since Jolie had Mo's direct contact number, he believed she could be trusted.

Ray told her he had ideas for exposing anyone inside and causing grief for anyone on the outside who was hacking. Today, he was assessing his current situation to decide his next steps. As they wrapped up the conversation, Ray added, as he was leaving, " When you call Mo as soon as I leave, please tell him that I will have an update Monday." Jolie consciously tried to control her laugh as Ray closed her office door.

Ray's office was Enrique's rendezvous point. Professional equipment ensured the phone app captured everything in Ray's office. All was clean. They were free to talk. Ray wanted to get Enrique out of the office just in case there were unexpected visitors. Grabbing a bite to eat checked that box. Ray's lunch haven was unrecognizable. They picked up a sandwich at a new gourmet food truck. Ray's bench was empty, as was most of the park. Ray taught Enrique how to use the environmentally safe paper bag as a tablecloth. The two brainstormed idea after idea. They kept narrowing and fine-tuning possibilities. Ray noticed that the park was becoming occupied by less-than-scrupulous individuals. He suggested they go back to his apartment.

They continued to discuss and adjust as they moved at a quickened pace. They could not stop brainstorming as they entered the building, took the elevator, and strolled down the hall to Ray's place. Ray noticed packages outside his neighbor's door. Ray told Enrique the story about meeting his new neighbor. One of Ray's comments was, "I would have testified in court that it was you." "I thought you must have won the lottery or something to that effect."

Ray opened the door to his apartment. He explained

to Enrique that he needed to get the key to put the packages inside the neighbor's apartment. "I forgot to tell you another coincidence. Not only do you look alike, but you also have the same Martinez name. Maybe it is some distant relative of yours," Ray said jokingly.

In jest, Enrique piled on, "Let me help with the packages. Maybe I will find a long-lost relative in one of the boxes."

Ray knocked, but there was no answer. He opened the door, entered the apartment, and scanned for a suitable space to place the boxes. Elias had already started to unpack. Dishes, glasses, and cookware were covering the kitchen counters. Ray could see into the bedroom where piles of clothes covered the bed. Books lined the shelves, boxes of pictures were arranged in the corner, and a dining table converted into a makeshift desk led Ray to realize this was organized chaos.

As they placed the last box out of the flow of traffic, Enrique looked around the room. There was a lone picture on the bookshelf that caught his eye. He could not look away.

"Ray, do you know your neighbor's first name?" It was fortunate that Enrique was standing next to a large sofa because as soon as Ray said, 'Elias,' Enrique's knees weakened, and he fell backward. He landed partially on the padded arm of the sofa, causing him to roll over onto his side. Ray rushed to help. Enrique's hand was cold and moist. Ray helped him to an upright position.

"What is it? Are you okay?" Ray knew the second question was stupid, but it was built into everyone's DNA to ask it. Ray's voice reflected a slight panic.

"That picture." He pointed to the bookshelf. "Can you bring me that picture?"

Ray rushed to retrieve the apparent stimulus for Enrique's collapse. The small, carefully framed picture was clearly significant. Enrique grasped the picture in both hands and held it as if his life depended on it. He pulled the picture to his chest as tears flooded from his eyes.

Ray had no idea what to do. Handling emotion was his Achilles heel. He waited as long as he could. "Enrique, what is it?"

Enrique released one hand from the picture to wipe away the tears. He switched the picture to the other hand to repeat the process, but the picture always stayed in his grasp. Enrique slowly reclined with the picture back on his chest.

"This is my family. Ray, Elias is my brother." Enrique turned the picture around to show Ray a photo of two young boys standing in front of their parents, posing for the camera. The picture had obvious signs of wear and tear.

Out of nowhere, Enrique asked, "Do you have his number? I am going to call him right now." Enrique had to release the picture, but Brinks Security could not have protected it better. Ray opened his contact list and slowly read the number, pausing with the dashes. Enrique's hands shook. It was an effort to enter each number.

There was great expectation as the sound of a phone ringing filled the room. It was like a choreographed move as they both turned toward the bedroom. The ringtone brought back childhood memories of the sole large black rotary-dial phone in the hallway. Enrique was in the bedroom first. The ringing stopped.

Enrique immediately hit redial. Bells started filling the room. The light from the screen filtered through the sleeve of a shirt sprawled on the bed. He threw the shirt out of the way. The message displayed Enrique's number on the screen. Enrique sat on the bed with total disregard for the layers of clothes. The ringing stopped.

Even though Ray was not good with emotions, he could see Enrique cycling through every passionate feeling. Enrique bowed his head. Ray could hear some indistinguishable whispers. He slowly looked directly at Ray. In a tone of consolation, he said, "Jesus lifted Elias to his place in Heaven."

More tears trickled off his cheeks and onto his shirt. There was no immediate effort to wipe them away. "The minute I realized the rapture had taken place, I asked Jesus to forgive me for my doubt, my rejection of His existence, and for my anger. My faith tells me He has forgiven me. I have not been in contact with my brother since the day of our separation. But I know we will meet again soon."

Ray was amazed at the comfort and peace Enrique projected as the remnants of his tears dried. Even though the disappointment was still harsh and blatantly evident, Enrique appeared to have made a miraculous recovery. Enrique picked up the picture and walked toward Ray without looking up. As he showed Ray, his narrative explained the picture's setting. Enrique strolled down memory lane with every inch. The detail was down to the tree in the background. He and his brother climbed the sprawling Sycamore in total disregard for their mother's directive to stay out of the tree.

Ray just let him vent. He knew that Enrique was really talking to his brother, sharing one story after another. A comprehensive family biography could have been composed from this worn yet beautiful picture. Enrique finally let out a long sigh and returned to the sofa, finding the perfect spot to unwind.

Ray calmly said, "I am going to my place to start working on some of the ideas we discussed. You're welcome to come over when you're ready. The door will be unlocked." Ray placed the key Elias gave him on the kitchen counter. "Why don't you stay here tonight?" Ray left and gently closed the door.

Before Ray inserted the key into his lock, his logical, solutions-oriented mind engaged. The pinball effect kicked in with ideas bouncing back and forth between the right and left brain. Mr. White Hair's words sprang into his mind one more time because this was way beyond coincidence. How is this possible? Elias had an excellent position with the publisher in Mexico. Elias's company announced the promotion about 2 weeks ago. The timing for wrapping up his current job, preparing for the new job, and organizing the move had to have been done at the speed of light.

And what are the odds that Elias got this apartment? As far as Ray knew, there was a waiting list. The manager is meticulous in interviewing and vetting each potential resident. Elias must have had a video conference. Maybe his company had some influence. Who knows?

Thoughts continued to race in his head. "There is something else in play, or this is one amazing coincidence. If God exists…" Ray interrupted his thought process. He could not imagine ever thinking that God might exist. For Ray, since the accident that killed his family, there was no God, or at least no God worth worshiping.

To follow a logical trail, Ray considered that a higher power must be involved. Ray picked up his self-talk where he left off. "If God exists and He made this happen, He must be some planner. The brothers would have had to follow specific paths over the course of decades for their lives and careers to intersect.

"But if that is the case, why didn't God just let them reunite? And why, of all people, would God put me in the middle of this craziness?" Ray started to ask himself another question but stopped. These questions, without logical answers, could go on forever. He thought out loud, "I wish I had gotten Mr. White Hair's real name and number. He has some explaining to do."

Ray refocused, and speculative revelations began to flow. We may be able to keep Elias alive. Ray could work in buckets efficiently. He preferred the word 'silo' instead of 'bucket' because he could store significantly more in a silo. One project did not interfere with another. Focus was the key. The problem was that this God bucket kept overflowing. The thoughts, speculations, and even the rare, deep feelings of emotion kept flowing into the other buckets.

Ray sat in front of his computer that was loaded and ready for action. His mind started coaching. 'Focus Ray! Deep breath. Again, deep breath. Bad Guys. Revenge.' After more self-encouragements, Ray began to let his fingers glide across the keyboard. Code started filling the page. The more he typed, the more confident he became that this idea might work.

He finished and returned to line one, slowing down to consider the what-ifs. After implementing changes, Ray prioritized a new set of options. More changes and one more review gave Ray the confidence to move to the next silo.

The next area of focus was the antithesis of the first. He talked this one out with the computer screen. He took on the role of the bad guy. "How might Ray discover this bug? How would he find it? How would he debug?" Some of the answers forced Ray back to square one for more adjustments. Ray kept reminding himself that this needs to be perfect.

Ray moved to his recliner where he could relax and let his mind organize all his thoughts. This move usually led to questions, possibilities, and solutions. He had lost all track of time. Mentally and physically exhausted, Ray leaned back to recline fully. He thought, "I should rest for a bit." His eyes closed. In the background, the screen saver turned black. Ray's mind emptied. He slept.

CHAPTER SEVEN

It was early Sunday morning. The fog of a dream state had lifted enough for Ray to realize he had spent the night in the recliner. He pressed a button just below the chair's arm and groggily said, "Upright." The chair obeyed and slowly retracted the leg rest while lifting the back to the perpendicular position.

The hinges on his front door desperately needed some lubrication. The irritating, high-pitched squeak pierced the room as the door opened. Ray was still in that state between sleep and the reality of the conscious world. He turned toward the door to see Enrique with a laptop in hand. "I knocked," he said in a way that stated it was Ray's fault that he just walked in. "Interesting thing about a door lock, you need to turn this little knob to make it work."

After the usual greetings and a generic observation of the sunrise angling through the glass doors leading to the balcony, Ray headed for the kitchen. The culinary area was separated from the living room by a long countertop lined with four swivel stools. "Coffee?" That was a definite yes for Enrique as Ray approached the coffee maker that any barista would envy. "What would you like? I can make… Enrique interrupted. A simple cup of strong, black coffee was all he wanted.

Ray slid the cup across the countertop while kidding Enrique about his lack of creativity when it came to the finer attributes of coffee. Enrique watched Ray push three different buttons, causing the machine to grind, gurgle, and begin blending coffee with the previously poured cream. Ray directed Enrique to the freezer. The top shelf featured custom-prepared gourmet breakfast selections prepared by a high-end restaurant. Ray told him to pick one out as he pointed out the microwave-oven combo that required an advanced degree to operate.

Ray placed three oranges in the automated juicer that began to hum and whirl. Enrique watched as juice and pulp flowed into a serving container. The orange peels dropped onto a lid that plopped open and snapped shut. Ray casually handed Enrique the glass of freshly squeezed juice. They sat at the table on the balcony, enjoying the food and the view. As they cleaned up, Ray finally had to ask how Enrique's evening went.

"First, thanks for suggesting that I stay there. I…uh, it was… It's hard to explain. There were more pictures. Not a lot but enough to give me insight into my brother's life. Elias was a good brother in the short time we were together. He had his ups and downs from what I could tell. Overall, it looked like his life was good. I regret that we were never able to have a family relationship. But, before long, we will reunite and have eternity to catch up."

Enrique made a slight turn in his story. "I also had a good talk with Jesus. You came up in the conversation. I know you think this is nuts, but I appreciate that you, unlike others, do not try to make me question what I believe. I am now at total peace with everything." Ray could not control a quick look of skepticism, but he was truly curious about where this was going.

"You were telling me yesterday about the Temple III project. I can tell you the Bible indicates that the Temple will be rebuilt." Ray interrupted and asked if there was anything in there about Mimtrin getting the contract. Enrique rubbed his eyes, shook his head, and grinned. "That comment makes it clear you need a biblical foundation right away. I asked the Holy Spirit to help me with that. I can already hear your next question: 'What did He say?' He could talk directly to me if He wanted, but that is not generally how it works. The Holy Spirit is the Helper that protects and guides us. He did help me pick out four books from Elias' library. I set them aside. We'll get them later." Ray wanted to ask, "Holy Spirit Librarian?" But instead nodded to acknowledge Enrique's efforts.

Ray confessed his failed attempts to learn something about the Bible. "I tried to do some research online. I typed in 'bible knowledge' and got an interesting result. But then the first verse referenced another verse that clarified part of the first verse but the information in the second verse needed clarification from a third verse… I just stopped. I did make a couple of helpful notes, but that was about it. This is more complex than I imagined. I need some quick basics and a plan of attack."

Enrique empathetically said, "Once you have a foundation your research will go from frustration to fascination." Before Enrique could continue, Ray shifted him away from any God or Bible-speak. They moved inside to the dining room table.

"I am looking forward to that talk, but now we need our plan of attack. I worked on an idea and played with some coding. I want to see what you think." Ray opened a file. Then, he shared his screen with Enrique. "Here's the concept. I will take Debbie's computer offline. You can insert this code since you know the spyware program already installed. When anyone opens the sharing program, their computer will power down. That person will need to call the IT help desk to get it fixed. I will tell IT that I have read about a trending upgrade glitch that shuts down computers. The story will be that I helped a friend with a fix. That would be you. If anyone calls for that problem, the help desk people will call me."

Enrique was multi-tasking. He was focused on the code and listening to Ray at the same time. It took him no time at all to grasp the plan. Ray asked, "So what could go wrong?" If an Olympic sport called Synchronized Programming existed, these two would have won the gold medal. Two hours had passed before the bantering stopped and the keyboards silenced.

Enrique asked, "How can we test this?" Ray sprung out of his chair and motioned for Enrique to follow. They went into the guest bedroom. Enrique smiled. "A minimalist would love this room. A tall, empty bookshelf on top of a storage drawer, nothing on the walls, and no other furniture."

Without saying a word, Ray moved toward the door. A remote control with a 6-by-8-inch screen was situated in a holder as an extension of the light switch. Ray took it out and tapped three icons. Two concealed six-inch-wide doors on either side of the bookshelf opened in tandem. Two rails, the full length of the bookshelf, slowly tipped forward. Legs extended from the rails, locking in place just before touching the floor.

A shelf from the storage area emerged and made its way

to the end of the rail. Three additional shelves followed and were locked in place. With the muffled sound of hydraulics, the bookshelf began to lower. Enrique instinctively reached for falling books, but felt foolish when he realized the books were a permanently attached facade. The mattress on the back of the shelves sat securely on the top of the shelves. Enrique sprawled out on the double bed and observed, "This is dangerous. Guests might not want to leave."

Appearing not to be overly impressed, Enrique sat up. He said, "When I lived with my uncle for a while, we had something like this. The difference was that my room was in a storage area. The mattress took up most of the floor space. During the day, we would prop the mattress against the wall and hold it there with ropes. The same concept when you think about it." Even though both laughed, Ray felt a slight pang of sadness but had no idea how to respond.

Without a word, Ray worked the remote again. The ceiling fan started a slow cycle, moving the air ever so slightly. Then pictures started to appear on the wall. Above the fan were small projectors. Ray's system featured exceptional masterpieces and was capable of displaying modern works, abstract pieces, portraits, or any genre of art requested by guests. Without a word, Ray tapped the remote a few more times. As he replaced the remote in its holder, everything reverted to the original position. Enrique surrendered. "You are a complete anomaly. I am still trying to figure out who you are."

"When you do, can you let me know?" Ray said it as a joke, and they both laughed, but Enrique sensed the request was genuine. Ray slid the left closet door to the right exposing a built-in unit of drawers and shelves. Laptops, Macs, and iPads lined up on one of the shelves. One monitor and two towers were on the floor. Ray grabbed one of the laptops.

More curious than amazed, Enrique asked, "Are all of these your old computers?"

Ray explained that this was one of his hobbies. He does business with a locally owned computer retail and repair shop, DigiWorld. When a customer wishes to upgrade to a more advanced model, George, the store owner, provides a service. He takes the old computer, securely erases all data, and delivers it to a recycling center for proper disposal. Ray saves computers from the store's digital morgue. He would operate to revive them. Some he could bring back to life and others just did not survive. For Ray, the effort combined relaxation and knowledge. Revived computers would be donated to schools on a tight budget in the store's name. The computers in his closet are alive but have not yet found a happy home.

Ray pulled a laptop from the shelf. He retrieved a charger from the drawer and headed to the dining room, which turned into a conference room as soon as they sat down. "This computer will be close enough to mimic anything at the office. Let's load everything we need and test what we have." The glitches were insignificant and easy to adjust. After only three attempts, everything worked as planned in the controlled environment. They were ready.

Ray drove to the office for phase two of the test. He was anxious to load Debbie's computer. Back at the office, he knew the security cameras would see him going into Debbie's office, but the story of managing her projects still seemed to work. Once he was done loading, he called Enrique. The remote test was ready to launch. They decided to use a clean PC on Enrique's side to avoid contamination from the previous trials.

Ray called Enrique to have him activate his side. When Enrique was ready, Ray started Debbie's computer. He had disabled her computer from the company's server and used his personal hotspot to avoid the company Wi-Fi. "I have the alert. I am going in," Enrique reported that his computer was in share mode.

Ray kept waiting for the happy-dance news. Nothing. Ray could hear the fan on Enrique's computer, but there was no communication. Ray listened to the keyboard. Nothing yet. "Okay, I am back in. You must have lost the signal." Ray looked, but there was only one bar on his phone.

"Go ahead and abort. I will see if I can find the login to the backup company server. I really hate to do that, but our options are limited." Again silence. "Enrique are you there?"

"No need to abort. My computer just shut down. The eagle has landed." Enrique thought they were ready to implement the plan, but Ray put a damper on that idea.

"Put everything to zero. Let's try it again. I just picked up another Wi-Fi. It's a strong signal, and I think I know where it is. Ah yes, Leticia's office. Stay on the line." Enrique put his phone on the table with the speaker on. He could tell Ray was on the move. He easily detected the sounds of drawers opening and closing.

He heard Ray murmuring undefinable words. Then Enrique heard, "There you are. Now, how do I find the door that opens this little tower of electronic wonders?" Ray had been looking for a box-shaped modem. He found a round tower modem that had been decorated as an achievement award. Enrique could hear Ray's shoes clomping on the floor in a quick cadence. The familiar clicking of the keyboard filled the gaps of silence. The last click was not just a keyboard tap. The sound resonated when Ray struck the last key emphatically. "I am glad Leticia did not take my advice to have random passwords."

Debbie was now connected to Leticia's Wi-Fi. A second test was performed after the computers were in their original settings. There was no delay this time. Enrique's laptop shut down as soon as he tried to worm his way in. Even though everything worked as planned, Ray wanted one more trial.

He headed back to the apartment. This time, he wanted to be home to see the grand plan at work. Satisfied they were on track, the two returned to the office.

They loaded the shutdown code in each computer that had been set up with the shareware. Ray sighed and asked, "Once I know who it is, then what?" After a deep inhale and slow, blowing exhale, he conceded, "I won't be able to answer that question until I know who this menace is."

From his office, Ray called Chas, who had just entered the building. He was on his way to his office to prepare for tomorrow's meeting. Ray updated Chas on the surveillance equipment and transmitters. The meeting highlights with Jolie Lange in Security were covered quickly.

Ray began to focus on the plan. "You should advise your staff that there is a computer upgrade glitch that will shut down a computer. It just turns the computer off but does not affect the computer itself. Let your people know that I researched the problem and know how to fix it. If it happens to anyone, have them call me. You need to give to the IT help desk that same story – they call me."

Chas started to ask a question, but Ray cut him off. "I will fill you in tomorrow at the meeting. I will only need about fifteen minutes unless you have questions, then it takes the time it takes." Ray shifted gears. "Who is responsible for hiring the maintenance company?" Ray wanted to know everything he could about that selection process. Chas had no idea but gave Ray the name of the Director of Operations, Dominic Sanders. That was enough to start a background check. Ray was looking for any connection between an inside employee and CPS Metrix Technology.

Ray wanted to wrap up this conversation. His to-do list was getting longer. "We will need to discuss the next moves. I have some ideas, but Mo doesn't want me screwing up one thing while unscrewing something else. I will update Mo and Paul later tonight. I will be in touch with anything urgent but, for now, we just need to wait."

After a slight pause, Chas added, "It seems like you worked your magic."

Once the call concluded, Ray checked the time. Mid-morning on a Sunday was normally set aside for relaxing and starting a new book. Since the word 'normal' seemed to have been erased from the dictionary, Ray and Enrique returned to the apartment to reassess their options.

Enrique had already started on an idea to slow the enemy's advances. Ray had a different priority for now and interrupted Enrique's work. "I have this meeting tomorrow and have no idea what it is or why I need to be there. What I do know is that I need some Bible basics." Enrique was glad to oblige and saved his work. "Let's go across the hall. Elias has books and materials there that I know will help."

Ray was amazed at how orderly the apartment was. Enrique had put the unpacked things away. Every box of brochures, handouts, and pamphlets had been opened and stacked by category in the living room area. The built-in bookshelves were lined with books and magazines published by Elias' company. Audio and video CDs were placed on the narrow shelves on either side of the larger shelves. It appeared as though pillars were holding the whole structure together. Only Dewey Decimal labels were missing.

The dining room table was covered with flyers, brochures, and pamphlets. There were booklets of assorted colors, but they all started with the heading 'Study Guide.' Enrique took the makeshift classroom over. "We can start with some basics. A structured approach will help eliminate confusion. Asking anything at any time, as you tend to do, is out. I am not a Bible expert, but I have successfully debated many theologians over the years. My mother made sure we studied at least once a day, and I mean every day. When I look back, I am amazed that nothing triggered the slightest desire for me to accept the spiritual side.

"My mother did not just teach the content; she taught us how to research. My missionary mother would tell us: 'This is what the Bible says, and I am telling you what it means based on my knowledge and the inspiration of the Holy Spirit. You will hear other opinions, and when you do, research to make sure the view is biblically based. Grow with what is and run from what isn't.' I would suggest you heed my mother's advice.

"I will follow in my mother's footsteps and give you what the Bible says. I will add my commentary based on what I have read and studied. Comments will also be based on what I believe and know. But mine is one opinion. About eighty percent of my knowledge was from my mother and the Bible study classes I was forced to attend. Reading and preparing to debate my college friends on biblical principles built on the foundation that had been laid. Now that I have Jesus in my life, I am seeing everything I learned from a completely different angle. I have a clarity that… It's hard to describe. Maybe one day the same will happen to you."

Enrique pointed to the dining room table. "See those materials. I scanned each as I was organizing. From one of the many piles, he extracted a four-page brochure titled 'Introduction to the Bible.' The design looked like a Sunday School handout that Elias's company would have sold to churches or study groups. Enrique just followed the flow. "This is for someone like you who wants an introduction to and basic knowledge about the Bible. I will give you more like this as we go. You will need to focus on these rather than your usual tech research. You will probably have tech withdrawals, but sticking with the plan will get you ready."

Before Ray could comment or question, Enrique started talking. Ray saw a man on a mission. "The Bible is divided in two distinct sections: The Old and New Testament. Imagine a book of sixty-six short stories written by forty different authors. Inside each book there are chapters and verses that are numbered making it easy to find the appropriate reference."

Ray, proud of his minuscule knowledge, said, "First Thessalonians 4, verse 16. The first book of Thessalonians, the fourth chapter, and the sixteenth verse. Believe me, I'll never forget that one."

Enrique was pleasantly surprised. He jumped forward. "Each book has its own set of information, but, as we will see later, the words in one book will relate to text in another book or several other books. These connections are designed to clarify, qualify, expand on text from one book to the other. As a bonus, the cross references provide proof that the Bible is true and accurate."

Ray jumped in. "That is what happened to me when I tried to search 'Bible Knowledge.' A reference led me to other passages that had their own set of references. I didn't know if I was coming or going."

"That is because every word, every jot and tittle, is meaningful, connected and accurate." Enrique saw a question on Ray's face. "From the beginning, when God's words were recorded on scrolls, every page copied needed to be exact and complete down to each jot, which is the smallest letter or stroke of any writing. When pages of a scroll were copied, if one letter was wrong when it was proofread, the pages would be destroyed. Sometimes a 10-meter scroll would be destroyed. The copy began over from word one."

"I guess that is why God gave us spell check," Ray said with a small laugh.

"Yeah. Papyrus paper was the major technological breakthrough back then." Enrique shifted from the outline. "As a preview we are now in a time when Jesus opens a scroll in Heaven. We are about to feel God's judgements as written in that scroll. These times were disclosed in several books of the Bible over thousands of years. Verses in Revelation easily connect to verses in Daniel, Ezekiel, Isaiah and other prophets."

Enrique stayed on track. "Back to the Bible. There are a total of sixty-six books. The Old Testament has 39, and the New Testament has 27. In that brochure I gave you, the books are listed in a table.

"The Old Testament starts at the birth of everything in the universe. The New Testament starts with the birth of Jesus. It continues with His life, death, and resurrection. The last book of the Bible is Revelation which describes all the events that leads to the next birth of a new earth. So, the

Bible starts with the first creation and ends with the next creation of a new heaven and earth."

Ray's brain was working overtime. His sarcastic question was, "So, all of this chaos is the new earth?"

Enrique was glad for the challenge. It gave him hope that Ray was engaged. "Almost. This is just the start. Come over here." They went to the balcony. "See that construction site over there. That new building concept drove the Zoning Commission a little crazy. In my other job, I delivered countless legal documents to developers and learned a lot I should not have known. Corruption is a daily activity. It is promoted to be the most striking landmark in the LA metro area. There will be retail, restaurants, offices, condominiums for purchase, long-term rental units, and time-share units that can also be used as luxury hotel rooms. All in one place." Enrique pointed to where an old, condemned building was being torn down. "What does that look like to you?"

Ray smiled. "I get it. Good point. It looks like chaos. Chaos that will become a thing of beauty."

Enrique continued, "But we have not yet begun to see the madness that is coming. Turmoil will not come close to describing Satan's evil and God's judgements on evil. I know you don't understand this right now. I don't understand as much as I would like to. There are still millions on earth that think the same way you do about the Bible, Christianity, and Judaism. Everyone still has a chance to understand and turn to Jesus… or not."

Ray looked like he wanted to ask a question but couldn't find the words. Enrique could sense Ray's dilemma and thought some clarification might help. "The concept is easy. Even though Jesus hates evil, He still loves people, including you. He will give anyone who has rejected Him the opportunity to have a place in Heaven through repentance and belief. I made my choice to confirm my relationship with Jesus. I know, without question, I will be with Him soon."

Ray noted a soberness and sincerity in Enrique's voice. His brain worked at full speed, trying to absorb what he just heard. He had spent his life rejecting "fairy tales" about religion. A short week ago, he would have laughed and looked at Enrique as another religious nut case. But in that short week, Enrique had become a friend and advisor. Ray, at the very least, wanted to respect that connection.

Enrique had no idea he was interrupting a different conversation in Ray's head. So he moved forward. "God, the Father, creator of the heavens and earth, has always had a long-term plan. The phrase "long-term" is for those who inhabit this earth. God has no time constrictions. The concept of time was created by God for humanity in Genesis 1:14-19." Ray refocused.

Enrique tapped on the brochure. "Back to God's plan." Enrique opened the 'Introduction to the Bible' brochure and pointed to a chart. "This lists the books, the authors, and the theme of each book.

CHAPTER EIGHT

Enrique hesitated as he thought through his lesson plan. "Neither of us is sure what you will need for tomorrow's meeting with the client. We do know you are going to need a solid foundation. I am going to try to stick to the highest of the highlights." Since we know you do not have much time, our crash course will be divided into three parts: the Jewish side, the Christian side, and a comparison and contrast in part 3.

A mild chuckle accompanied Ray's smile. "That is exactly the way I would have organized something like this."

Enrique was anxious to begin with part 1. "There are 24 books in the Hebrew Bible, called the Tanakh. When first created, the books were meticulously crafted scrolls. You would have looked at the scroll as one long sequence of code. Members of the Sanhedrin knew every scroll in great detail."

Ray blurted out his first of what would be many questions. "Sanhedrin?"

Enrique kicked himself for inserting terms without a quick explanation. Getting through the information Ray needed would be impossible if he had to stop every other sentence. "The Sanhedrin was like the Jewish Supreme

Court with 70 judges led by the High Priest. There were two main schools of thought. Sadducees were by-the-book legalists. Pharisees knew the laws but included oral tradition in their interpretation. You probably would have enjoyed watching those debates."

Ray wrote down two quick notes. "I love a good debate. I will check that out…if I ever have a minute to myself."

Enrique shrugged, then picked up where he left off. "The first five books of the Tanakh hold considerable importance within Judaism. Jointly referred to as the Torah, these texts are regarded as fundamental teachings and unquestionable instructions."

Ray interrupted Enrique's train of thought. "This sounds like it is going to be important information that I will need to know. But I have a meeting tomorrow and I know the Temple is going to be central to the discussion. How does this relate to the Temple?"

Enrique smiled, leaned back in his chair, and gazed into space. "Okay. So much for an orderly discussion, but I see your point. The good news is that I can tie things together. The information in the Torah is directly related to the Temple. The first five books are Genesis, Exodus, Leviticus, Numbers, and Deuteronomy. Moses authored these books under God's direction. God often spoke directly to Moses. He gave Moses laws for all Hebrews to follow. The laws were a structured guide on how one's life with God should be lived. The Ten Commandments are the most well-known."

Ray interrupted again, "I think I have a better than average memory, but I don't see how I am going to remember the names and sequence of books in the Tanakh or Bible. Do you think it is necessary in the short time I have?"

Enrique gave an understanding nod. "There will probably be one or more Rabbis on the selection committee. Knowing these particular five might come in handy. The best way to remember the books in the Torah is with the purpose. **God Explains Life, Not Death.** The first letter of each word is the first letter of the five books in order. Genesis – God, Exodus - explains, Leviticus - life, Numbers - not, Deuteronomy – death. The handout gives you the gist of each book. I think you should prioritize this one."

Ray conceded that he may need the Torah books in his memory bank. "I think you are right on that. Your memory trick will make it easy. I will need to read this information later. What's next?"

Enrique picked up as though the sidebar conversation never happened. "The balance of the Tanakh includes narratives of historical value and life lessons. Prophecies are also a major element. There are prophecies that we know are true because they have already been fulfilled. Other prophecies in the Tanakh will be fulfilled in the very near future."

Enrique gave Ray some time to finish taking his notes. He was concerned that Ray would want to know which prophecies, but those questions did not come. Ray looked up and nodded. Enrique continued. "Think of the text in the Tanakh as a family with young children. Children do not understand concepts like nutrition, hygiene, or right and wrong. Parents teach and set the rules."

Ray added, "You know I have about two hundred questions, but I understand you are trying to keep me focused. Can you hold your tutorial for a minute?" Ray stood up and walked out. He returned with his laptop. It was firing up as he walked back in. Ray moved some of the materials on the dining room table to make room for his workspace.

When he finished typing, he announced, "Okay, I am ready. I started my question list."

Enrique regrouped, "Okay, the connection. Even from the very beginning, God allowed His children choices. He set the boundaries and taught them right from wrong, but His children are not puppets on a string. They can decide whether or not to follow the rules. He has given you that same ability to choose to follow Jesus…or not.

"The Jews were growing up but still not old enough to understand the rules for living a Godly life. The same applied to the rest of the world. God saw that things were moving in the wrong direction. After freeing the Hebrews from Egyptian slavery through a series of miracles, God gave Moses Ten Commandments to give to the people – the principles to live by. There were many directives from God prior to the Ten Commandments, but these ten are directly relative to the Temple."

Ray stopped typing and looked up. "My parents would drag me to church. I took the paper cover off one of my father's Bibles and wrapped it around whatever book I was reading at the time. People would tell my parents how cute it was that I would read the Bible during the sermon." Ray paused and smiled as he reflected on how clever he thought he was. "From my childhood I picked up thou shall not lie, murder or steal. It was like those were really the only three."

Ray paused again as another flashback interrupted his train of thought. "As a child, I was a creative storyteller. Other people saw some of my stories as lies. It may be my own defense mechanism, but I don't remember that any of my stories hurt anyone. What I do remember is that I was told by some muckety muck at the church that God would punish me and I would burn in hell if I ever lied again.

What exactly is that?"

"Well, whoever told you that just broke the third commandment that says you must not misuse the Lord's name." As he was talking, Enrique was rummaging through a couple of boxes. Ray did not know if Enrique was speaking to him or talking to himself. "I know I saw that booklet somewhere. Ah, here it is!" Enrique handed Ray another booklet titled The Ten Commandments. Ray opened it up to the first page. As a speed reader, Ray could have zipped through the information in no time. Enrique noticed that Ray stayed focused on one page.

The Ten Commandments – Exodus 20:1-17

And God spoke all these words: I am the Lord your God, who brought you out of Egypt, out of the land of slavery.

1 You shall have no other gods before me.

2 You shall not make for yourself an image in the form of anything in Heaven above, on the earth beneath, or in the waters below. You shall not bow down to them or worship them; for I, the Lord your God, am a jealous God, punishing the children for the sin of the parents to the third and fourth generation of those who hate me, but showing love to a thousand generations of those who love me and keep my commandments.

3 You shall not misuse the name of the Lord our God, for the Lord will not hold guiltless who misuses my name.

4 Remember the Sabbath day by keeping it holy. Six days you shall labor and do all your work, but the seventh day is a sabbath to the Lord your God. On it you shall not do any work, neither you, nor your son or daughter, nor your male or female servant, nor your animals, nor any foreigner residing in your towns. For in six days the Lord made the heavens and the earth, the sea, and all that is in them, but he rested on the seventh day. Therefore, the Lord blessed the Sabbath day and made it holy.

5 Honor your Father and your mother so that you may live long in the land the Lord your God is giving you.

6 You shall not murder.

7 You shall not commit adultery.

8 You shall not steal.

9 You shall not give false testimony against your neighbor.

10 You shall not covet your neighbor's house. You shall not covet your neighbor's wife, or his male or female servant, his ox or donkey, or anything that belongs to your neighbor.

After more time than he would typically spend on a page, Ray said, "This is not something I can grasp without doing the research. Time is not something I have at this point. Initially, this upcoming meeting sounded like I would just be filling an empty chair. However, Mo was adamant that I should at least have some understanding of this project from a Jewish and Christian perspective."

Ray sounded frustrated when he said, "This is stuff they

say I need to know if I am going to work closely with both Christians and Jews. I need to be fluent in Biblical language! Not gonna to happen."

Enrique was enjoying every challenge of this conversation. One surprise after another was keeping Enrique on his toes, ready to react to anything thrown his way. "Our lessons for today are foundational. The handouts I will give you for your own research will allow you to get focused." Ray wanted his old life back but got Enrique's point. "Let's take a logical approach. When you break things down, it is not that difficult. You may need a seminary degree for the deep dive, but for now the basics will suffice. This booklet has some of what you need for better clarity. You will have later today to sift through the information I'm giving you. Let's keep going." Ray had no words. He surrendered to reality with a nod.

"First, know that the Ten Commandments were supernaturally carved into two stone tablets. Those tablets are a major reason the first Temple was built. Second, it is easier to remember these ten rules when you understand why they were given." Once again, Enrique needed to take a detour with the handout as the map. "Look at it this way. Instead of seeing ten, break them down into three groups. The first three commandments represent your relationship with God. The following two represent your relationship with your family. The last five represent your relationship with decency and your fellow human beings.

"The first three are simple directives from God for your relationship with Him. One, there is no other God. Two, don't make one up. And three, don't use God's name to promote your own agenda.

"The following two are family-related commandments.

First, love your mom and dad. Second, God took a day off and wants you to have one. On that day, he wants you to take the time to reflect on all the blessings He has given you. Appreciate your family, friends, and everything you have been given.

"The last five are common decencies for your relationship with fellow human beings. First, don't murder anyone. The Bible talks about the fine-line difference between murder and killing someone in self-defense. That is a discussion for a different time. Second, don't cheat on your spouse physically, mentally, or emotionally. Third, don't steal. Fourth, don't lie. Fifth, don't be envious or want other people's stuff or lifestyle. You have been given what you need and more will be given when needed.

"Many believe, and even teach, that if each person obeys these rules, it guarantees a place in Heaven. There are major flaws in that argument. Humans are not perfect. Humans break the laws in the Bible that result in sin. When we get to the New Testament, I will let you know what Jesus says about the laws. As a teaser, He said, no person, regardless of power, money, title, or piousness can come to God the Father through external acts." Enrique could see the wheels turning in Ray's head.

"Even though the Ten Commandments represent the top ten list, there were many other laws embedded in the Old Testament – over 600. Many of those additional laws related to rituals designed to seek God's forgiveness for the rule breaking that was done. As I said earlier though, it is the tablets with the Ten Commandments which are one of the primary reasons for the first Temple."

Ray was listening and typing at the same time. His hands froze on the keyboard. "A primary reason. I am sure you will explain that. That primary reason is one of my primary issues. I don't get it. If God is all powerful, why doesn't He zap the bad guys and then take the good guys to Heaven? That would sure fix our problems trying to expose who is behind the product sabotage."

Enrique pursed his lips, closed his eyes, and gave a quick, short nod. "Because of your disbelief, what if you were considered to be one of the bad guys?" Ray had no response. "The real answer deals with moral will. Remember, I said that we are not God's puppets. He has given everyone the ability to decide between right and wrong, to believe in His Son or not. Once the Tribulation period starts, people will have, at most, 7 years to commit, one way or the other."

Ray noted, "The world has always been crazy in one form or another throughout history. I can't remember it being this bad, but surely it will shift back again. This Tribulation you keep telling me about seems awfully extreme for a world that naturally ebbs and flows."

Enrique did not hesitate to respond. "That is definitely the worldview, but not the Godly view. There is no balancing out at this point. The reality is that we are now in the end times." Enrique seemed to stare into space. "Let's try this. Maybe it will help you understand what the tribulation period is about." Enrique stopped to quickly organize his thoughts. "Imagine yourself as a parent with a teenage daughter who is addicted to drugs. You try to help. Your daughter agrees to stop, but she doesn't. The usage gets more severe. You try educating her about the lives of others who are abusing drugs and the sad state their lives are in. It still does not work. She steals from you to pay for her addiction and lives a dangerous life.

"Finally, you have an intervention where you watch your

daughter being taken away to a drug rehab center, kicking, screaming, and crying. Your heart is breaking because you love your daughter. You know she is going to go through painful times. She is cursing you for putting her through this. Your conclusion, however, is that the intervention was the only way to help her understand and have a chance to live a long, healthy life.

"Toward the end of the treatments her mind gets a clear picture, and she realizes the pain she has caused you and others. She asks for your forgiveness, which you gladly give. Then you tell her there is a room in the house for her. She will be joyfully welcomed home." Enrique sighed. "The Tribulation will either be punishment for those rejecting God, or a healing opportunity for accepting God. It is a choice between eternal misery or unending joy."

Committed to getting back on track, Enrique continued the lesson. "Back to the Temple. Now, you need some background on Moses. It pains me to condense this discussion, because the five books of the Torah, written by Moses, are the heart of Jewish life. You can read the details about Moses in Exodus starting in chapter 2. Enrique handed Ray another study guide: Moses – The Journey Home. Enrique outlined the contents. He then targeted the discussion to what he felt Ray would need.

"Moses was born in Egypt during a time when Pharaoh had ordered all newborn Hebrew males to be drowned in an attempt to control the expanding male population. He wanted to reduce the possibility of a Hebrew army forming. Moses was saved from that fate and was raised as an Egyptian. He was found out and avoided execution. His escape route took him into the desert, where he, once more, almost died. He was saved by a farmer, worked on the farm, and married the farmer's daughter.

"God spoke directly to Moses. He was told to go get all the Israelites out of Egypt. They had been in slavery there for many years. God was ready to lead them to the land he had promised them long ago. On the journey, one of the stops was Mt Moriah. That is where God gave Moses the Ten Commandments. As the trip continued, it was important to protect the tablets."

"To protect these stone tablets, Moses ordered the construction of a container. God gave the specifications. The chest is called the Ark of the Covenant. A tabernacle, in this case a portable tent, was designed to protect the Ark of the Covenant during the journey. This tabernacle is directly related to the construction of the first Temple. The innermost room, the Holy of Holies, was designed to replace the tent and house the Ark of the Covenant.

"Along the forty-year journey, Moses disobeyed God's directives. For those indiscretions, Moses was not allowed to be that triumphant leader entering the promise land. He turned the leadership over to Joshua, his loyal servant. From Mount Nebo, Moses was allowed to see the land that would become today's version of Israel, but he was not allowed to set foot on that soil."

Enrique paused to see if Ray needed clarification on anything, but Ray indicated he would hold his questions for now. He was eager to hear Enrique's ongoing words of wisdom. Enrique handed Ray another booklet titled 'David.'

"It may seem like I am randomly shifting subjects but stick with me because it all connects. The next piece of information you need concerns David, of David and Goliath fame. David is considered one of the greatest leaders in Israel's history. Put First and Second Chronicles, First and

Second Samuel, and Psalms in your notes. You will find more there. Also, when you read, remember twists of fate are often God driven."

Ray jumped in. "Meaning that coincidences are not always just coincidences."

Enrique was glad to see that Ray was back on track. "Exactly right." Enrique marked the booklet to make it easier for Ray during his own research. "David became King after Saul. David issued the mandate to build the first Temple. He acted as the pre-construction project manager although he would not be the one to build the Temple. God had told David he would have a son who would complete the Temple. He was to name that son Solomon."

Enrique pointed to Ray's laptop and told him to note 1 Chronicles 22. He recommended that Ray read the entire passage. "David chose Mount Moriah as the site for the Temple; the same place Abraham took his son Isaac to be sacrificed. God stopped that ritual. I'll tell you more about Abraham and Isaac at another time.

"When David died, Solomon became a great King. Just as God had told David, Solomon had the Temple built. Once the most inner room, the Holy of Holies, was completed, the Ark of the Covenant, which now held three key items, was placed in that innermost room. In addition to the Ten Commandments, Aaron's staff was the second item placed in the Ark."

Ray grinned while challenging Enrique. "A walking stick. Seriously? That must have been some ornate piece of wood."

Enrique knew another short detour was needed. "These were not just walking sticks. They were tools used to guide the sheep or fight off predators. This particular staff was blessed by God." Enrique opened his Bible. "Imagine you are with the Israelites that just escaped captivity. You are being led to the promise land by Moses and his brother, Aaron. But instead of a straight line, you keep wandering in random patterns. At a certain point you might question your leaders."

Ray's body language said, "Obviously." Ray put on his logic hat. "I probably would have called for a vote of no confidence - if that is what they did back then."

Enrique nodded. "Basically, that is what happened. There are 12 Tribes of Israel. You can learn how that came about later. Eleven of the twelve leaders wanted a change of leadership. So God decided to put an end to this rebellion. He told Moses to have the leaders of each tribe bring their staff, inscribed with their name, to a meeting. The staff of each was stored overnight under heavy security. Aaron represented the tribe of Levi. Moses told everyone that they would know who God voted for because that person's rod would sprout buds. Keep in mind, this is a dead piece of wood.

"The description of what happened starts in Numbers 17:5. Aaron's staff did not just bud; it sprouted flowers and produced fresh almonds. Everyone else just had ordinary sticks to pick up. God had made His point. The vote of confidence was blatantly apparent. Aaron became the High Priest and began formalizing the religious structure.

"That stopped the whining. Verse 10 is where God tells Moses to put Aaron's staff with the Ark as a reminder that God is in charge. Make a note to read Exodus 4 and Numbers 20 to get a more complete picture.

"The third item was a golden pot that contained Manna. During the forty years traveling after escaping slavery, they faced harsh conditions. To help with the lack of food,

God miraculously provided the Israelites with 'bread from heaven,' called 'manna.' The manna appeared each morning. The Israelites were given specific instructions on the gathering process." Enrique pointed to Ray's computer and told him to see Exodus 16:15.

Ray asked, "Manna? What is it?"

Enrique replied, "Exactly." Ray was confused. "The Israelites trekking across the wilderness saw the food and asked, 'What is it?' Moses told them, 'It is the bread that the LORD has given you to eat.' The literal translation of the Hebrew word manna means, 'What is it?'

Ray smiled, looked down, and shook his head. "Okay, now you are telling me God has a sense of humor." Ray looked back up. "So, what is this miraculous food?"

Enrique chuckled. He decided to skip the humor comment to maintain some semblance of focus. "One description in Exodus 16:31 says, 'It was like coriander seed, white, and the taste of it was like wafers made with honey.' Whatever it was, God provided what they needed to survive the journey."

Enrique kept going before Ray came at him with a barrage of questions. "Back to the Temple. The building was large, and the courtyard was vast. The building was oblong, with three rooms of equal size. The vestibule had a beautiful porch as the entry. The Holy Place was the main room for religious services. "Solomon completed the first Temple in 957 BC."

Ray's fingers continued to blaze across the keys. He stopped to ask. "So obviously that Temple was destroyed, or there wouldn't have been a second Temple built. What happened there?" Before waiting for the answer, Ray held his hand up like a kid in school. Enrique smiled and acknowledged Ray's request. "I get that the Old Testament is all about the Jews. So how do we really know that the Jews are the chosen people?"

Enrique's short answer was, "Because God sent his Son into this world as a Jew to save the Jews as well as the Gentiles." Even though Enrique knew the answer was much longer, he figured his response would need to suffice for now.

CHAPTER NINE

The question was a perfect transition for Enrique's next phase. Ray appeared to be buying in, not all in, but even a little counted. Enrique wanted to tie into Ray's pragmatic side. "Since we do not know who is on the selection committee, I think it is reasonable to assume the participants are well versed in every historic and religious aspect related to the Temple. This is actual history, not just Bible stuff. So, let's continue our condensed history lesson. Around 722 BC, the Assyrians invaded the Northern Kingdom of Israel. As a side note, at this point in history, Israel was divided. Most of Israel was in the north and Judah was in the south. We can't go into all that happened to create the division, but you need to know there were essentially two separate kingdoms. There were several reasons the Assyrians did not take Judah in the south. One of those reasons was that a plague hit the Assyrians. A coincidence? In 612 BC, Babylon overcame the Assyrians. That included capturing Israel in the north.

"The Babylonian Empire now reigned. In 586 BC, the Babylonians captured Jerusalem and destroyed the First Temple. The invaders took whatever they determined was valuable. They took many Jews captive and enslaved them in Babylon. Daniel, a key player in this part of history, was taken captive."

Enrique popped out of his chair. Ray watched as he pointed to the bookshelf, then to the table, and finally to the boxes stacked in the corner. His hand waved like a metal detector searching for a nugget of gold. Then the movement stopped, and he went to a box. He found the prize and held it up. "More homework." He handed Ray a booklet with a statue on the front cover. "This next section will be the lightning round for the next 500 years."

Ray was amused. "I wish you had been my World Civilization professor in college. She would have taken five semesters to get through five hundred years."

"Well, this will not be a liberal arts lesson. It will be a Biblical arts lesson that will answer your question about the Second Temple.

"The Persian Empire is next. Shortly after conquering Babylon, King Cyrus released the Jews from captivity after 50 years of slavery. It is interesting, at least to me, how God involves non-believers to work His will. The Jews were allowed to return to Israel. They looked forward to returning to the worship services and rituals that were central to their relationship with God. Sadly, they returned to a decimated Temple." Enrique paused and sifted through his notes. "Sorry, I am looking for my notes on Cyrus."

Ray jumped in. "I know a little about Cyrus. I authored a paper about him in college. He took a different approach from all previous monarchies. Instead of putting his own leaders in charge of the regions that he had captured, Cyrus established an early form of a republic. He allowed local leaders to stay in charge if they followed specific empire-wide rules. He stressed the need for education, culture, infrastructure, and services to improve the quality of life in each community. The government structure was like that of the our Republic without a Congress to make laws. Cyrus still made the laws."

Enrique was mesmerized by Ray's summary of the history of the Medo-Persian Empire, culminating in a major defeat at the hands of Alexander the Great. When Enrique refocused, he asked, "Did your research include the Persian control of Israel?" Ray had not concentrated on regional control. "Well, let me add to your wealth of knowledge. Zerubbabel became the leader of the tribe of Judah in 538 BC as the Jews migrated home. Cyrus appointed him as Governor of Judah. Shortly after the appointment, Zerubbabel began rebuilding the Temple. Cyrus approved the reconstruction.

"The Babylonians destroyed the first Temple in 586 BC to the extent that the foundation took Zerubbabel two years to repair. Samaritan turmoil delayed construction for seventeen years.

"Two prophets, under God's direction, Zechariah and Haggai, arrived in support of Zerubbabel. They encouraged the people to act. Four years later, in 516 BC, the Temple was ready for worship. The Jewish holiday of Passover was finally observed in the Second Temple."

"We are leaping forward about 554 years to 70 AD. As a reminder, all this history of the world's empires was foretold in the Bible thousands of years before any of it happened. When you have time, research Daniel's interpretation of the Babylonian monarch King Nebuchadnezzar's dream about a statue of a man. The prophetic dream describes four empires: Babylonian, Persian, Greek and Roman. The last three did not exist at the time of the writing. And people say there is no God."

Ray clicked the finishing key of his notes with some emphasis. He kept staring at the keyboard. His hands were still poised to continue typing, but there was no movement. He was paralyzed, at least for the moment. He finally blinked and looked up. "This is not right. I have not dedicated myself to a magazine subscription for more than a year. The Jews stayed loyal, generation after generation, through all of this. The Christians have stayed loyal to Jesus for 2000 years." He looked at Enrique. "I should not be on this project."

Enrique bowed his head. Ray could see Enrique's lips moving, but there was no sound. He suddenly looked up. "My friend, what you just said makes me believe, more than ever, that you should be on this project. That comment was not the pragmatic, problem-solving Ray I know. That was one of Satan's minions casting doubt. Satan does not want you on this project because he knows that Jesus does."

Ray did not say the words, but he thought, "Nice try, but that really didn't help."

Enrique restarted. "Nebuchadnezzar's dream was an amazing prophetic message spanning about 1500 years." Enrique detected doubt as Ray returned focus to the keyboard. "Ray, Mr. Realist, I have good news and bad news. The bad news: I am not a psychic. The good news: I do know what is coming. It is all in the Bible. If God spoke of four world empires thousands of years before they occurred, Jesus revealing His next moves for Earth should not be a surprise to anyone."

Ray started with 'Yeah, but...' when Enrique interrupted. "Do you believe everything that I have explained so far? Everything can be backed up by historical documents and archeological finds."

Ray said, "I am accepting what you tell me at face value, for now. I cannot dispute anything without doing more research." Ray could not help being slightly defiant. But it really does not matter what I accept as true. It is what the Jews and the Christians believe that counts. I need to respect their convictions so I can work with both."

Enrique replied, "I agree with all but one thing. It matters what you think. Just as important, it matters what you believe." Enrique then picked up where he left off. "Okay Ray, we are coming into the home stretch toward the Temple."

Enrique was compassionately firm. "I am confident that your research will verify what we have discussed. But for now, to eliminate distractions, assume that everything is true. And if all is true so far, why wouldn't the next set of prophesied events be true?"

Ray said, with surrender in his voice, "You are not going to let this go, are you?"

Enrique hesitated as if waiting for someone else to join the conversation. "I have no idea why Jesus wants you on this project. I have no idea why He wants me to help you. But it's happening. Let's continue getting you ready for your meeting."

"A dog with a bone. Okay, what happened to Temple II? Go." Ray readied his hands to type.

Enrique said, "Before that, I have been thinking about this selection committee. The notion is that everyone on this Temple III project will know that God is in charge. That must be factored in your preparation. For sake of argument, I would go with the assumption that there are born-again Christians on the project until proven otherwise. They will trust that the Rapture is the sign that Jesus is coming back."

Ray's curiosity struck again. "Until proven otherwise?

Do you think there might be counterfeit Christians on this project? If I were in charge, I would want to make sure everyone in a position of influence was properly vetted."

Enrique did not anticipate that question. "These are not ordinary times. Prolific liars are pawns of Satan, whether they know it or not. Just look in your own backyard. Whoever is behind the sabotage has obviously deceived you and anyone who should have known."

That comment was a reality check for Ray. He sighed. "Great. You have just expanded my suspect list to, oh, I don't know, EVERYONE." With a smirk on his face, Ray pointed two fingers at his eyes, then quickly turned them toward Enrique. He repeated the action.

Enrique smiled. "Okay. If I suddenly burst into flames you will know you were right. In the meantime, can I get back to the lesson?" Ray smiled and repeated the I-am-watching-you gesture.

Enrique mentally checked where he was in the discussion. "The Jews do not believe in the concept of the Rapture, but they do believe in a resurrection. I would assume the Jews on the committee might look at people recently disappearing as a sign that the *first* Messiah is about to come. Again, until proven otherwise. I think sticking to those views will allow you to stay focused. It could also keep you on track during any discussions with the panel. Don't let paranoia break your focus."

Enrique suddenly realized he had been holding a Bible during that little interlude. He loosened the grip and gently placed the Bible on the table. "Back to the Second Temple. Herod, Caesar's appointed King of the Jews, remodeled the Temple II to Solomon's standards in 20-18 BC. By now, Judea was part of the current-day Israel.

"The First Jewish Revolt against the oppressive Roman rule began in the year 66. The Roman legions surrounded Jerusalem and methodically chipped away at the Jewish stronghold. By year 70, the troops had breached Jerusalem's outer walls. In defiance of official orders, the Temple was set on fire. The soldiers brutally murdered those who hid in the Temple and survived the fire. Riotous ransacking happened when the attackers saw the riches of gold, silver, and gems. They trampled one another to confiscate what they could. The scouring ended with the burning and ultimate destruction of the Second Temple. Even the stone walls fell.

"The people of Israel were now scattered. The name Israel lived on, but the country had died until Israel was resurrected as a nation in 1948. According to rumors on the chat site I use, Temple III is a real possibility. Those behind the project want it to be rebuilt to the glory and grandeur of Temple II. There is one major roadblock—the Dome of the Rock. The Muslim shrine was built on the Temple Mount in Jerusalem in 691.

"The Temple Mount, located on Mount Moriah, is the holiest site for the Jews. The Dome is also on, or very near, the 'Herod Temple' destroyed in 70 AD. Evidence suggests that the dome is located on the site of the Holy of Holies. Psalms 48:2 and Isaiah 4:5 call it Mount Zion. It is also the third-holiest site in Islam. The Muslims know it as the Sacred Noble Sanctuary."

Before Enrique could make the transition to the Christian Bible, Ray's phone rang. Just before hitting the decline button, Ray noticed the call was from Chas. He held up the wait-a-minute finger. Enrique responded with, "Go ahead. I'll grab a couple of bottles of water."

Numerous possibilities flashed through Ray's mind as

he accepted the call. "Chas. What's up?"

Chas was all business. "We just found out that the three-man committee coming in tomorrow knows information about our recent updates on the language module. Those improvements have not finalized and should not have been discussed with anyone. Mo received an email asking for any significant changes since his last meeting with the group leader. One of our changes was specifically noted. I know you are just getting started with your investigation. I just wanted to find out if you have anything."

Ray could sense the concern. "Everything is in place. If the code works as planned, I should have a starting point as soon as someone attempts a hack. There is a possibility that whoever is behind this might come in today. I would doubt it. They would need to sign in. It would be too risky. But, I will do a sanity check later just in case."

The concern remained, but Chas was only slightly disappointed. "That is what I figured, but I had to check." Chas spent 10 minutes updating Ray on the changes to the language module that prompted Mo's email. After Ray confirmed he understood the situation, Chas shifted the subject.

"Mo wanted me to check to see how your Bible research was going. He knows you won't be a world-famous theologian in this short time, but I would like to relieve some of his concern."

Ray jokingly said, "Let Mo know that you just rudely interrupted my tutorial. So If I am not up to speed it will be your fault."

Chas laughed. "Nice try." Chas grasped something Ray just said. "So you have a Bible coach?"

Ray looked at Enrique as he set the bottle of water on

the table. "He is a teacher extraordinaire. Unfortunately for him, there is not much to work with." Enrique realized he was the target of this conversation. He nodded in agreement.

Chas chuckled. "This guy must have the patience of Job."

Ray said, "I wouldn't know. Job is not in the lesson plan for today."

Enrique declared loud enough for Chas to hear, "And we are not going to be distracted by any questions about Job, are we?"

Chas laughed again. "I don't know who this guy is, but I already like him. Gotta go. Call with any updates. Otherwise, I will see you tomorrow."

Ray explained the call. Enrique asked if they should conduct additional tests. "No. I think we have done all we can do at this point. If all goes as planned, the games will begin tomorrow." Ray took a sip of water. "When today's lesson is done, we can consider options. For now, let's stay focused."

Enrique smiled. "That will be easy for me. It's your focus I am concerned about." Ray had nothing to add. He could only use a circular hand motion to let Enrique know the lesson could resume.

"Okay, **Part 2**. Enrique made sure Ray had the correct materials handy. "Christians revere the Temple as the place Jesus began teaching at Passover when he was twelve years old." Enrique looked at the time. He looked at Ray while taking a short, deep breath. "I am going to need to adjust the plan. There is too much to explain about the New Testament at this point. Let's move to part 3 where we can make some comparisons and discuss the differences. What we discuss will cover the much of the Christian side anyway."

Ray typed in '**Part 3**' and was ready for whatever was next. Enrique pointed out the appropriate page in the handout. "The first five books of the Old Testament, the Pentateuch, are the same as the Torah. Remember, these books were written by Moses."

"The **Torah** is the beginning of all creation. It is also the beginning of the Hebrew nation in the land of Canaan. God promised to bless Abraham and said his lineage would form a great nation. God said He would bless those who honor Abraham and curse those who don't. That same covenant includes the Israelite people and the Jewish religion. The Torah began what many describe as the **Era of the Law**.

"The first five books of the New Testament, collectively called the Gospels, introduce a new beginning. Instead of the birth of a nation, Matthew, Mark, Luke, and John describe the birth, death, and resurrection of Jesus. The Book of Acts is a continuation of Luke's book. It was written from a historical view. This began the **Era of Grace**.

"Critics of these five New Testament books say it proves the Bible has flaws because the story about the same events from each author is not consistent. If the critics knew anything about hermeneutics, the theory of interpretation, they would realize it is the same story told from the unique perspective of each author."

Ray asked, "So it is like four witnesses to an accident. Each witness would have a slightly different take on exactly what happened."

Enrique resisted the urge to expand on that observation. "That is the general idea. Since Luke had no first-hand knowledge, his books are more like a reporter interviewing multiple witnesses on the scene. In today's world, Luke would have won a Pulitzer Prize for his work." Ray understood but typed several questions into his list. He nodded, indicating he was ready for whatever was next.

"There are also direct correlations between the **last book of the Tanakh** and the **last book of the New Testament**. The last book of the Tanakh is **2 Chronicles**. This book highlights themes of restoration, the temple, and the hope for a future leader. Revelation is the last book of the New Testament. It foretells of a newly revived Earth. The book also leaves us with hope for a phenomenal new Heaven and Earth.

"The Septuagint, sometimes referred to as the Greek Old Testament, is the earliest translation of the Hebrew Bible. There are 24 books in the Tanakh and 39 in the Old Testament. "

Ray's analytical mind jumped in. "So the Old Testament is not really the same as the Tanakh."

"Yes and no. The writers of the Old Testament made changes primarily for organizational and readability purposes. The content is the same.

"The Old Testament architects split certain books of the Tanakh into two books. For example, Chronicles in the Tanakh is one book, but there are two in the Old Testament: 1 Chronicles and 2 Chronicles. The same applies to the books of Samuel and Kings. The 13th book of the Tanakh are shorter narratives of the Minor Prophets. That book was divided into twelve books in the Old Testament. Thus, 24 books of the Tanakh became 39 books of the Old Testament."

Ray's half-empty glass attitude kicked in. "When they split the books, the transcribers could have made changes to the text." Enrique assured Ray the changes were strictly logistical. No one changed the words. Ray could not resist throwing down a challenge. "Lucky for you, I don't have time to try to prove you wrong."

Enrique patiently responded, "Here is an idea for you. Once you become fluent in Hebrew, instead of trying to prove me wrong, why don't you try to prove me right. It will be easier once you change your perspective."

Ray laughed. "Fluent in Hebrew. That's funny." Ray's thought process changed his expression. "Perspective. Interesting word. We may be looking at the product sabotage and leaks from the wrong direction. We will know more tomorrow, but…"

Louder than normal, Enrique said, "Stop! Don't even think of going there right now. You need to focus on your meeting. After tomorrow, you can take your pick of rabbit holes to go down." Ray knew Enrique was right. His hands hovered over the keyboard, signaling it was time to move on.

"Since Jews do not believe that Jesus is the Messiah, they do not accept the New Testament. Based on their interpretation of prophecy, Jesus does not satisfy the criterion to be the Messiah. Christians, on the other hand, believe that the Old Testament is foundational to the New Testament. They constantly cross reference the New and Old Testaments. Christians believe Jesus completed the Old Testament Messianic Prophecies. Other prophecies are yet to be fulfilled."

Ray jumped in. "Was that difference of opinion about the Messiah enough to want the guy crucified?"

"Before I answer, let me throw a little more fuel on the fire. Type in your notes Matthew 5:17-20. Jesus said he fulfilled the laws as a result of His coming. Jesus made it clear that salvation comes by faith, not by good behavior, animal sacrifices, or any outward rituals. Jesus taught that upon

His death and resurrection, we are released from those laws so that we serve through the Spirit and not by Old Testament laws."

Ray sat quietly, pondering what Enrique had just said. "Alright. I am a member of the Sanhedrin, and a smart, but common man, comes to a meeting and tells us that those 600-plus laws no longer apply."

Enrique responded, "Basically, yes."

"So the Ten Commandments are out?"

Enrique said, "As far as a law is concerned, yes." He paused, digging deeper into Ray's question. "I think you are struggling with this because you are missing a piece of information. It is referred to as the Law of Christ. A scribe of the Sanhedrin asked Jesus what he considered to be the greatest law. You can find more about His answer in Mark 12:28-30 and John 13:34. I am paraphrasing, but Jesus told the man: The Lord God is one. With all of your strength, love the Lord your God with all of your heart, soul, and mind. Second, love your neighbor as yourself.

"If you think about it, the Ten Commandments still apply. No other God, no idol, no disrespect. The second command is to love others. That includes your parents. If you truly love others, you won't murder, commit adultery, steal, lie. Instead of being envious of others, you will be happy for them. The Sabbath Day was set aside with specific guidelines. Even though strict adherence to that law is not required, churches all over the world have Sunday services. And, if you really think about it, that law is obeyed because you are praising God every day, not just one."

Ray said, "Now I understand why they wanted Him dead. One guy blows up thousands of years of belief. No laws means no lawyers. No lawyers means no power. No power means no money. But, then again, it seems before setting Jesus up to die, they should have at least formed a committee to study the options."

Enrique smiled. "Yeah, so where were you when they needed your help?"

"Exactly! I probably could have fixed everything." Even though Ray had more questions, the one he asked was, "What's next on your lesson plan?" Instead of waiting for an answer, Ray finally lifted his fingers from the keyboard. "You know how the Temple wall collapsed. That is what my brain is doing right now." He looked at the screen, hit a few keys, and closed the computer.

"I knew none of this. I will need some processing time." They both agreed and decided to take a break.

Enrique rubbed his eyes to refocus. "Okay, here is the deal. I will organize these materials, but it will be up to you to do your own research. Indirectly, the Holy Spirit will know when you are ready for more and provide the information you need."

Ray stared blankly at Enrique. His silence prompted Enrique to shift his focus from the materials and look up. His mind began to rewind the conversation. With a soft laugh, he said. "Okay, this one is on me. Holy Spirit. Right?" Ray grinned. Nothing more was needed. "This is one you will absolutely need to know." Enrique did not want to get into a full-blown discussion of the Trinity, but another handout from the heap Elias had might stimulate Ray to learn more. "Put this on your research list. I can explain more later. Do not stray from your goal for tomorrow's meeting."

Ray sarcastically replied, "Yes dear." Ray tilted his head back ever so lightly. As he ran his fingers through his hair, he said, "We still need to deal with moles. Come on over later today. We can talk while we have a bite to eat. I have several meal options in the freezer." Ray made a half turn toward the door but quickly reversed. "Thanks for all of your help." Ray headed across the hall.

CHAPTER TEN

During the lessons on Sunday morning, sunshine filled Enrique's apartment. The afternoon water-laden clouds now darkened Ray's unit. The lighting system Ray had the owners install offset that issue. As the door opened, Enrique knocked as an afterthought. He wasn't sure why he bothered since Ray had told him to come in when he was ready. But there he was. Ray had already organized all the material from his tutorial with Enrique. A pink file folder labeled Temple III held packets of papers. Paperclips of varying colors squeezed documents together. The red, green, yellow, and silver clips hung together like teammates.

The apartment smelled like a pizza parlor. Ray had just removed the second of his custom-made, individual-sized pizzas from the air fryer. The first pizza was already dominating the room with its aroma. The pie's diameter was perfect for a late lunch. Enrique did not realize he was hungry until the mouth-watering scent left him no choice.

"Come on over here. I cleared a workspace for you." Enrique quickly concluded this would be a working meal. Ray was anxious to work on the mole and hacker problem but wanted to address an unrelated idea first. The theory had popped into Ray's mind out of nowhere, but he was not sure what Enrique's response might be. "Were you able to round up the Elias documents we discussed right before I left?"

"This pizza looks great." Enrique was ready to eat but knew he first needed to get Ray to disclose whatever he had up his sleeve. "Yeah. Right here. I also brought his wallet. The strange thing was, I found it on the dining room chair next to his keys. What's up?"

"First things first. Jump in. The pizza is as good as it looks. There are drinks in the refrigerator. Help yourself."

Ray opened the skinny wallet. He thought, "I like this guy already." No excess nonsense. He removed the items in an orderly manner. Ray lined up the four money cards: one credit card tied to a Marriott membership, one debit card from a Mexican bank, and one company credit card. The Marriott and Company cards were from the same bank. One additional card was the thickness of two cards. Ray tugged on the top edge, and it slid out. It was a flash drive embedded in what looked like a health club membership card.

Other documents included a company group health insurance card, an auto insurance card from a Mexican insurance company, and what appeared to be a company security access card.

There was a picture of a woman with two children in a plastic sleeve. It appeared to have been in the wallet for some time. The boy looked to be an early teen, and the girl was a bit younger. Ray handed that to Enrique. He first cleaned his pizza-covered hands. When he focused, his eyes scanned every inch. He held it like a fragile glass sculpture. "This must be his family. I recognize some things in the background. I wonder if he was living close to our parent's old house?"

Ray found the words 'must be' curious. Why would Enrique use those words? Ray let it go for now. He needed to stay on track. Ray finally got to the item he needed. It was a Mexican driver's license. Ray faced Enrique. He held the driver's license at arm's length, as if he were going to hand it to Enrique. Ray nodded his head and put the license on the table. He picked up the passport and repeated the process. Next came the computer-chipped photo ID security card—same routine. Finally, Enrique had to ask. "What are you doing?"

Without answering, Ray continued his scavenger hunt through a stack of file folders. He found one titled 'Transfer.' When he opened the file folder, the expression on his face looked like he had just discovered a pot of gold. A letter of transfer, a Visa with no restrictions from the US Embassy in Mexico City, and a list of company employees at the LA office. The big find was a brand-new Social Security card, paperclipped to a copy of Elias' birth certificate and the law firm-initiated application. Two letters were also attached, one to a senator and one to a congressman. They had requested assistance from the local Social Security Administration to expedite approval. Ray was sure there was a hefty donation to their political campaigns for their support.

Ray turned back to Enrique. "You can put the picture down. It is not going anywhere." Enrique complied but kept it in a prominent position. Then Ray extended his hand to shake Enrique's. It was as if they were meeting for the first time. "Elias, I want to be the first to welcome you to the United States."

Enrique shook his hand and, with a smile, said, "I think I overtasked your brain this morning."

Ray became energized. "Remember, I told you that I thought it was you moving in last week? I truly could not tell the difference from a distance. Driver's licenses and passport photos are not the best reflection of what someone really looks like. Anytime I need to show my driver's license picture, I know they run me through the system, thinking I appear like a criminal because of my photo."

"Still no idea what you are saying." Enrique was confident Ray had lost his mind.

"It is simple. Tomorrow you are going to go to the Department of Motor Vehicles and apply for a California Driver's License. You have the official forms of ID. You only need two for a driver's license, but you have a minimum of three. Once you have that license with your picture, opening other accounts will be easy."

The lights came on for Enrique, but the concept had not completely set in. "You want me to assume Elias's identity?"

"Yes! It's brilliant if I do say so myself. It solves most of the identity issues you have."

"What about his family? I don't know anything about them. I had to cut all ties with them for their protection. The incriminating evidence I have is the only thing that keeps me alive. At least that is what I thought until I saw Captain Guiterez. I am not sure what he is up to."

A brain flash just brought the answer to Ray's earlier question. Enrique looked at the picture and said about Elias, "Must be his family." Just in case Colonel Torres decided to renege on their deal and go after Enrique, he had cut all ties with his friends and family to protect his brother. He did not want the Mexican military to use anyone as leverage to make him give up his files. Whether true or not, Ray had to assume high-ranking officials were tracking Elias and watching for contact from Enrique. Since leaving the military, neither brother knew anything about the other.

Ray held up his wait-a-minute finger. He had to think. "You are right. We need to think this thing through. Let's take the same analytical approach we used before planting the surveillance bug." Ray's finger was still pointing upwards, but now it was wagging like a metronome. He was trying to find the right rhythm for problem-solving. "Family could cause us to go to plan two…or no plan at all."

Ray handed Enrique a notepad and a pen. "Brainstorm. Start listing everything that will disconnect you from Elias. New credit card from a different bank, new checking account, new whatever. Let's keep what we can, but nothing that could be tracked. Check to see if he used automatic payments on his credit card. If he did it will make the transition easier."

"Ray, my man, you are morphing from Mr. Realist to Mr. Devious."

Ray laughed. "No. Still Mr. Realist. Define problems, research as needed and solve problems. I have used the 'mini-max regret technique' so often it is just second nature."

"Okay, I don't know that one."

"It is our what-could-go-wrong exercise. You look at how to minimize the maximum regret – mini-max. If you continue to use Elias's credit card and make payments, for example, it will give the appearance that he did not disappear. But why is he not showing up for work if he is still around? Since it is a Christian company, most everyone working there should have disappeared anyway." Ray caught Enrique's curious expression. He noted, "It is a logical conclusion based on the pattern of people who disappeared. There may be other explanations, but I am holding on to the vanishing Christian theory for now." Ray noticed Enrique's disappointment with that 'other explanations' comment but ignored it. "We need to ask, 'What could go wrong?' Then we need to decide what to act on, modify or abort."

Enrique was still doubtful. He picked up the pen but could not bring himself to start writing. Ray recognized the hesitation. Ray shifted the discussion to a different need. "Were you able to get into Elias's computer and phone?"

"That was easy. My brother was always predictable. The day he got his first new computer was May ninth, 1996. For him it was a major event. He commemorated the day with his security code. As he learned more about security, he would subtract one. The date of 5996 becomes 4885. The six-digit version is 5/9/1996 or 480885. I got it the first time."

Ray grinned from ear to ear. "I love it. I think your brother and I would have gotten along like you and I do. It is a shame you had to sever ties to him and his family." Enrique did not change expression, but that last statement released a sadness he had been able to suppress until now. On the other hand, there was some comfort when Ray acknowledged the bond they had formed.

Since Ray had no clue about Enrique's internal and emotional thought process, he forged ahead. "Have you looked for any personal information?" Ray figured that the search might not have happened with all the other sorting and organizing Enrique had done.

"I just did a quick scan but did not open any files. I guess I was not ready to go there." Ray asked Enrique for the notepad and sent Enrique across the hall to get all communication devices. When Enrique returned, half the page was filled with a list of issues affecting identity changes. Action items needed to follow each issue. Enrique went to his dining room table workspace, opened the computer, and tapped the appropriate keys. The screen saver Ray saw was an ancient-looking scroll. The words were in Greek, but he somehow recognized them as John 3:16.

"Find anything you can about his personal life. I know this will be hard for you but do your best. Let me know if you need to stop or want me to take over." Ray could see Enrique had come to terms with this highly unusual scenario. "First, add to this list I started. Then, I will find whatever I need for a deep dive search. My assumption, which may prove false, is that the family disappeared just like Elias. But then again, you are still here, so I need to factor that into my search. See if you can find his wife and kid's email addresses and any social media. I will start with what I know."

Ray's first instinct was to go for Elias's driver's license. He placed it next to the computer and started typing. For the next twenty minutes, the only sounds in the room were the keyboards ticking, the refrigerator compressor kicking on, and some external noises through the open balcony door. Ray broke the silence, but his eyes never left the screen. "I found someone still active on social media sites. Do you know Hernando DeSilva? Could he ID Elias?"

That caught Enrique off guard for just a moment. "Uh, yeah. My uncle married Bernadette DeSilva. No, I need to rephrase that. They did not officially get married. They lived together, but everyone thought they were married. Hernando is Bernadette's son from her first marriage. I was in the army when they moved in together, so I don't think he would know much about me. Nando, as we called him, is a nasty piece of work. I am surprised he is not in jail. It would make sense that you could find him. I cannot imagine Elias would have had anything to do with Nando. How did you find him?"

"He was named as one of the six pallbearers at your uncle's funeral. I don't know why exactly, but I decided to check each person on the guest list. There were only thirteen that I could find at the funeral. Six of them were pallbearers. The search went quickly. What you said filled the gaps for me." Ray glanced up to see an unusual expression on Enrique's face. "What?"

"I did not know my uncle died. Remember I have not been in touch with anyone in Mexico. No one would have been able to let me know." Ray leaned back in his chair and closed his eyes. It was one of those 'I just screwed up' moments. "Ray, there was no way for you to know that."

Ray nodded and got back on track. "Let's keep Nando on our 'go wrong' list just in case. When I have time, I'll do a deeper dive." Ray's comprehensive search turned up nothing. That, in itself, was significant. "I have what I think will be good news for you. There were no social media posts for Elias's wife or children after the day everyone disappeared. The church had its own chat room. Again, nothing. The family must have vanished as well. We will go with that."

Enrique sighed. "Then they are together in Heaven." Ray felt Enrique's relief. Maybe there is something to all of this, he thought. Ray's realism quickly patched that crack, although some cracks were becoming significant, maybe beyond repair.

The two reviewed everything. Ray thought Enrique's transformation would be safe without an unexpected Nando surprise. Ray took a deep breath, combined with some momentary relaxation. "Let's call it a day. I want to clean up some loose ends, then do more research based on what you helped me with today. It will be hard to prepare things for tomorrow since I am unsure what is on the agenda."

"If you need to check with me on anything as you get ready, let me know. I will go through more files and pull out anything that could impact our plan. Oh, I forgot to tell you. All the furniture is rented under the company name." Enrique added, "While you do your thing, I will be working on an idea I think we can implement against the bad guys. You will probably want to be more devious than me, but we can talk tomorrow."

As soon as Enrique left, Ray's focus turned to a folder labeled 'God's Path Materials'. The file contained both informational and logistical documents. He was amazed at the size and number of Christian distribution centers. The website provided an array of written, audio, and video educational materials. Ray did not bother counting the number of translations available. The comprehensive product line was remarkable.

The company is headquartered in Mexico City, with distribution centers across Europe, Asia, Africa, and the United States, including coverage in Canada. The company that employed Elias is privately owned, which means Ray would need to put in extra effort to gather information about the individuals behind the company and its financial situation. It was not a priority at this point, but now he was curious and wanted to learn more.

Elias appeared on the company's website, Facebook, and LinkedIn pages, but he had little exposure across any of them. His picture was at least five years old, which Ray thought was odd. As part of the job, Ray generally thought sales and marketing people were self-promoting, or 'networked', to use a more politically correct term. His posts looked like they came straight from the PR department with no real personal touch.

The only personal social site was Truth Social. Ray felt it was necessary to search for active friends on the social media site. It did not take long since there were not that many. To be overly cautious, he explored the friends of the friends. All but two were his wife's friends. There were no photos of him with his family on his profiles, another oddity Ray could not explain.

Acquaintances with no close ties would not be able to tell the two brothers apart. Ray deduced from his research that the close friends also disappeared, but he had to assume that some were still around. Ray thought, "Elias must be like me and wanted nothing to do with all the nonsense on these social sites." But why would he want to keep such a low profile?

Elias had just moved into the apartment. Why no family? The apartment would have been tight for a family of four. That probably meant the family was not coming in the near term. He was perhaps scouting out the area for a more permanent location. Or was this just a temporary assignment? Questions just kept leading to more questions. Something did not add up. Then he thought out loud, "You need to stop this, Ray. You do not have time for this right now. But if something is wrong, you must find it before Enrique morphs into Elias."

Ray put all of that aside and focused on today's Bible introduction. Enrique had given him plenty of resources. After several hours of preparation, he stopped. Ray only needed about 4 hours of deep sleep to start the morning fresh.

Ray returned his focus to the bad guys. He was anxious to see which computer would be impacted by the bugs he planted. With Enrique out of pocket to manipulate the spyware when the computer shuts down, Ray's Bureau of Investigation would be fifty percent short-staffed. Adjustments to the plan implementation would need to be done solo for the first time. Which application to apply would be up to Ray. He had to have his options ready for Mo to avoid any doomsday scenario.

Manually writing down ideas on a notepad was not Ray's standard operating procedure. Since he needed to think outside the box, a different approach might impact his thinking. After balling up and throwing sheet after sheet of rejected ideas in the general direction of the trash can, he kept one page with potential. He stared intently at the page, daring it to contradict the possibility of success.

The page was full of random thoughts. The laptop screen was now in full view, and the keyboard was poised for action. Then Ray began. If the keyboard could think, it would believe two people were typing simultaneously. The mouse went into action, highlighting and moving key components to some logical order. He read his work from top to bottom, but it still did not feel right. Something was missing.

He thought about an idea he had written on one of those crumpled papers near the trash can. Ray went to the pile of papers on the floor. He was disappointed after spreading and reviewing the pages he had smoothed out. The idea was just not there. He was about to throw the stack away when he spotted the only ball of paper that had hit its trash can mark. He had found the one page he needed. "Come on!" he thought out loud. "There is no way some super force would have made that shot." He shook it off. "I think this whole God thing is starting to make me crazy."

But then again, it was the missing piece of Ray's plan.

He headed back to the keyboard. After several internal arguments, some additional research, and a final self-congratulation, he finished the plan on draft four. Without missing a beat, he started coding. Ray saved the work on his computer, then on a flash drive.

It was just after midnight. Ray wanted to get the flash drive to Enrique. He knew that since Enrique reported for work at four in the afternoon, his sleep schedule started at two in the morning with a wake-up time of nine. He would complete any deliveries assigned by Maria or conquer his daily chores. By two o'clock, he would stop at home, eat, and don his uniform.

Ray was afraid he had already disrupted Enrique's circadian rhythm, but he thought that if there was no response to a light tapping on the door, he would withdraw to work up a plan two. Fortunately, a light shone on the threshold. A complete knock ensued. Enrique opened the door and thrust a flash drive toward Ray, who had mirrored the move. They each handed off their version of a brilliant plan. As if it were composed, they harmonized, "Let me know what you think." Nothing else needed to be said. They retreated to their refuges.

After fifteen minutes of reviewing Enrique's formula, Ray stepped into the hall to see Enrique standing in the open doorway with his laptop. They moved to Ray's place. The two were in sync to the point of finishing each other's thoughts. They finalized the plan to install their spyware on any computer that goes blank.

Monday morning came faster than Ray thought it would. His alarm was set for 5:00 AM and was programmed to play soothing classical music. If this were a typical day, he would have gradually ascended into the real world, gone through his morning ritual, and enjoyed the twenty-minute walk to the office. Today, he stopped the alarm from doing its job several minutes before it was supposed to. The standard routine was not on the agenda.

Arriving at the office earlier than usual, Ray was poised like a leopard focused on picking off its prey from a grazing herd. Because of their global exposure, Tech Support, housed on the ninth floor, provided 24/7 service. He was convinced they would be ready. Ray had opened his laptop in anticipation. Ray reviewed the plan one last time and was mentally prepared for one of three options: This will work, almost work, or it will be back to the drawing board.

Ray had replaced the middle drawer on his desk, which typically stored pens, pencils, paper clips, and other things he was averse to using. The more practical, retractable keyboard with various adjustment options now fills that space. He logged on to the company system, reviewed his task list, and started working. The two deadlines on the list just needed a few tweaks. Today, if an alarm bell sounded, the other tasks du jour would have to wait.

Ray plugged in a flash drive with his notes for today's meeting. Since he had no idea what to expect, he focused on Bible references to the Temple and connected secular historical facts. He assumed the mindset of the Construction Project Manager. He also accepted that he would need to fly by the seat of his pants. For Ray, mentally preparing for the unknown was vital to staying focused.

Maria came in, placed her oversized, black-and-gold leather bag on her chair, and headed to Ray's office. "Good morning." Her intonation did not match the words. Ray's standard reply lobbed the ball back to Maria. "Here is Leticia's laptop. I left her iPad there. Hopefully, she will be using it soon. Her standard logon did not work. I was going to do some work on her computer to avoid the need to transfer files back and forth. The remote access worked fine on my laptop.

"When I left Saturday about noon, Leticia was still in an induced coma. The good news is that she is making progress. We may know today if they are going to gradually bring her out of the coma."

"That sounds positive. Do you have a specific contact at the hospital? I am going to a meeting today and would like to update Chas."

Maria looked surprised. While she handed Ray a business card for the contact at the hospital, she said, "I don't have anything on the calendar. Mr. Jenkins has been letting me know about meetings so that when Leticia returns, I can update her. We are doing our best to stay optimistic."

"This one just came up Friday. I think I am just a placeholder at this point." Ray knew that was not exactly right, but he was not one hundred percent certain that it might not be the case. At least, that is how he justified stretching the truth.

"Do you know what it's all about?" That question raised a small red flag. Why is she so interested? But since he knew she was somewhat of a control freak, he accepted her questions as reasonable.

"I was told I would be filled in when I got there. I am just hoping it is not a waste of my time. You know how much I despise blah-blah-blah meetings. If there is anything Leticia needs, I will update you on what I find out." That satisfied Maria's need to know. She just nodded and headed back to her desk.

Within five minutes, Ray heard, "What is going on with

my computer?" Ray thought, 'Can't be.' He was out of his office in a heartbeat but maintained his controlled demeanor. "Has anyone been on my computer while I was gone?"

Ray was ready. "Not that I saw, and I was here all-day Friday. What's wrong?"

"I tried to open my computer twice. The first time I opened a file, the computer just logged off. I opened it again, but as soon as I logged on, it shut down again. Is anyone else having this problem?" The second time was a surprise. She would have needed to reopen the spyware. It could be a cache problem. He made a mental note to check with Enrique.

"Not that I know of." Ray said as though he had just had an epiphany, "Wait! I think I might know what is wrong. It has something to do with a recent update. I read about it just last week. If it is what I think it is, I am pretty sure I know how to fix it."

Ray noticed Maria's coffee mug was empty. That was sacrosanct to start her day. "Why don't you get a coffee? You should also update Chen about Leticia's condition. If this glitch is what I think it is, the fix should be easy, but it might take several minutes."

As soon as Maria left, Ray worked at warp speed and planted his spyware. He removed the code that caused the shutdown. Maria was still meeting with Chen. Ray dashed to his office. He needed to know if everything was working before Maria ended her update with Chen. He could see her standing in Chen's doorway.

He quickly typed the password while keeping an eye out for movement. He hit enter - password error. The next time, he forced himself to be more focused. Ray coaxed the screen: "Come on, come on, come on." Then victory. He was in. He hustled back to Maria's desk.

Only now could he begin to process what was happening. He did not have Maria on the radar. She was making her way back to her desk. Fortunately for Ray, she was a social animal, taking the time to pause at one cubicle and then another. She was more than likely updating everyone on Leticia's condition. He was also sure, at least now, that her version would be fake news.

Ray was standing next to Maria's desk as she approached. "Done. It was exactly as I thought. I am going to try to research more just to make sure I didn't miss anything. I just needed to pre-empt the boot and install the patch. Go ahead and reboot. Let's make sure everything is working."

The logon screen appeared. Ray asked Maria to take another step. He moved around to the front of her desk, giving her the appearance of privacy. He needed to appear credible. "I would like you to open exactly as you did initially. I want to make sure there is not another program or virus causing the problem." Ray could see the concern on Maria's face.

Maria had a dilemma. If she opens the share program and it causes the shutdown, how can she explain that away? If she does not open the share program but tries later and there is a shutdown, she knows Ray will want to take a deep dive to see the problem. She saw that Ray noticed her hesitation.

Quick thinking prevailed. "Sorry, I am trying to remember the sequence." She decided there would be trouble one way or the other. Her best hope was success. Maria logged on. So far, so good. While holding her breath, she made the final click. She exhaled slowly. It worked. Just in case Ray wanted to see what she had done, she immediately got out of the shareware.

"I am up and running. You are the man. Thanks." She could not see Ray's relief or tell that Ray was giving the fist-pump move that a golfer makes after sinking a twenty-foot putt to win the tournament. She could not know because it was all in his head.

Reality struck. Ray had one more hole to play in this golf tournament. Can he see Maria's computer? Is Enrique's shareware version going to work? He grabbed his laptop as he was sitting down. Multiple taps on the keyboard. His pinky finger hovered over the 'enter' button. Tap. Ray could see Maria's screen. That generated the second fist pump.

The next move was to wait until she was away from her desk. The upcoming meeting was imminent, but there was still time. He was about to check on another installed feature when the phone rang. He barely had said "Ray here," when he heard, "This is Paula. I manage the Help Desk. I was told to call you if someone's computer shut down for no reason. It's Tina Aguilar. Her desk is close to the conference room on the ninth floor. She acts as a floater. After everyone disappeared employees jump in where needed."

"Okay." Ray calmly replied. "One shut down happened just a few minutes ago on Maria's computer. I was able to repair it. I can be right there. Please let her know to keep the computer off. This is a glitch in an update. I need to drop some information off on my way."

"I'll be glad to let her know. Ray, are you going to let us know what's going on?" Paula said it more like a statement than a question.

"I will, but I have a meeting and I am not sure how long it will take or what might become a priority. So, it might not be today. Chas will be in the meeting I am attending. If there is an opportunity to update him, I will." Ray gave Paula his cell number. "For now, just call me. I know you are short-staffed as we are. And I am sure with some research you would be able to make the repair. I will be saving you a lot of precious time." Ray was not ready to commit until the last shutdown happened.

Ray was taking the shortest route between two points to get to Jolie Lange. He wanted to update her, but, more importantly, he wanted them to be allies, not foes. Her support would be vital. Just outside her office, Jolie was conversing with someone when she spotted Ray as a man on a mission. He passed the previous guest as she was leaving. There was no 'hello, how's the family' discussion. "Come in." She went around her desk and sat down. She expected Ray to take a seat, but he stood. "You called it," she confessed.

"Yes, unfortunately, or fortunately, depending on the glass being half empty or half full. I have always been a half-empty glass skeptic. Maria, Leticia's admin, and Tina Aguilar are the targets. I fixed Maria's and installed a fail-safe code if an immediate shutdown of this reverse sting operation should be needed. It should work with Tina as well." Ray was not ready to expose the spyware installed. He wanted to be the only one going under the bus if it came to that.

Jolie wrote down the two names. Then she wrote, Sophie. Ray knew Jolie was already ahead of the curve. Sophie, HR Director, was the first step. Ray added, "I suspect they were both hired around seven to eight months ago. Did they come from the same agency? Do they…"

Jolie held up her hand. Ray knew to stop. "I've got this. I understand that's a phrase you use." Ray smiled. "When am

I going get the whole story?"

"When Mo tells me to make it a priority. This is a very fluid situation. I don't even have the whole story. Currently, I am reacting more than acting. That will change soon. Maybe today. I promise you that you will know what I know when I know it."

"Another thing, Miss I-got-this, you will want to write down Dominic Sanders, Head of Operations. Do you know him well?"

Words flew out of Jolie's mouth. "I know who he is, but the question is why."

"Because he hired the current maintenance company about seven months ago. That company has new owners as of ten months ago. The former maintenance company had been with us for five years with few complaints. There was no reason to terminate their contract.

"About six months ago, the new owners, under the guise of doing their due diligence, found some wiring problems. They brought in their electricians to make the repairs instead of using the electrical contractor we currently use. Why would Dominic allow that? I don't know Mr. Sanders. Maybe he delegated everything. If I am right about the Tina and Maria hire date… It just seems that the dots are starting to connect. Who influenced, introduced, or…" Ray caught himself. "Sorry, you have this." As Ray started turning to leave, he asked, "Any large purchases made by Dominic recently? Just thinking out loud." After Ray was out the door, Jolie smiled, looked down, and shook her head.

Ray's next stop was Tina's desk. He replicated the repair. Similar to Maria, Tina was instructed to repeat the login sequence. He saw a controlled but similar angst that Maria had when she was asked. Another success. His office was next. Ray had modified the algorithm by one digit to isolate the two desks for tracking and recording purposes. He logged on again, typed the new access code, and hit enter. Curiosity replaced the fist-pump. He mumbled, "What's next?"

As soon as he knew the coding worked, an unusual observation dominated his thoughts. Both Maria and Tina typed nothing. To get in, they clicked the shareware link. That almost invisible icon must come into play. These two do not have the technical skills to pull off a complex login. They are pawns on this chessboard.

Ray knew chess pawns played a significant strategic role. He also knew that pawns are easily sacrificed. Suspecting that Captain Gutierrez might be behind this, Ray imagined that more people could disappear, and not in a biblical way. The question popped into his head: "How can I use my opponent's pawns? How can checkmate happen before those pawns are sacrificed?"

Ray returned to reality when the phone in his shirt pocket vibrated against his favorite silver-plated pen. He had forgotten the phone was in his shirt pocket. The text message was from Chas. "Where are you?"

"On my way. Two computers shut down." Ray waved at Maria as he blasted out of the office.

CHAPTER ELEVEN

The meeting was about to begin at Martinelli's law firm. As Ray entered the large conference room, he spotted Chas talking to two people he recognized from the Mimstruct Pro introduction. Close by, three people huddled, reviewing a document. One of the three, from his appearance, was an Orthodox Jew.

Standing by the conference room's back door was another cluster of three people. A stately man wearing an impeccable suit was directing the other two. Ray guessed he was one of the law firm's partners of Martinelli, Sakowitz, and Martinelli. One person would not be staying for the meeting. He had the traditional white shirt, sleeves rolled up, with a blue tie. The third could have easily been a Miss America finalist. Whatever her title, Ray knew the blue-tie guy was no match for her influence on the suit guy.

Ray spotted Mo isolated as much as anyone could be isolated in a conference room full of people. Mo was having a serious conversation with a man in a dark blue suit. It was the only coat in the room that was buttoned. The suit was tailored, not as a fashion statement, but as a functional tool of the trade. He did not recognize this man, but Ray instinctively knew his role fell into a category only Mo understood. Ray suspected this guy was security but would keep an open mind on that one.

Chas caught Ray out of the corner of his eye. He waved Ray over to a spot he had reserved at the expansive oblong table. When he knew no one was paying attention to them, Chas asked, "Where are we?"

Ray's response, "I know where the fish are…well at least two, Maria and Tina. We just need to throw them a line and set the hook when they take the bait."

Chas told Ray to have a seat and that he would be right back to give him the lay of the land. Chas headed toward Mo and the other man. Chas kept his part of the conversation brief, but Ray could see it was meaningful. Mo's friend glanced Ray's way but quickly returned to the conversation.

Chas returned and sat next to Ray. He pointed out the three men reviewing the document. Aylwin Goldberg was clearly the Orthodox member of the trio, as Ray suspected from his beard and attire. Benjamin Ableman was the Conservative delegate. The Kippah was the clue for Ray. Ethan Cantor, the third, was unknown until Chas explained. He represented the Reform denomination. Ethics eclipsed the law. These three represented the organization planning to build the third Temple.

Benjamin was the Chair of a large committee working on the Temple III reconstruction project. This particular sub-committee's goal was to bring the best project management software for a full committee vote. A simple majority vote would suffice. The team's recommendation ensures approval. To Ray, Benjamin would be the ultimate decision-maker.

The tie-guy had left. Miss America tugged at her skirt and sat at a table easily accessible to the table-top podium at the narrow end of the conference table. Ray guessed that this was a two-minute warning. When he silenced his phone, the clock flipped to 9:58. Ray impressed himself with that two-minute warning guess.

Mo and his colleague headed toward their seats on the other side of Chas. Ray moved in their direction. "Ray, this is Calev Macron." The two shook hands and used the standard 'nice to meet you' lines. Mo told Ray, "I heard from Jolie this morning. Whatever you are doing seems to be working. After this meeting, we will meet in the conference room across the hall." That was it. Mo took his place. To Ray's surprise, Calev left the room.

Ray spotted the first name on the agenda, Bernard Martinelli. He began, "If everyone could please be seated, we can start." A woman appeared seemingly out of nowhere. She must have come through the back door to the conference room. She greeted no one and sat down next to Miss America. She placed three different-colored file folders to the left of center, then positioned her Mont Blanc Skywalker JFK Special Edition Pen on the provided notepad.

Ray planned to take notes on his laptop but noticed that Miss America was the only one at the table with an electronic device. He never thought he would ever be glad there was a notepad available. Ray removed the Skywalker, Mont Blanc Space Blue Metal ballpoint pen from his shirt pocket and placed it in a similar position on his notepad. The corner of the mystery woman's lips tried to form a smile when she noticed what he had done, but she retreated quickly to her serious demeanor.

"Thanks to everyone, especially our friends from the Temple Mount Institute, for being here for our second face-to-face meeting. As great as web meetings are, so much more can be done when we are sitting around the table together. This has been a long two-thousand-year journey. A journey that now has its destination in view." Bernard reviewed the agenda.

Although Mo was confident Mimtrin was the frontrunner, Ray replacing Debbie was a big unknown. The objective for today was to determine if Mimtrin would be one of the two finalists. Mo thought about coaching Ray to listen, observe, and give the shortest possible answers. He did not bother because he knew it would do no good.

Bernard continued. "Because of the recent phenomenon, Mimtrin has brought in Ray Ferrari to replace Debbie, one of the many that disappeared. Mo has assured me that Ray has stepped in and has already been an asset for the project." He unexpectedly turned to Ray. "Would you like to tell us a little about yourself?" Chas and Mo just realized they could not exhale.

"Sure, be glad to. The first thing you should know is that I am not important, but this project is. You three gentlemen are essential. On the personal side, I am married to my job. My wife is my computer. My children are projects. I take them from infancy, nurture them, and educate them. And when they mature, I will have another child. My friends are my books, technical magazines, and research. Many people think that is sad, but I am happy. Many of those same people cannot say that.

"My skill set is defining and solving problems. I could give you a list of credentials, but credentials don't generate results, people do. I will be glad to answer anyone's questions, but that is it in nutshell."

There was dead silence in the room. Benjamin examined Ray for a moment. "Welcome to the team, Ray." Chas and Mo's sigh of relief was brief. The next inhalation was trapped again when they heard: "Is there anything you would like to know to get you up to speed with this project?"

Ray's immediate response allowed for another exhale. "Debbie was a talented, integral part of the team. I am reviewing her notes. From a Mimtrin perspective on the technical side, I am ready. On the particulars of this project, I am here to learn from your perspective. I am not shy. I will ask what I need to know." The leaders in the room exhaled. The relief was again temporary. "Actually, there is one question that will help me focus on today's meeting. Which Temple will be your model for the rebuild?"

Ray did not notice the visual daggers heading his way. His focus was on the answer. Benjamin responded, "That is an excellent question. Before I answer, why do you ask?"

Ray was matter-of-fact with his response. "It will help me focus and prioritize the project. Keep in mind that Chas has put together an exceptionally talented team. Because of his proactive approach, the gaps left by the recent disappearances are being filled by equally talented, and in some cases, more experienced people. Duplication of effort is not an option."

Ethan jumped in. "Are you Jewish?" No was the reply. "Are you a Christian?"

Ray clarified, "I consider myself a realist. I respect your belief in God. I respect your need for an appropriate place of worship. I do not rule anything out, but for now I need to deal with the tangibles."

Ethan flipped the script. "From everything you have said, I believe you are a straightforward man. But understand, as a people we have been working on this in one form or another since 1948 when we got our nation back. We have been told a lot, from truthful men, with no tangible results." Ray gave an understanding nod.

Aylwin's skepticism required a test. "Tell me, which Temple would you advise us to use and what would be your 'tangible' focus?" Chas was aware that Ray knew nothing about the Bible and was about to interrupt. Where Ray would take this was up in the air. Sticking to the agenda would be the saving grace at this point. He started to turn to Bernard when Mo stopped his hand from going up.

Ray nodded his head. "Ah, a hypothetical gotcha question. Good. Before I answer, do you have a budget for the rebuilding of a Temple?" All three nodded. "Am I right to conclude that the numbers are not finalized?" Again nods. "Can I assume this budget is not unlimited?" Again nods.

Ray looked at Aylwin. "I am going to guess you are voting for Solomon's Temple. That is the temple that God engineered. Is that correct?" He smiled and nodded. "Good. Let's assume that is the choice. Let's assume that we follow the preparation David made for Solomon. Let's just use one item as the example."

Everyone in the room focused on Ray, but nobody knew where he was going with this line of thought. "Admittedly, I am not a Bible scholar. So, quoting exact verses is not in my skill set. One that did stand out to me was 1 Chronicles 22:14. In that, David left Solomon assets, a budget of sorts, in gold, silver and other materials. One hundred thousand talents of gold and a million talents of silver. Let's use gold and silver for this example.

"Using seventy pounds per talent as a round number, we have seven million pounds of gold. Multiply that by 16 ounces, and we have one hundred twelve thousand ounces. At four thousand dollars per ounce, which is low, the gold portion of the budget is four hundred and forty-eight billion dollars."

Ray was making these calculations in his head. Aylwin was writing, trying to follow Ray and fact-check his numbers at the same time. "Follow that same logic with one million talents of silver at twenty-five dollars per ounce on the low side, you would get… twenty-eight billion dollars. The total budget in gold and silver would be $476 billion.

"Then we would need to factor in all the other materials, bronze, cedar, iron, and jewels. To make it easy, let's assume that the materials cost rounds up to seven hundred billion dollars. That is what it takes to replicate Solomon's Temple in materials alone. Am I close?" Ethan revealed that Ray's numbers were amazingly close, considering his limited knowledge of the project.

Ray rattled off several other sets of numbers. He looked at the three. There was no argument at this point. "Now, to your tangible results question. We can easily assume your goal is to come in under budget. The costs I used were spot-market prices, which can vary worldwide. The Mimstruct Pro has an AI component. The program can analyze trends to search for the best market price.

"It can be programmed to automatically buy the gold at the best price. Timing is everything with spot markets. On the way to the meeting I was talking to Ariel, our person leading the AI development. She said that the testing has generated a range of savings from five to eight percent depending on the sourced commodity. Assuming the low end at 5%, the savings on the gold talents would be…$22.4 billion dollars. Even the best AI system cannot guarantee a savings in a volatile commodities market. The result, at least until now, is that our AI has outperformed two major commodity brokers on the same day for the same products in a mock trading day. Did that answer the tangible part of your question?"

Aylwin was a temporary statue. Then he set his pen on the pad full of notes. "I am about to say something that I have never said in business meetings that require negotiations. That was impressive. Now see if you can impress me with the other part of my question."

If anxiety levels could be measured, Chas would have set a new record high. Mo was running various meeting-saving scenarios in his head, depending on which direction Ray took. Chas's lips moved soundlessly, reflecting what was on his mind: "Ray, don't blow it now."

"I will answer in an advisory capacity. The caveat is that I do not have the significant amount of research that you have. I am also going to guess that you do not have Solomon's astronomical budget, although I would not rule anything out. Let me walk through my logic with the information as I understand it. Feel free to correct me if I am too far off.

"Solomon's Temple and Herod's Temple have the same set of financial problems. Herod's Temple is a name that I personally think was a slap in the face to the Jewish people." As soon as he said it, he realized he may have overstepped. Ray apologized for the editorial comment and moved forward in the same breath. "There may be more accurate engineering specifications for Herod's project, but other non-construction related issues will impact the original plan. We know that Herod claimed to be a Jew, but he was a traitor to the Jews when he sided with Rome during the Jewish Hasmonean dynasty conflict. The Roman Senate declared him the King of the Jews. Another slap in the face." Ray caught himself again but skipped the apology.

"To appease the leaders of the Jewish communities, Herod convinced Rome to approve the remodeling of the Second Temple. It was ultimately good for the Jews, but everyone knew Herod was covering his backside and basking in his egotistical glory. So, the optics of a third Temple using Herod's design could create problems you do not need.

"We know, however, that Herod did not build the second Temple. Zerubbabel did. He was in the first wave of Jewish captives in Babylon that were allowed to return to Israel after Persia defeated Babylon. Cyrus appointed Zerubbabel as Governor of Judah in 538 BC. He started to rebuild the Temple immediately. Zerubbabel experienced resistance and the ultimate withdrawal of Persian support. In the Book of Haggai, the Lord blessed Zerubbabel. Hold on one second, I wrote it down." He started to open his phone.

Benjamin jumped in. *"On that day, declares the LORD Almighty, I will take you, my servant Zerubbabel son of Shealtiel, declares the LORD, and I will make you like my signet ring, for I have chosen you, declares the LORD Almighty."* Benjamin added, "Zerubbabel was indeed blessed."

"Thank you." Ray continued, "With the help of two key prophets, the Temple was completed in 516 BC. But it was far from the glorious structure that Solomon built. The Temple was modest but functional. This Temple fulfilled the needs of the people."

Ray put his phone down. "I think if Zerubbabel's Temple was good enough for God, then it might just be good enough for Israel. It would be built faster, be within whatever budget you may have, and, most importantly, your worship services with rituals and traditions could begin sooner. You could expand some areas of worship in the design without breaking the bank. You could add to the Temple as resources are available. But, in my humble opinion, that modest start would represent major renewal for Israel."

The three sat silent. Aylwin was stroking his beard as he stared somewhere in space. Benjamin locked his fingers and closed his eyes as one might in silent prayer. Ethan looked straight at Mo and nodded. Benjamin then whispered to the other two before saying, "Excuse us for a couple of minutes." The three stepped into the hall.

Bernard was a bit confused and tried to fill the gap. "Everyone, help yourselves to the refreshments. As a warning, those almond scones are addictive." Chas and Mo sat in silence. No one moved, except, of course, Ray. He sauntered over to the table, retrieved a sparkling water, and picked up one of the addictive scones. Ray noticed that the lady with the fancy pen was packing up. She put the colored files in her notebook, then disappeared through the back door. Ray was going to find out who that was before he left the building today.

Just about the time Ray had finished his quick break and returned to his seat, the door to the conference room opened. The three calmly repositioned themselves at the table. Benjamin started. "Bernard, we would like you to skip the first two sections of the agenda. Chas, we would appreciate it if you would discuss the updates from our last meeting and the additions to the software you are making.

"As you know, we have already met with one other firm. Next week, we are meeting with another. Sorry Mo, we are cutting your part, but it is not necessary at this point. We want to see what the next group has to say, but we can tell you now that your company will be one of the three finalists." Mo nodded a thank you.

As Chas gathered his presentation and stood, Aylwin looked at Ray and said, "I am still voting for Solomon."

Ray smiled and responded, "I would have bet the farm on that." That removed some of the stressors from the equation. The rest of the meeting focused on functionality and logistics. Chas went through each module, emphasizing the modifications made specifically for this project. He explained how each component was interconnected. Ray used this opportunity to catch up on the project's status. His participation from that point on stayed limited to clarification questions.

After the meeting, Benjamin cornered Mo. "One request for planning purposes. Assuming the overall committee chooses your company, we would like Ray to be the project manager and liaison. He made a few mistakes in his presentation, but as he said himself, he is not a biblical scholar. On the other hand, we have never had anyone with a better understanding of our wants, needs and goals. It seems we might need a realist on our team." The five-hundred-pound gorilla on Mo's back jumped off and ran away.

"For timing purposes, Israel could potentially sign a treaty in the next ninety days. The Temple is a major sticking point right now. One of the deciding factors for selection might come down to which company can be ready with a full package by then. I am not sure who this Amir Acee is, but his political influence is rising faster than Barack Obama's ascent to power from obscurity. We know Amir is trying to stop a three hundred sixty-degree Muslim assault on Israel. This will be a major test to see if he is the leader everyone in the press seems to think he is."

Ethan stopped by to shake Ray's hand. "Thanks for your input today. So, just curious, what would you call this third

Temple?"

Ray, without hesitation, said, "Call it what it is: Yahweh's Temple."

Mo, Chas, and Ray moved across the hall to a conference room. It was unexpected but not a real surprise to Ray when he saw Jolie stationed at the 12 O'clock position of the round mahogany table. The maroon leather chairs were the perfect complement with the added touch of the same wood arms and legs. Each of the three placed any materials they had at the first available spot. Ray chose to sit next to Jolie. Before starting, they took advantage of the cornucopia of food and drinks on the matching credenza. What would typically be bookshelves sitting on top of the base, with three sets of file drawers, was instead a cabinet with enough alcohol to stock a busy tavern.

Ray picked up a bottle of water. He asked Jolie, "Can I get you anything, water, Perrier, or…" He looked at the selection, looked back at Jolie, then back to the selection. "A glass of the twenty-one-year-old Balvenie single malt scotch?"

Ray could see Jolie focused on the bottle. With a longing sigh, she said, "Drinking from their bottle would be the only way I could afford a chance to experience that scotch. But, I'll have to pass, thanks." She looked curiously at Ray, trying to figure out how he knew she was a scotch drinker. Maybe a lucky guess, but knowing Ray, it was an educated deduction.

Bernard stepped into the room, not to participate, but to make a statement. "Just wanted to let you know that I will be in my office while you are here in case you need anything. The green button on the phone over there is my direct line. I also wanted to let you know that both Essie and I thought the meeting went very well."

Ray piped in. "I assume Essie is the lady that was sitting opposite of us. I did not get a chance to meet her. Can I ask who she is?"

"Essie is a valuable asset of this firm. She is much more than a lawyer. She does our jury selection. She has two PhD's in psychology and her dissertation for one of them was on reading people. She converted the dissertation into a book that did pretty well."

"Essie Bevelhimer? 'It Is Not Just What They Say.' Is that her book?" Ray waited for the acknowledgement. "I read that book; it was brilliant." The others in the room just stared at Ray with that who-are-you look. "So, no offence to your opinion of the meeting, if she thinks it went well, it went well. Please let her know I am a fan."

"I will be glad to let her know. I am sure you two will meet at some point." Bernard was on his way out but turned back for a brief moment. "Any questions, green button."

As soon as the conference room door closed, Mo started. "First things first. Jolie is busy and just needs the same status that we need on the devices found in the office. Ray, you are up."

Ray nodded. He took the opportunity to jokingly throw a zinger Jolie's way. "Is your computer working?"

"Nice try. It is working just fine, thank you."

"Were there any more shutdowns?" The response was no. Even though Ray suggested no one spend any time on this, he knew Jolie would ignore that recommendation. "Did your person, whoever you picked, figure out what I did?" She shook her head no. Her glare could have penetrated the wall of a nuclear missile silo. "Obviously, you respect and trust who you picked. I will be glad to walk him or her through it. Who will I be meeting?"

"I could give you her name, but she won't respond if you use it. She goes by Tera, as in terabyte." Ray knew exactly what she meant. Geeks, especially hackers, have a handle they use. Anonymity and reputation are the driving forces behind the name. If someone exposes a corporate executive, politician, or another person for corruption, they attach their handle to ensure their real name cannot be traced.

"An independent contractor. Brilliant move." Ray looked at Mo. "I don't know how much you pay Jolie, but it is not enough." Ray started to update everyone when Calev Macron entered the conference room. After apologizing for his tardiness, he took an empty chair. Calev was introduced as the owner of a company that provides cybersecurity and monitoring for Mimtrin.

Ray started at the beginning, walking through the entire process. Ray told them about the spyware he embedded into the two computers. "My next goal is to determine where the information they captured is going. Once I know, I will be able to thwart any plans they may have." Ray looked at Mo. "As you said, screwing up something while trying to un-screw something else could be a problem. I have designed a preliminary code, but I would like to test something first."

He double checked his notes. "Chas, I would like you to send an email to Mo. The subject line should be 'Client Meeting - Important.' The email will reference an attachment, but there will be no attachment. Mo, you will respond saying you did not get the attachment, please resend. Then add a question like: Is this in reference to the upgrade AI algorithm patch?"

"That should get their attention. I will follow the email. Once I know the recipient, plan one initiates. We will attach a bug to the file you referenced in your email. The type of file attached will depend on timing and what we want to do next. If I am right about who it is, the file will contain a revised AI algorithm that would interest them. It will have one easy-to-find, blatant error and three buried errors that are difficult to find. If they follow protocol, they will catch the obvious and think they made the fix.

"If they catch the obvious glitch but not the others, their test will fail. Then they will look for another error. That will take time. If they find all three, the only algorithm they will get from us is one they probably already have. I would need to work with Ariel on that. Surprisingly, I found no spyware on her computer or bugs in her office."

Mo asked, "If you have plan one, what is plan two?" Ray's answer was simple: "Blow up their entire system." Mo's response was quick. He had already considered that option. "That causes other problems if we get caught…or even if we don't. If the client discovers we were behind any sabotage, our credibility and contract for the Temple project will be gone."

Calev joined in. "You said you think you know who it is. Can you update me on that?"

Ray looked at Mo. "Sorry Ray, you should have met Calev earlier, but we did not have time to talk. Calev worked with me in Israel. He has a security company, SyberSek, with multiple locations. When we are done here, you will be going to Calev's Cave, as I call it. He will update you on his background before you spend time trying to figure out who he is. Cyber security is his specialty, but his company is multi-faceted."

Ray looked at Jolie with an almost indistinguishable nod. He had just figured out who Tera worked for. Then he focused on Calev. "It is in the start-up menu. Your company probably looked there but might not have gone deep enough. The strings are woven through different layers."

Calev asked, but in reality, was demanding to know. "And how did you know where to find it? Did you help create it?" Ray locked his eyes with Calev. The other three in the room were one hundred percent fixated on the conversation.

"No. I just modified it."

"Then who told you where to find it and how it was built?"

"I am not going to tell you that right now."

Calev was clearly agitated. "That is not your decision. It is mine."

CHAPTER TWELVE

Ray knew the first power-play shot was fired. He fired right back. "First, this is not the military and your holier than thou attitude does not play with me. Second, it is not your decision. Third, Mo might think you are some kind of genius, but I do not trust you to start investigating people I know, those I've corresponded with or, someone I met at a conference. If you truly had a handle on things, you would have already figured out what I did. If you were to screw around investigating any names I might give up, lives could be at risk!"

Still glaring at Calev, Ray stood up. "Did you know about Maria or Tina before this week? How is Dominic Sanders involved? Has anyone tried to find out who installed the VOR on the roof? Did you even know there was a VOR on the roof? If you knew who installed it, you would know he is not a maintenance worker. What was Leticia doing in Colorado? That is just the start. And if I am wrong and you did know, why didn't you stop it? As far as I am concerned right now, you are part of the problem. The chance that I am giving up any of my multiple sources to you is zero."

Ray stayed focused on Calev. Ray knew he was at least eighty percent right. "Well? Update us." There was silence.

Ray looked directly at Mo. "You can fire me right now, but I am not answering to this guy."

Mo recognized that Calev had been busted. Mo said, "This is not going in the right direction. Calev, can we talk outside?"

As soon as they left, Ray jumped into action like nothing had just happened. He asked Jolie whether anyone had been captured on the security camera on the roof. She indicated they spotted someone working on it, but he was wearing a hoodie and sunglasses. There were only a couple of facial shots, but they were not good enough for facial recognition. She opened her computer. While it was loading, Jolie said, "Thanks." Chas could not officially say anything, but Ray could tell he was not a member of Calev's fan club.

The pictures came up. Ray verified that the second camera had been perfectly repositioned. He had Jolie open those images. She had forgotten about that change. She rewound to the day the camera was changed. The fast-forward mode engaged. And there he was. The man in the hoodie was purposely avoiding the primary security camera. By his movements, they realized that he did not know about the second camera.

Ray had Jolie isolate three frames that generated a reasonably clear picture. She could not text, but she could email. Ray gave her his private email address. He went to his phone and downloaded the images. He made a call. "Sorry to wake you. Go to your email. Open the three files. Tell me what you see." There was a pause, but it was not long. "It is him. Good. Go back to sleep."

About that time, the door to the conference room opened. Mo and Calev returned and took their seats. Ray was checking additional footage to see if he could get a better image.

Mo started the conversation. "These are trying times for everyone." Ray raised his hand.

"Sorry for interrupting. He is sorry; I am sorry. In reality, neither one of us means it. We do not have time for this so let's just move on. Calev, you probably could use some leverage with the Mexican CNI. Yes? No?"

Calev still did not like Ray, but he immediately had a new respect. "Leverage is the name of the game in this business."

"Arturo Guitierez was a captain in the Mexican Military Combat Engineer Division. He had his own information technology team that embedded security devices into buildings. When I gave Jolie a heads-up about the VOR, she adjusted the angle of one of the roof's cameras, leaving the primary camera unchanged. He knew about the main camera, and he avoided it like the plague. He was obviously unaware Jolie had made the change. The second camera caught an image.

"The CNI in Mexico would be very happy to know where this guy is. I am guessing one or more of the cartels would like to know his whereabouts as well. If he is taken out, I predict the head of our snake will be cut off. Whoever the people are behind this will have a serious problem." Ray could see that Calev had to restrain himself from initiating a complete interrogation. Mo's little talk had sunk in.

Mo looked at Calev and shrugged. "I told you Ray has skills no one understands." Mo made the next move. "I think everyone in this room recognizes that this is the team, repeat, team, which will drive us to the goal of Temple III. Share with each other and play nice."

Mo turned to Ray. "You mentioned Leticia's name as a suspect and made some points that could justify that conclusion. Take her off your list. You will know more after she recovers. For now, no need to waste your time looking into her." He paused and focused directly on Ray for emphasis. "You have to trust me on this." Mo stood. He looked at each person at the table. No additional words were needed.

Mo knew today was a game-changer for Mimtrin. "Chas, take over with the next steps. I have other issues to deal with right now. I am not sure I will be back before you finish up. Thank you everyone for your efforts today."

He opened the door to the conference room, but instead of leaving, he turned around. He looked at Ray and gave him the come-with-me wave. Outside, Mo told Ray, "Stick to plan one for now. Let me know what you find. Calev will not interfere. But know this, he will be taking over the sleuthing part. I will need you to focus on other things. Plan to meet me here tomorrow at 2 PM." There was a brief pause. "Good job today. I am bringing a defibrillator to the next meeting. I think my heart stopped two or three times today."

Ray smiled. "Full disclosure. I will probably be wearing an adult diaper." Mo just nodded like that might be another option. "I will be here at two tomorrow. Quick question before you go, how well do you know Bernie?"

Mo rolled his eyes, "Bernie has been with me from the time Mimtrin was a concept. Now what?"

"It's probably nothing. There might be something Bernie should know if he doesn't already."

Mo asked, "I will be seeing him before I leave. Any messages?"

Ray pointed his wait-a-minute finger. He pulled the phone from his pocket, scrolled, and tapped twice. "I made a note. Do they do immigration work here? Wait, here it is, Samson Englebright. Does he work here?"

Mo was even more confused. "The name sounds familiar as a new hire about a year ago, but I know nothing about him. And, as far as I know, this firm is strictly corporate law. Why?"

"You should wait to say anything until I confirm, but I thought I heard Maria refer him as an immigration lawyer. If, and it is still a big if, he knows Maria, we might want to know more about that connection. I will let you know asap. If I am right, maybe I can throw this bone to Calev."

Mo looked intently at Ray for a moment, trying to decide what to say next. Instead, he just turned away, slightly shook his head, and moved toward his mission. Before returning to the meeting, Ray made a fast call to Maria. "Hey, it's me. I am on a quick break, but I wanted to meet the lawyer you mentioned to see if there is anything I could do to help Enrique. What was his name?"

"His name is Samson Englebright, but he is not the lawyer that will be the one doing the work. He finds specialists based on the client's needs. Samson makes all arrangements."

Ray played along. "So, if I wanted to pay for part of his expenses, who would I need to pay. I am just trying to think through the best way to help."

"It depends on the form of the payment. Most of the transactions are cash. The firm he uses the most is the easiest for cash. Enrique, for example, would take the cash with him to the first meeting. But Samson could give you the account number to transfer funds. PayPal or Zelle is the recommended method of payment."

Ray said, "Thanks. That gives me an idea of what to expect. I don't know if I will be able to see Samson today, but I will give it a shot. Thanks. I have to go." Ray returned to the conference room. On the way, he checked to make sure the entire conversation was recorded as planned.

As he entered the room, he nodded at Calev. The conversation picked up where it left off. "Ray, to answer your earlier questions, we had suspicions but no hard evidence until Jolie came to us. Tera was put on the project. She is a genius, but like a baby with a stuffed toy. Take the toy away and she starts screaming." He looked at Ray. "She would have figured out what you did."

Ray nodded in agreement. "If you and Jolie respect her talents, I have no reason to question her abilities. I look forward to meeting her."

Jolie laughed. "You and Tera are a match made in heaven, and you haven't even met."

Ray responded, "A match maybe, in Heaven, yet to be determined." Jolie found that comment revealing. Ray walks and talks as a believer should, but he does not believe. He even noticed my Bible. Curious.

Everyone went full disclosure, although there was always an ace in the hole that each could play if needed. Everyone has a secret. Calev admitted he knew nothing that would have indicated that Maria and Tina were involved in anything nefarious.

Calev explained that he left this morning's meeting after being introduced to Mimtrin's potential client. At times, Mo used Calev as a prop to give the future clients confidence in the security of any disclosures. Calev also wanted to make sure Ray's comments about Maria and Tina were addressed.

Chas filled everyone in on the potential problem with Maria and Tina. "When they were first hired, Calev had met with Sophie Humphries, who, as HR Manager, signed off on the clerical hires. Calev reviewed her notes and the files on both.

"Sophie Humphries runs standard background checks of all hires up to a certain level. Calev's company runs checks on upper-level hires and anyone who would be directly involved in confidential matters. Since Maria and Tina recently came to America, there was not much in the system. She could have called previous employers in Mexico, but since she does not speak Spanish, it would have been more trouble than it was worth. Sophie took the word of the employment agency that sent them in.

"Everything was in order. They both had their asylum requests approved by a court which allowed them to obtain work visas and Social Security numbers. A letter of recommendation from the law firm that handled the process stated that it had conducted due diligence before assisting with the work visa. The resumes were impressive, but there was no real way to verify their backgrounds."

Chas closed his eyes and ran his hand through his hair to his neck and around to his cheek. "In hindsight, there was a possible red flag. A citizenship application was already in each file. At the time it looked like the two were both diligent and ambitious to become citizens. Now, it looks like there is political influence and money behind those efforts."

The only red flag for Calev was the speed at which they made it through the system. The normal waiting period to appear before a court is 3 years. They needed someone who could pull a lot of weight to accelerate the process. Calev was planning to investigate further, but it had not been a priority until now. Calev reviewed Sophie's notes with the information she remembered from the interview. What seemed to be immaterial quickly became relevant.

Calev explained, "When I left the meeting this morning, I put one of our investigators on it. Turns out we already had information on the two from an investigation done by one of our network partners in Mexico City. But there was a complete disconnect between that investigation and Mimtrin. Unless we had explicitly asked, there would have been no reason for that agency to know the two were potential hires. Even so, we would not have bothered them for clerical positions.

"Both lived in Mexico City. Even though they lived only three blocks apart, they did not know one another. They came with the caravan excursion to the US border, where they entered close to San Diego. The cartel that controlled that area was paid extra and moved both to the front of the line. I will get to the money part after a little more background. Tera obtained the Borter Patrol intake interview notes for both Maria's and Tina's asylum applications." Calev started with Maria.

"Maria was an accounts receivable clerk for a large real estate developer, mainly rental properties and condo projects. The company had its own finance department that secured loans for buyers. Debtors were required to buy a life insurance policy for the amount of the debt they owed, plus 10%. The company was the beneficiary of the balance due plus expenses. Thus, the ten percent.

"Maria was the first point of contact for someone behind on their payments. The stress of that job was getting to be too much for her. It was her job to decide if the client could pay. If so, they worked out a double-digit interest loan on the back debt. If the client could not pay, she assigned the client to a collection agency owned by the developer under a different corporation.

"She asked for a transfer to a different desk. She was assigned accounts receivable at the life insurance company. While reviewing the files to become familiar with her tasks, she noticed that the insurance company's headquarters was adjacent to the collection agency. She did a quick search out of curiosity. The developer owned the life insurance company under a third corporation.

"She also noted there was a very high percentage of 'accidental deaths' of those debtors who were assigned to the agency for collection. Maria wondered why a company would insure someone when there was a high probability of that person dying. You would just be paying yourself. When she put two and two together, it added up to money laundering with no regard for the sanctity of life.

"One day, on her way home from work, a black sedan pulled beside her. Two men in suits got out. They flashed badges and said they were from the SAT (Servicio de Administración Tributaria). Our IRS. She was ordered to get in the car. The two agents took her to an office building for questioning about the real estate operation. There were no signs indicating she was at an SAT facility.

"A third man entered the room. The first two men left. He told her that someone had reported that she was looking at files she had no authority to see. He wanted to know what she found. She told them that she was only trying to learn about her new job. The man suspected she had inadvertently discovered a link between the companies. She told them what was in the files she saw but said they looked legitimate.

"He told Maria the company has a life insurance policy on her. Recovery of training and development expenses justified the policy in the event of death. If the company finds out she was snooping around, she was told they may want to collect on that policy.

"But the man told her that he likes the way she thinks." Calev turned to the notes on his iPad and began to read from Maria's transcript.

"Man." He scrolled down. "Maybe we can help one another. We are investigating some bad people in the United States. I can get you in and fast-track your asylum request. You go to an assigned lawyer, who arranges for your identification and a bank account. You will go to a specific employment agency that will get you a job. You will be employed by the company under investigation while working for us. We occasionally will ask you for operational information. Nothing dangerous. We pay for everything and you get bonuses for information. Win-win." Calev put the iPad down. "She agreed.

"Tina's interview with Sophie followed a parallel track to Maria's. She had worked temp jobs even though she did not need to. She lived with her boyfriend, who had a great job as a dispatcher with a transportation company. He earned a good salary, and, according to him, the company was generous with cash bonuses. Her resume looked good due to the variety of clerical positions she was assigned through the temp agency. Her reviews were excellent. Of course, there was no viable way to check all of this.

"Tina explained that she had entered the United States through the open border for a better life. She had been concerned about her boyfriend's financial dealings and needed to get away from that environment. She was directed to the same employment agency as Maria and the same law firm for all paperwork. Not much more was in the file.

"Tera worked her magic and hacked into the Border

Patrol surveillance camera archives. The best we could tell, they probably met for the first time while in line for asylum at the check point. They both were wearing the same red and white hat noted in the surveillance pictures. This was a standard technique for the prepaid reception party to recognize them as they entered. Again, illegal, immoral and/or unethical but nothing flag raising for a clerical job."

Ray asked if Calev knew the law firm name. "It should be on the application." Calev scrolled through the screens on his iPad. When he stopped, he smiled and shook his head. "The name is Alfa and Best Law. The Alfa is spelled with an 'F' instead of 'PH', using the Spanish translation of the word. They are under investigation for fraudulent practices related to their specialty, personal injury suits. My firm investigated and debunked two separate injury claims for our insurance clients. Most of their lawyers left the firm when they were forced to become immigration specialists."

As soon as Calev mentioned the law firm both women used, Ray suspected that this might be the firm that would take Enrique's case. Ray thought about investigating Samson, but at this point he had way too much on his plate. Ray announced, "I think I have a new stuffed animal for Tera."

Calev smiled, but it was not one of his fake smiles like the ones he used with customers or with someone he was trying to suck into a conversation. This smile seemed sincere. "Is this a stuffed bull with horns or a teddy bear?"

"I think I will let Tera tell me. There are only three options: Bear, bull or no bull." Ray walked through his thought process, stopping intermittently to answer what-if questions. "I don't believe Samson, Alfa, or the employment agency is a decision-maker. I don't think we are even close to the head of the snake. We need to follow the money."

Ray added, "I was just thinking it would be nice to know where the next client meeting for the Temple Institute will take place. I have a concern that it might not be worth the risk to find out. Even the smallest mistake could be a blow to our plan. I will leave that ball in your court." Calev assured everyone that no risky actions would be taken.

The conversation switched to a review of the morning's meeting with Chas. He formally assigned Ray the task of coordinating with Ariel Weizman, Director of Artificial Intelligence Development. He texted her as a heads-up that Ray would be involved at a high level. Next steps and communication plans were finalized. Chas and Calev left together.

Jolie and Ray were the last to leave. "Ray, are you a Christian? Have you converted?" Rays face spoke a thousand words. "Sorry. If you don't want to tell me, that is fine."

Ray's tone let Jolie know that he was perfectly fine with the question. "I have always said that I am a realist. What made you think I converted?"

Jolie was a bit gun-shy at this point. "You noticed my Bible. You would be the first person who spotted it that had not converted. I also heard you had a command of the Temple history from a biblical perspective. I just thought…"

Ray interrupted. "I can see how you got there. Mo told me that I needed to understand the Bible from both a Jewish and Christian perspective. My extremely limited knowledge is practical by nature. I have an associate, actually a friend, who is tutoring me. He came from a Christian family but he never bought into any religious doctrine. That kept him from the rapture. I am not sure how all of that works. He says he is not a biblical scholar, but he is a wealth of knowledge."

Ray paused. Jolie had something to say, but she waited to let Ray finish his thought. "My friend told me that when he turned to Jesus, he experienced a sense of peace. He said he is still looking for his ultimate mission. For now, he believes Jesus has given him the mission to help me. He will need a lot of help from Jesus if he is going to work with me!"

Jolie almost said "Amen" to that but decided to explain her change of heart. "I do understand. I was never a believer, but I met the love of my life, or so I thought. He was a devout believer. I went to church with him a few times. After each service, I knew for sure I was going to hell. Fear of God was always the message. Guilt was another tool they used for donations. This particular church is in a shopping center, which was appropriate since it might as well have been a retail operation.

"We got engaged, but I needed to go through some orientation before the pastor would agree to marry us. The pastor explained my 'duties' as a wife and future mother. After all that, I was told I needed to take classes to be baptized. I drew a line in the sand. I was done being programmed. My fiancé asked me to return the engagement ring.

"I figured if that is Christianity, I wanted no part of it. My fiancé did not want a life partner; he wanted a Stepford wife. When I called my bridesmaids to explain what happened and tell them everything was off, they were relieved. My Maid of Honor told me she got a letter from the church asking her to meet with the pastor. I knew nothing about that.

"It's not that I didn't believe in the possibility of a higher power; my exposure to Jesus was not at all what I would have expected. Other than a few Christian friends trying to explain that was not the Jesus they knew, I never really pursued any religion until everyone disappeared.

"Then something very odd happened. I needed to pick up a new computer. The guy I use for all of my personal equipment had boarded up his store because of looting across the city. He moved all of his inventory and repair equipment to his garage. His house is just around the corner from the church I told you about. The route back to the office took me by the church. Two men were boarding up the opening. I was curious, so I stopped to see what was going on.

"One of the men, Pastor O'Donnell, I recognized as an assistant pastor from my visits there. I never had a chance to talk to him during my so-called orientation. The 'holier-than-thou' pastor, my words not his, had the stained-glass windows disassembled and packed up. Several ornate and expensive crosses, figurines, and other valuables were also packed up. The safe was open when the assistant pastor arrived that morning.

"The senior pastor said it was for protection against evil perpetrators. Turned out that in the middle of the night, he had loaded a truck with the goods and took off. The assistant pastor found a note saying God had called the pastor to establish a new church near the great mountains. God would guide the leaders, as He guided Moses, to the final destination.

"Basically, he had ravaged the church and left the place with limited resources. Pastor O'Donnell said he wanted to try to keep the church active. It appears that several of the deacons and directors missed the rapture. They had a prayer meeting that morning. They asked Jesus to forgive them and lead them in a new direction.

"Pastor O'Donnell asked me to forgive him for not standing up to the Senior Pastor. He felt responsible for breaking up my plans for marriage. I told him it was a blessing in disguise. He stopped what he was doing to take the time with me. He explained that the rapture had just occurred. All true believers were taken, but those who remain can still have a place in Heaven. After two hours, that seemed like fifteen minutes, I prayed with him. Actually, he prayed for me. I asked Jesus for forgiveness and committed to work to help others accept Him as well."

Ray remained silent as Jolie, searching for what to say, went deep into her own mind. "Here is my problem: I don't know how to help others. I don't know what I am doing. I think I made a promise I can't keep."

Ray started to say something, but he took a few seconds to think it through. His standard response before he turned and left would have been, "Good luck with that." He started with a caveat. "My friend told me some things I will need to paraphrase since my knowledge base is close to zero. Mary had no idea what she was doing when she became pregnant with Jesus. When Jesus said, 'Follow me,' the disciples had no idea what they were doing. But they followed. David, a shepherd, had no idea how to be a King, but he was one of the greatest ever. They all had one thing in common. They trusted God."

Jolie was stunned. That was the perfect advice she needed, but it came from a guy who says he is not a believer. "Ray, thank you. I am not sure how you do it, but you can quickly put things into perspective." After a slight pause, she said, "But I still need to learn so I can talk to people like you just spoke to me. Can your friend help me?"

"He would love to if he could. It's complicated but I will ask. What about Pastor O'Donnell?"

Jolie noted, "He is organizing some classes that he wants

to start next Monday. Maybe you could bring your friend. I will find out what time. The more the merrier."

With an apologetic tone, Ray let Jolie know, "He works nights right now. I am trying to fix that. I will let you know. And, by the way, I liked how you snuck the Bible study in the conversation. Who says you do not know what you are doing?" They left the law firm offices together with substantially more questions than answers.

CHAPTER THIRTEEN

Ray was listening to a local news channel on his drive to Calev's Cave. His GPS constantly interrupted him, directing him to turn here and there and warning of police presence or a disabled vehicle. The reporter, who lives in Mexico, was describing a cartel war. "With millions of people gone due to the unknown phenomena, cartels throughout Mexico are fighting for territorial control. Even though hundreds of civilians have been reported missing or killed in the crossfire, there has been no state of emergency declaration from the President. The military is on full alert.

"According to a confidential source, the military is taking a defensive posture to protect government and key infrastructure facilities. Local police forces in many areas have been depleted. Citizens are starting to form militias to protect their communities. Senator Menendez has been extremely critical of the military strategy, saying if they do not get control, a civil war could tear the country apart."

Ray told the lady on the radio to change the channel to another station. There was no good news there either. An overly dramatic reporter spun his field report. "I am standing in front of the Englewood Safeway on Market Street. People are waiting in line to get in. Guards at the entrances are armed. Only a certain number of people are allowed in at a time. I spoke to a shopper loading her car. She told me most of the shelves were empty. I was able to talk to the Store Manager. He said the main problem was the shortage of employees across the board, not just at the store level. At the corporate level, about thirty percent of the employees, buyers, accounts payable and receivable, warehouse, drivers, and other operational people disappeared. This is just one store struggling to keep its doors open. We can only hope this gets resolved before people take matters into their own hands. Back to you Rita."

Ray turned the radio off. No news was better than bad news at this point. He was getting close to his destination. The GPS lady announced, "Your destination is ahead." Ray was looking for an office building but only saw a small warehouse. At the loading dock, there was a pup trailer at one door and a box truck at the other. He did not recognize the company name on either. The warehouse doors were closed. There were two passenger vehicles. An SUV and a van were parked in front of the building near the office entrance. He pulled into the closest available space and double-checked the address. Although the GPS lady was likely correct, he decided to try a different map application. For that one, he had to turn left in two hundred feet, and his destination would be ahead. As he approached the front door, he heard the buzzing sound indicating the door lock was disengaged. He went into a small reception room. A phone was on the wall next to where the receptionist would have been. A sign that read "Dial 9 for Assistance" was taped next to the phone. He heard another door buzz, so he took that option. He was dumbfounded by what he saw: an empty warehouse except for a few racks and a non-operational forklift.

He heard a ding sound to his left, and he saw the elevator doors opened. Calev held the door and called to Ray, "This way." Even though the abandoned warehouse was dusty and debris-filled, the elevator was spotless. "Welcome to my world. I must apologize. I forgot you were not aware of our setup."

"I have to admit I thought I was lost. So far, I am impressed with your clandestine approach to the facility. I can't wait to see what's next." The hydraulic-driven elevator inched slowly to a soft landing. The doors opened. Ray thought he was walking into an electronic heaven. Three massive monitors on the wall opposite the elevator mesmerized him.

One monitor was tracking the movement of a vehicle. The middle screen had an aerial view of the Temple Mount and the surrounding area. There were buildings highlighted in yellow and some in pink. The other screen was divided into three sections. Each section contained a picture of the Temple participants from the earlier meeting. Next to each picture was a bio.

There were four workstations to the left. Each had three large monitors that were more effective than cubicle walls. The chairs looked similar to his custom AI designer chair. Even though the room was designed with an open concept, the lighting could be adjusted for each area. To the right were two standard-looking offices. One was likely Calev's office, and the other was empty. Ray figured somebody had disappeared.

"So can I assume my picture was up there at one time?" Calev gave a confirming smile. "Can I also assume that Tera resides in the far-left corner?" Calev wondered how Ray figured that out but didn't think now was the time to ask.

"Good guess. I will introduce you after a quick tour." Calev started with a high-level overview but made the mistake of pausing after the first three sentences. Ray's questions were immediately inserted into the conversation. Calev realized he was not dealing with a client who was there for a dog-and-pony show. Ray focused his questions on Mimtrin's overall security.

They moved to Calev's office. Before sitting down, he tapped the phone's screen and asked Tera to join them. Ray was unsure what to expect, but imagined the standard geek attire, tattoos, multiple piercings, and an attitude. When he heard, "Yeah, Boss," he turned to see an attractive forties-something woman dressed in what Ray considered professionally casual. No jewelry and limited make-up, not that she needed any.

Even though Ray tried to hide his surprise, Tera said, "Don't let the look fool you. I am still a nerd at heart." Ray was even more surprised. Most geeks he knows don't have body language skills unless they studied as he did. When he finally smiled, Tera said, "Oh good. I knew you were in there someplace." She smiled as Ray extended his hand. "Ray Ferrari, a fellow member of the nerd society." They shook hands. Her grip was stronger than he expected. He could feel her confidence.

Tera wasted no time. "So, your code. Talk to me. The opening menu?" Calev just realized he had lost control of the conversation. They both made themselves at home in Calev's office before he made the offer.

Ray was happy to update Tera. He first provided a quick background to make sure they were on the same page. He started with the formula on the whiteboard in the conference room. "There was an algorithm on the whiteboard that

I saw in the room next to the scheduled meeting. The door should have been locked. I knew enough about the project to spot three errors. When I looked at the board closer, the smudge marks and slight changes in handwriting indicated that these alterations were intentional.

"In hindsight, someone may have been in there when I walked by. Each conference room in that hallway has a back door for catering personnel when there are large, extended meetings. That is speculation, but it is a possibility."

Calev jumped in. "There are security cameras at the caterer's entrance. The one facing the parking lot is obvious and could be avoided. Only an insider would know about the camera covering the exit from the inside. I can get the footage; I will let you know."

"That's interesting. I have been back there and missed that one." Ray picked up where he left off. "I am sure Chas told you about the consultant hired as the Mimstruct Pro project manager, Bryan Thorton, who just happens to be the son of Warren, the owner of CPS Metrix Technology, Mimtrin's biggest competitor."

Tera decided to add to the conversation. "When Chas alerted us, I started my research. Your information on the shell companies was an invaluable start. It saved a lot of time and led me to a deeper dive. Warren is obviously in control. Well, obvious to everyone except the IRS, FTC, SEC, and FBI. I hit a wall in Mexico."

"Mexico? You are well beyond what I found." Tera could see the wheels turning in Ray's mind. "Do you have information on Arturo Gutierrez?"

Tera indicated Arturo was next. "I am trying to connect the dots. What is Warren's business in Mexico? If Arturo is working for Warren, maybe that's how Arturo gets paid. I don't know. I will find the connection. Can you tell me any-thing about Arturo that you think might help?" Ray walked her through everything that led him to find the spyware. Arturo was in that discussion, but Enrique was not.

Tera concluded, "The maintenance company. Jolie's in-put makes more sense now. We are all over that one. I was told to avoid your contact, and I will respect that request. I would like to know why."

"There are people who would like to see him dead. It might be a moot point anyway. He is concerned for his safe-ty and might be leaving soon. He will vanish, and because of the mass disappearance a few days ago, no one will think of looking for him." In his mind, Ray justified the 'leaving soon' comment. It was Enrique's identity that would be leaving. If Tera researched body language with the intensity he did, she would know subconscious expressions cannot be hidden.

"I have no doubt that you could find him, but it would be a huge distraction from the problem at hand. The results would be inconsequential. He is considered a friendly and not an enemy that needs to be destroyed. We need to focus on beating the invaders at their own game." Tera nodded as the point was taken.

When Tera stood up, her Bic pen slid to the floor. Ray moved to pick it up, but Tera was too fast. Ray could see a necklace slipping from behind her blouse as she stood. It was a cross. She quickly repositioned her necklace. As though nothing had happened, she said, "Let's go to my desk. Show me everything and tell me your plan."

After Ray and Tera reviewed the options, he realized that his two-man army with Enrique was fighting with sticks and pitchforks compared to the nuclear-grade computer power Calev had at his disposal. One wake-up call was when Tera said, "You know we are Mimtrin's cybersecurity company under the name of SyberSek." Ray assumed that, but he always preferred facts over assumptions.

"Cody works at that desk over there." She pointed to the space in the opposing corner. He saw the young man, maybe in his late teens or early twenties, centered on his little world. "He is a prodigy. Every time there is an attack on Mimtrin, he is on it. He researches the breach attempt and writes code for your system to catch, remove, and block future attempts. The attempts have radically increased in the past year."

"Cody would not have known about our situation because the spyware was an inside job. I want to thank him on my way out." Ray asked, "Have you found any consistent sources of the attacks?"

"That is the interesting part. About eighty percent of the increase has come from the same source. But they are very sophisticated in the way they route the attacks. Let's say you attempted to hack my computer. I would figure out who you are, hack you, and blow up your computer. If you routed your attack on me through someone else's computer, I could only blow up that computer, which probably belongs to some unexpecting amateur with no sophisticated cyber protection."

Tera tapped the keyboard several times, and the big screen on the right changed to a world map with dots and lines going in random directions. Ray knew he was seeing an attempted hack that had been tracked to a source. This particular attack involved five points across three countries. Ray talked through what he understood while pointing to the screen and tracing the route. Tera loved working with a knowledgeable peer.

"This gets me to a starting point, or at least a primary one. Now watch." Tera tapped again, and the screen layered six color-coded attacks for differentiation. "You can see from this there are two common points. Denver and El Paso. From El Paso, it goes wherever. Then all end in Denver."

Ray pursed his lips, nodded, and said, "CPS Metrix Technology! But they are located outside Denver."

Tera nodded and said, "But PreciseCo Security, LLC has an office in Denver. They are, at least on paper, the security company for CPSM. PreciseCo Security is one of the companies owned by Warren Thorton." Tera admitted, "I am not one hundred percent sure, but everything points there. Starting about a year ago, there were multiple attempts. About six months ago, the number dropped. Everything you have explained solves that dilemma for me. Since they could not get in from the outside, they had to invade from the inside."

The two discussed options to go on the offensive without the source of the attack being blatantly obvious. Ray considered sharing Enrique's flash drive, but since he was unsure what was on it and did not want to stoke Tera's curiosity, he passed on the idea. Tera mentioned that Calev occasionally uses one of her fellow hackers, Rekah, for special projects. Testing the CPSM security might be one of those times."

Ray stood up. "I have to go. I need to review my plan and talk to my contact…that you will not try to research." Ray paused again for emphasis. "We will talk tomorrow. I think we can attack on multiple fronts."

Tera stood, knowing the meeting was over. The thought popped into her head that Ray could be a chess master, always thinking several moves ahead. Cody's workspace was on the way to the elevator. Ray stopped where he could be seen in Cody's peripheral vision. "Cody, thanks for your great work for Mimtrin." Cody looked up at Ray with a quick smile and immediately re-entered his reality. Ray easily got the point and continued with Tera toward the elevator. As they approached, the door slid open as soon as Tera was in range. She escorted him through the warehouse and out of the building.

As they stood in the sunshine, each took a deep breath. There was a strong eastward breeze that brought the Pacific Ocean's freshness. "Tera, it has been my great pleasure to have met you. I am looking forward to our next meeting."

In mutual respect, she said, "Until then." She returned to the cave. Ray's next destination was the office. His head was spinning faster than the wheels of his car. While waiting for the green light signal to appear at one of the multiple intersections, a thought came from nowhere. Ray laughed and said to the invisible man beside him, "Rekah. Hacker spelled backwards. Clever."

As soon as he walked through the seventh-floor doors of the Mimtrin Offices into the maze of cubicles, Ray was bombarded with questions from workers about their projects. For two of the analysts, after several quick keystrokes, he resolved their issues faster than a pit stop at the Indy 500. The other two were learning moments. He took each through a series of questions that allowed them to work through the problem. "Now you will never need to ask me about this again," was Ray's standard declaration as he walked away.

He finally made it to his home away from home. The phone was rapidly flashing. In his mind, the lights were screaming for him to check the ten messages showing on the screen. As he listened, he knew eight of the issues had already been handled. One call that needed attention was from Jolie. The other was someone from the help desk. No name was given. He started with the latter. "Help desk. This is Barry. What is the issue?"

"Barry, this is Ray. Someone from your group left a message for me. Did another computer shut down?"

"Shut down? No." After a short pause, he said, "Oh, you are the guy that fixed the glitch. Good work on that. I didn't make the call, but Paula wanted to talk to you sometime today. She is in her office meeting with Jolie, but I will let her know you called."

"Barry, would you let her know I just returned to the office and must stomp out a few fires? I am guessing an hour max." Barry confirmed that he would get the message to Paula. Ray had second thoughts. "Barry, scratch that. I am on my way right now." Ray put Enrique's flash drive in his pocket. He headed to the Help Desk offices. As he dashed from his office, out of the corner of his eye, he saw Maria standing up. He was not ready for her. He picked up the pace and kept going.

Through the soundproof picture window in her office, Paula saw someone coming. She had no idea it was Ray since she had only met him by phone. She said something, and Jolie turned. She confirmed it was Ray. Jolie gave him the come-and-join-us wave. After the formal introduction, Jolie got right down to business. "I am updating Paula now about the hack." With a smile, she nodded toward Paula. "She knows if she discusses it with anyone but you, Chas, or me, I will have to kill her. As a quick update, Tina and Maria are still the only incidents."

Paula asked, "Are you going to show me how to make the fix?"

Ray did not hesitate to say, "No." He looked at Jolie. "Was part of the discussion my spyware?" Jolie gave the affirmation nod. He turned back to Paula. "It is not that I do not trust your abilities, but as Jolie has told you, I am putting spyware in the spyware. We have never worked together, so I do not know your skill set, but I guess it is extensive. If you are working with Jolie, the bar must be high. Have you written algorithms and code?"

Paula responded, "In a previous life."

Ray made a mental note of that answer. He would look into that previous life as soon as he got a chance. "The embedded spyware took me about three hours to figure out. It took me about six hours to write and test my code. It is not worth spending the time on something that might never reoccur. When we eventually clean those computers, I will make sure you are on the front line." That comment allowed Paula to close that project for now.

Jolie asked about the cave. Ray gave her the highlights but stayed somewhat vague, not knowing Paula's part in the scheme of things. "You were right about Tera. I am meeting with Mo tomorrow to discuss additional options she put on the table. I will give him my opinion but will only move with his call. I am sure he will be in touch with you. We must be ready to implement the plan by late next Monday or early Tuesday. We know the Temple III committee trio will meet with CPSM Tuesday afternoon."

Jolie shifted subjects by asking, "Remember the restart of the church we discussed at the Monday meeting?" Ray's nod said yes, but he figured there was an agenda behind the question. "I hope you will be able to find some time for the

Monday meeting at the church. Paula will be joining us. I sent you a text with the information."

"I can't promise anything. Much will depend on our tests. But it is on my calendar, and I don't put things on it unless I intend to keep the appointment." Ray was happy to cross off the remaining two phone messages in one meeting. He bid his farewell and headed out.

Ray was prioritizing his action items on the way back to his office. Maria intercepted Ray just before he could sneak into his office. "How was the meeting?" Ray continued moving to his place behind the desk. Maria stood in the doorway, waiting for his response.

"It was interesting. Prospects were there to discuss features of the new Mimstruct Pro platform. I was just there to answer technical questions. I don't think there is anything for you to note. The law firm has all of the information. Chas will be able to update Leticia as needed when she returns. We may not even get this client."

Maria looked puzzled. "I thought Leticia said a deal was about to close."

Ray acted uninterested. "That may be, but they told us they were still shopping." Ray changed subjects. "Any news on Leticia?"

"Bringing her out of the coma is progressing slowly, but they are optimistic. Do you know who the competitor is?" Ray knew she was fishing for something to report. He did not want to overplay his hand or miss this opportunity to plant distracting information.

"No, and that information is above my pay grade anyway. From the bits I heard, it sounds like a company in Israel partnered with someone in Europe. They filled each other's technological gaps that were needed to be competitive. At any rate, they are talking to more companies. Two, I think." Ray hoped that would end the conversation. After a slight pause, she retreated to her desk. He immediately opened his laptop, logged on, and activated the spyware. Her screen was now his screen.

Maria closed the company site and opened Google. She logged in as Ma Dentro and opened a Gmail account. Ray thought to himself that the name was a total lack of imagination. "Maria Inside" translated from Spanish. Seriously? She typed, To: Jefe@tek.iq.biz. Subject: Renewed competition. The body read: The Israeli competitor may not have been ruled out. A possible partnership puts them back in the running. No name. I will see what I can find out. Let me know if you already know. The client is still shopping.

She cleared the sent folder, closed Gmail, and reopened the company site. She made a quick 360-degree scan of the area to see if someone had seen anything. Acting normally after each message took a conscious effort until her nerves finally settled. The price she was being required to pay for her new life in the US was taking an emotional toll.

As Ray was writing a text message to Tera with this contact information, Maria closed the company site again. She opened her Gmail. There was an email with the same subject line, but it was not a reply. They were careful to cover their tracks as much as possible. The message read: We know who the Israeli company is, but don't know anything about any partnerships. Are you sure?

That email was deleted. A new one began. "Ray was at the meeting. He was not part of the discussion but overheard the conversation. His impression was as I stated." The reply: Find out exactly what he heard! Maria's turn: I will try. He was sure there was no decision and that two other companies were being evaluated. That ended the exchange.

Ray mumbled, "How did she know to open her Gmail? Text is the obvious answer. But these people seem to avoid the obvious. Burner phone? Maybe. Probably. But why not just text with that phone? Maybe the company policy restricting personal cell phone use in the office area might raise a red flag? No." Brainstorming was one of the techniques he used to solve problems. Ray knew to stop speculating when thoughts were at the edge of logic, or he would start to see ghosts. This dilemma was just another unwanted addition to his to-do list.

Ray checked in on Tina. He had set up a file folder. Anything saved or deleted would be copied to that file. Ray opened Tina's screen. She was on the company site. He checked the folder. When he saw the activity list, he thought, "She is amazingly efficient." Too bad she's a mole. The time-stamped order sequenced all of the work she had saved or deleted. Ray sorted the extensive list by logging on and logging off now that he understood the process. Anita-Onuwave was her email address @yahoo. Tina, with an extra 'a' spelled backward, on the nueve, nine. Ray wondered how these two were chosen and who gave them the names to use. But then again, they have been doing this for at least six months without being noticed.

The receiver was different from Maria's. Mudir@UNsanDLe.org/1jf9m2b. The only message to Tina was: "Get Jenkins' notes from the meeting!" The reply: He has not come back to the office today. I will ask if he would like me to help with meeting minutes or organize his notes for the day.

Things were starting to fall into place. Ray's glass-half-empty attitude kicked in. He used pessimism to avoid overconfidence. Too many people seemed to know what was going on. It would be easy for someone to slip and alert the enemy. Ray's sense of urgency to find the source of all of this was growing.

Even though Ray's office was free of surveillance equipment, he took the precaution of going to the stairwell halfway up to the eighth floor. From that isolated spot, he called Tera. After giving her the names and addresses, she said, "I have an idea. Give me access to your laptop. It will save me hacking time." She could imagine Ray's droll smile. "I will use it as a portal. As you know, 'deleted' doesn't really mean deleted. Maybe previous emails will give us more clues."

"That's brilliant. I am just irritated that I didn't think of that." Ray paused. Through the phone, Tera could feel dendrites and axons firing in Ray's brain. "I think I can make it easier for you. It's about four o'clock. Maria can leave early for… whatever reason. I will give you the IP, etcetera. The firewall will be disabled, and you can navigate away."

"Perfect." Tera went silent for a few seconds. "One slight detail poses an issue for me. My part could still take some time. I committed to help a friend tonight. His church was vandalized. A couple of computers were stolen. Among other things, they damaged the wiring, modem, and router. The guy is clueless regarding technology, but he needs to be operational. He has a meeting tonight at 7:30. I told him I would see if I could get him up and running. So… if you could step in, that would allow me time to focus."

The phone went silent for longer than usual. Ray was mentally scanning his to-do list and reprioritizing. It was going to be another late night for him anyway. Finally, he said, "This is a priority. I can take care of that." Tera gave him the address and all pertinent information. The church was only about twenty minutes from his apartment building. He would need to stop by to pick up his tool kit, which included just about everything he needed. He had some cables, modems, and routers hoarded in the storage unit in the parking garage. He could also resurrect three computers from his stash. Mentally, he was organized.

After Maria left for the day, Ray implemented the plan, focusing on her computer. He verified that Tera was in. Access to Tina's computer was the next to be infiltrated. His next move was to set an appointment with Ariel to discuss a fake update to feed CPSM. He dialed her extension and caught her just as she was leaving for the day. Ray needed those latest updates. His plan required precision and speed, two words Ray could not usually put together. Ariel was already late for another meeting, so she suggested nine o'clock tomorrow, which was perfect for Ray.

Finally, Enrique's flash drive. With Maria gone and Chas out of the office, Ray figured there would be no more covert emails today. He inserted the drive into his laptop. Enrique had made several notes. The code was designed to implement small but disruptive changes to specific algorithm strings. They would be part of most normal operations.

The changes would impact downline sequences. Their analysts and programmers should focus on those issues. Fixing all affected areas once the problem is identified would be relatively simple for a skilled programmer. Unless they are true pros, it would take precious preparation time away from CPSM's presentation on Tuesday. The real genius is the backside. The virus will erase itself once its code is activated to fix the anomaly. They will think it was a glitch. They could find the breadcrumbs, but it would take a monumental effort. By the time they figure it out, it will be too late for their presentation.

After reading Enrique's notes, Ray reviewed the code that would tell the computer what to do. He only made three notes and had two questions. He was ready for Enrique when he arrived for the night shift.

Ray was a bit anxious about going to the church. Not because it was a church but because he had no idea what he would find when he arrived. He had thought through all the cables he might need. The equipment needs were already organized in his head. The plan was to take tools to cover a myriad of possibilities.

Most of the people in the department had left for the day. Ray decided to go into the ten-minute version of his deep relaxation mode before Enrique showed up for his evening shift. For Ray, this was not just relaxation. He directs his brain to archive meaningless information, shelve pertinent information for easy access, and connect historic and current information to provide solutions. He stopped sharing this technique with people when he realized it was less effective for them. Others were missing information on mind-brain functions that he had acquired from one of his obsessive research projects.

The challenge is to get the bad guys to open the file. Those are the dots he wanted his brain to connect. Plan one success was the ideal. Ray always had plan two and usually plan three in his hip pocket. At this point, plan two was to hack and destroy. Enrique would be running everything through an IP address disconnected from Mimtrin in every way. He still had the login to one of the bogus sites set up in Mexico by the military intelligence. He had already tested his access and was prepared to enact plan two.

The timing was perfect as Enrique announced his presence. "Did you get a chance to review the code?" He was too anxious for the hello-how-are-you standard greeting.

"I did. It's great. I made a couple of notes and have questions." Ray and Enrique brainstormed the modifications once Ray understood the code's logic. Their time together was limited. They agreed to a few modifications for Enrique to make. Two programmers working late were still typing away. Ray had a mild case of paranoia. He thought it might be best to have Enrique begin working his maintenance job. Ray also made a note to check what those two were working on.

With a smile, Ray declared, "I am attending church today." He saw the surprise on Enrique's face. "Don't get too excited. I am helping a colleague's friend, who happens to be a pastor. I will repair damage to their computers and network caused by vandals at the church. There is some meeting tonight, and they need the systems to be up and running."

"Maybe the pastor will introduce you to Jesus. He will be attending the meeting as well."

Ray sarcastically noted, "I hope to be gone before the meeting starts. So, I will most likely miss Jesus today."

Enrique just shook his head. "That's not the way it works. You may miss Jesus, but He won't miss you." Ray had to smile. Enrique added, "You do know I am not going to stop."

Enrique made an enthusiastic shift. "Okay. I have something to show you." Enrique took the wallet from his hip pocket. Opening it slowly for dramatic effect, he extracted what, at first, looked like a credit card. He flashed his new Driver's License. "Yo soy Elias Martinez."

Ray replied, "It is a pleasure to meet you, Elias." Ray hurriedly said, "Let me see." Ray was impressed. "I am glad you smiled in the picture. That differentiates your photo from the passport. Any problems?"

"Not really. I was talking to a rookie that said I had to turn in my Mexican license. A supervisor quickly overrode him. I will try to set up a checking account tomorrow and deposit the money I have saved for the lawyer."

"Elias." Ray's tone reflected both happiness and relief. "Knock on my door when you get home. I will probably be up. If I don't answer, call me. I will have the ring tone at max volume." Ray looked past Enrique and noticed some movement. "Looks like you have company again. You better get going. Quickly, there is one more thing you need to do. Create a resume for Elias. Make it look good and tie in with your technical background. It will make it easier to answer interview questions. I will see if I can get you a meeting with HR. Don't hold your breath, but maybe."

"What am I applying for? Analyst in this department?"

"That works. You better get going. I need to leave anyway."

Ray made his way to the underground parking lot. As the door to P3 opened, Ray saw Chas pulling into a parking spot immediately ahead. Chas got out of the car but did not close the door. He saw Ray and waved him over. "Hop in." Before Chas got back in, he plugged his Tesla Model X SUV into the charging station. Even though the interior was massively impressive, Ray focused on the electronics. He wanted to start playing with the large monitor but thought better.

As Chas entered the SUV, he asked, "How was your visit to the cave?"

Ray filled him in with all the pertinent details. "It looks like plan one is in play. Your email to Mo to smoke out Maria and Tina's contact will not be needed. I already gave Tera the email addresses and access to Maria's computer. Hopefully, we will know more tomorrow."

Chas stayed laser focused. "Calev has more information, but he will call you tomorrow about whatever it is. Sounds like you are almost ready. I will be at your meeting with Mo tomorrow. I hate to cut you off, but I need to make a call. Oh, and thanks for your suggestion. I was able to obtain the signal jammer. No matter what happens in the next few days, we will sweep and clean the building on Tuesday evening." Ray was about to say something when Chas held up the infamous wait-a-minute finger. "Monday and Tuesday will need to be perfect."

Ray nodded in agreement but added, "You should know that Tina was ordered to get your notes from the meeting." Surprised, Chas asked how he knew that information. "The code I planted is working. You may want to go along with some generic notes. Make sure to add their decision is currently down to three companies. I already planted that one with Maria." Chas wanted to continue but knew tomorrow would be easier. They each went their way.

CHAPTER FOURTEEN

Ray made his way to the church address. He knew the street and that general area but did not remember seeing a church. The map lady told him, "in 200 feet, turn left." This can't be right. That is the Yellow Palm Shopping Center. There is no church building there. Ray thought the lady on the radio was wrong this time. But he was obedient to the map goddess.

The strip center is relatively small. The anchor location, and by far the largest occupant, is Trainer Jane's Health Club. Ray drove slowly by a small pharmacy with bars on the door and a boarded-up picture window. Then he passed a dry cleaner, a Chinese takeout, a physical therapist, and an insurance agency. The end unit came into focus. Panels of wood covered where the window would have been.

Ray could see that the large backlit sign was painted over. The "Disciples Church" still could be seen in the background. Still, the freehand-painted "Enduring Philadelphia Church" on the panels dominated the sign. There were plenty of parking spots available. He helped himself to the nearest one aimed directly at the entrance. Since he had no idea what he had gotten himself into, he left everything in the car until he could survey the landscape. The door was unlocked, so he wandered in.

The space was much larger than he expected. The seats were nicely padded, burgundy folding chairs. Although they were not permanently fixed, there was no indication they had ever been moved. The skewed chairs along the central aisle were the exception. Three large frames on the wall had several fluorescent bulbs mounted along their sides. The only outside light would have come from the large display windows consistent with the shopping center's design. Those front windows were now covered with large sheets of plywood. Ray guessed that these lit frames mimicked the windows. He noticed fragments of stained glass piled up in the corner. He could only imagine that those pieces were part of religious images in mock picture windows.

Ray turned toward the voice that called out. "Hello." Ray saw a taller-than-average man, best guess mid-thirties. His light complexion stood out against the all-black attire. "Hello. You must be Ray." He extended his hand. "I am Pastor Patrick O'Donnell, but you can call me Red." He ran his hands through his reddish hair." With a big smile, he said, "I'm not sure how I got that name."

Ray formalized his side of the introduction. "Red, how can I help you today?" Ray scanned the room. "I see you have been vandalized, but this looks orchestrated."

"Worse than that. We were betrayed. The previous Pastor must have started his plan after the Rapture. On Sunday night, he absconded with equipment, statues of the saints, our gold-plated cross, and the cash to be deposited from the service collection. He even took the beautiful stained-glass murals, except for those pieces on the floor.

"He and two elders packed up during the night and were gone before I arrived at eight the next morning. I found a note that read, 'We will send for you to join us when our new church is established in Utah.' But, other evidence confirms Colorado as their destination. I do not care. Those three will need to explain themselves at the Judgement Seat of God. We now are being led according to His will."

There was a reflective pause. "God is good." Red could see Ray's confusion. "There were two boxes they forgot or had no room to pack. They probably did not know the boxes contained silverware, silver dishes, and goblets used for honored dinner guests. Honored for the previous pastor means they bought the church's endorsement for their business. Sorry, donated money.

"The adult son of one of those honored worshippers had been trying to buy this complete set in the original cases dated 1792. Earlier today, I had the set appraised at $250,000. He just paid us $300,000 to keep the set from going to auction. Before the Rapture, at auction, the set was appraised for and could have sold for close to a million dollars. This money gives us a chance to rebuild our church. Did I mention God is good?"

Red watched Ray for a reaction but only saw skepticism. "Why didn't I take the set to auction? Hold out for a million? The short answer is that the market has been flooded with Christian antiquities since the Rapture. Many auctioneers don't want to touch anything Christian. We now have seed money to build a new church with biblical values. We are going one hundred eighty degrees from the hellfire and brimstone leadership that controlled the congregation. I bought into that system and the exhilarating rush of power that came with it. In reality, I really did not believe what I was teaching. The words merely justified the ends to the means. That is why I am still here. Jesus has forgiven me now and has shown me a new way.

"We are going to be teachers, not preachers. I grew up in a Bible church that taught people the words of God. Everyone was taught how to believe, not how to perform rituals or bow to some authority. This Enduring Philadelphia Church will be a refuge for those wanting to know Jesus. People need to hear from God directly. As I said, God is good."

Ray walked over to the control room behind a wall at the back corner of the church. A large, tinted window allowed someone to see out but no one to see in. Ray could tell that the people disassembling were amateurs at best. The panel that controlled the sound and lights was still intact. It would have taken up space they did not have. Ray returned to the sanctuary, scanned places a novice would have missed, and then approached Red.

"Is Xfinity your service provider?" Red confirmed it was. "You have a perfectly good Xfinity modem on the shelf with other outdated equipment. I will need to install two routers to make sure you have total coverage. Instead of just unplugging, they cut several wires." Ray did another visual sweep of the room. "I can do some patchwork, but I doubt I will have everything ready before you start tonight. I may need to be working while your meeting is going on. I don't know how many computers you lost. I have two laptops that need a home. That should be enough for now. You should plan to hire a tech company to make permanent fixes. I will email you a name that could help with that."

"Ray, you are a Godsend." That was the second time he was told that in a matter of days. Ray decided not to editorialize at this time, but Red noticed a slight wince on Ray's face when he said that. Red immediately knew - Ray is not a believer. "I do not know how many will be here tonight, maybe only five or six. I will let them know you are helping us. You are welcome to stay. The topic is understanding the love of Jesus in times of chaos."

"Sounds interesting, but I will probably pass." That confirmed the Pastor's observation. Red, however, was not planning to give up on Ray. "I need to grab my gear and get to it."

It was taking Ray much longer than he thought it would. The wiring was extensive and outdated. The damage was widespread, making connections challenging at best. Thieves had made clean cuts, but there were tears in the cables where they tried to rip the wires from the studs. For Ray, repairs were not the problem, but time was. He mentally surrendered to his commitment and was determined to complete the task.

Ray watched as people started coming in. The number of people was double what Red had anticipated. As a people watcher, he enjoyed the dynamics. One couple walked in the front door, looked around, and left. Two minutes later, they came back in.

The meeting started even though the electronic equipment for the visuals was not ready. "Welcome, everyone. Thank you for coming." Red took a few minutes to make everyone aware of Ray's presence and the fact that he may wander in and out. He explained the new vision of the church to teaching instead of preaching. Anyone could ask a question at any time. "With that in mind, let us open our session with a prayer." Before he began, a hand went up. Ray stopped working for a minute. He wanted to hear the exchange.

A man wearing a t-shirt with Eddie's Bar and Grill was acknowledged. Ray knew he was not Eddie, but, for Ray, this would be his name for today. "This is my first time in a church. I have seen people praying. They must be praying to somebody."

At the other end of the row, a lady in a long skirt and a blouse with every buttonhole filled said, "God. Jesus." Eddie's look at her indicated that the response meant nothing to him. Ray gave her the name Button.

A man sitting in a chair away from Eddie was wearing a cap with the Titleist logo. Ray thought of a golfer, so he put the label Arnie on him after the great Arnold Palmer. Arnie said, "My wife drags me to church almost every Sunday. The congregation would regurgitate the Lord's Prayer. I only heard 'blah be blah, cha, cha, cha Heaven. Do-do-do Kingdom come. It was so rhythmic that my wife had to poke me so I wouldn't go into a trance." Several others hesitantly nodded in agreement.

Ray was thoroughly enjoying this. He could see people wanted to laugh, but newcomers were trying to decide if it was okay to laugh in church. Red took care of that when he laughed and said, "Praise the Lord. I love your participation. Here is what we are going to do tonight. Grab your chairs, and let's move them to a U-shape. Instead of the advertised topic, we will talk about prayer tonight."

As everyone was getting organized, Red went to a table at the back of the room and returned with handouts. Ray thought they looked like the ones Elias sold. Another coincidence. He handed each a brochure titled The Lord's Prayer. Further down was another title, The Sinner's Prayer. "We have several pieces of information for you in the back. I would recommend 'Bible Basics' as a starting point." Ray recognized that name. "Please keep asking your questions as we go through this handout." Ray had no intention of joining the group, but he dramatically slowed his work pace to listen in.

Red surveyed the group about their religious experience. Eddie was just one of four who had no background. All admitted hearing about God taking all those people who disappeared, but that could have been science fiction for all they knew. Five of the twelve went to church out of obligation to family members or peers. They had essential awareness, but only through osmosis, not through study. That group had family members who attended Sunday services. Family and friends were taken with the Rapture.

Three were Catholics. They attended Mass regularly but still seemed to know little about the Bible. One said he just followed what the Priest told him to believe. He admitted that he was only there because he saw two tattoo-covered teens leaning on his car. He decided to pop in until the coast was clear. The in-and-out-of-the-door couple said little, but they were curious. Their crosses told Red they were probably informed but not well enough, or they would have been taken in the Rapture.

"I know what I am about to say will generate many questions. I am going to ask you to accept the foundational information for now. You will understand why as you learn more." Red explained, "To have a common starting point, accept that Jesus is the Son of God. There are many reasons that God sent His Son. The main one is that Jesus took responsibility for the world's sins. You and I are human beings, mortals. As hard as we might try, we are not perfect.

"We make mistakes. I am not discussing math errors or putting too much salt in your food. I am talking about the mistakes we make with our fellow human beings. Things like lack of compassion, hate for others, verbal abuse, and lies. I am talking about mistakes we make with our internal belief systems. Thoughts of greed, lust, envy. Translated, we sin."

A heavy-set man toward the back stood up. "Sounds like you are no different than the other talking heads. You are a sinner! You are going to rot in hell! Repent! I am tired of all of that. This is why I didn't go to church. My friends consider me a nice guy. I am considered a professional and fair plumber by my clients. Why would I want to go some-place just to be labeled an evil sinner?"

Red was calmly understanding. He confirmed the man was a sole proprietor plumber who did everything from minor repairs to complete remodels. "So, if I had the sink draining slowly, you could fix that." The man's expression indicated that it would be a no-brainer. "If I repaired it, would I be called a plumber?" The man snorted, shrugged, and shook his head. His expression said, "Of course not."

"But I did fix the problem. One time. What if the drain slows again, and I fix it a second time? Am I a plumber? What if I tighten a joint to stop a leak? Am I a plumber? Obviously not. So when I say that you sin, I am not calling you an evil sinner. We all sin in different ways because we are not perfect. Some may put that sinner label on you, but that is not what you will hear from me. Only Jesus can for-give your sins and help you resist future sin.

"With that said, some deserve to be called sinners. If you fix pipes and leaks and deal with all sorts of plumbing issues daily, you deserve the title plumber. A person who lives by stealing day after day deserves the title of thief. One of the Ten Commandments is that you shall not steal. That person who repeats the same sin over and over deserves the labels of thief and sinner; that is who they are. That is what they do.

"If that thief does stop, asks for forgiveness, and never steals again, Jesus will forgive that sin. Should he be called a thief if the person never steals again? Let's say you decide to do only carpentry work. You will start calling yourself a carpenter because you no longer do plumbing work. You could do plumbing work, but that is not who you are after the career change. The forgiven thief, just like you and me, will commit other sins and need to pray and ask for Jesus' forgiveness.

"During the days before Jesus, the Jewish people had rituals, animal sacrifices, and periods of self-sacrifice to atone or compensate for those various sins. But then, the next week, season, and year, these atonements must be repeated because sin is constantly present. God decided that only one sacrifice was needed to take on the world's sins.

"God sent His only Son, Jesus, to be born of a virgin, to live a perfect life, to teach the blessings and love of God the Father, to establish a new era of grace, and to die on the cross. But that death was only temporary because three days later, he arose and ascended into Heaven to sit at the right hand of His Father. With that ascension, you can be assured that your sins will be forgiven as a believer in Jesus.

"There is a catch. There is only one thing that God asks of us. That is to believe in Jesus with all our hearts, souls, and minds. Honestly believe. All of your friends and family that disappeared, they believed. If you believe in Him and live according to His words, you can pray and ask for forgiveness. You, too, can find a place in Heaven." Plumber, as Ray will call him from now on, eased back into his seat but kept his arms crossed to block any perceived attacks.

"This brings us to the question of prayer. You are not the only ones that have had questions about praying. The disciples following Jesus didn't understand and asked Jesus how to pray. This is what He taught." Red opened his handout as a guide for others to follow. He read the Lord's Prayer.

Our Father in Heaven, hallowed be your name. Your kingdom come; Your will be done on Earth as it is in Heaven. Give us today our daily bread, and forgive us our debts, as we also have forgiven our debtors. And lead us not into temptation but deliver us from evil. For thine is the kingdom, and the power, and the glory forever.

"For those that heard blah blah blah, let's break this down." There were several chuckles and some smiles. The group was quickly warming to Red's approach.

"**First**, Our Father... God the Father created the heavens and Earth in six days and rested on the seventh. He created man and woman. Those were His only two choices. Adam and Eve were His children. Everyone born after that is part of the miracle of God's creation. Each child, including you, is His child. He is OUR Father. All of us. And, His love for us is patient, kind and unending."

A hand went up. The lady wore a white blouse with a blue logo just above the pocket. Ray strained to see "Parmont Labs." On the other side was an official-looking badge. He spotted the name, Ruby. Ruby's badge was surrounded by words too far away for Ray to read. "As a scientist, I cannot accept that any god could create the universe in seven days. Especially when science dates the Earth as 4.5 billion years old."

Pastor O'Donnell gave a nod of understanding. "God is love, spirit, and light. There are multiple references to those three words anytime God is described. You can look up 1 John 1:5, *God is light.*" Red realized he was already talking past the basics. He took the time to explain the concept of books, chapters, and verses. "Now put your scientific, analytical hat on. If God is light, He exists at the speed of light.

According to Einstein's Theory of Relativity, what happens if a person could travel at that speed of light?"

Without hesitation, Ruby replied, "We are obviously speaking in hypotheticals because that would be impossible. At the speed of light, mass increases. It would take infinite energy to reach a speed of approximately 670 million miles per hour. If someone could reach that speed, time for that person would theoretically stop. Looking at it a different way, thousands of years at a normal speed could pass by while that person stood stationary. Essentially there would be no time for that traveler."

"Exactly. God is infinite. In Genesis 1:3, God said, *Let there be light*. For God to be able to create light, He must be beyond light, beyond infinity, or anything your mind, my mind, or Albert Einstein's genius can fathom.

"God started creating the universe. That led to our solar system, which in turn led to the creation of Earth. That allowed for the creation of mammals, sea life, reptiles, insects, and every other creature on Earth. He created the concept of time for us mortals.

"In Ecclesiastes 3, the Bible says that *to everything there is a season, a time for every purpose under Heaven*. In 2 Peter 3:8, the Bible says, *With the Lord, a day is like a thousand years, and a thousand years is like a day*. The word 'like' is important when interpreting symbolism. In this case, a thousand years could be *like* a billion years in human terms. Then again, it is God. He may have only needed seven days, seven hours, seven minutes, or seven seconds. The fundamental point is that God has no clock. He perfectly created everything in His time." Ruby was still skeptical, but that answer sparked a desire to learn more.

Red looked around and paused long enough to see if

there were any other questions before his next point. "**Second**, which art in Heaven… To state the obvious, God the Father is in Heaven. This means that you can assume there is a Heaven. Revelation 7:14-17 describes Heaven. No hunger, thirst, physical pain, or tears are found in Heaven. Only love and joy."

A man sitting across from the Pastor asked, "This might be a technicality, but why use the word 'which' and not 'who'? God the Father sounds like a person." Ray thought it was interesting how the man posed the question. Justify first, then ask. Ray decided to call him Justin Case.

Red patiently explained, "A man or woman can only be in one place at one time. God is spirit, and just as light is everywhere at the same time, God is omnipresent. To be able to do that, He cannot be a person."

"Okay." Red heard the word and anticipated what was coming next. "But, Justin emphasized, "God created us in His own image, didn't He?"

Even though the Pastor was pleasantly surprised at the questions, he knew he needed to stay on message. A condensed answer would suffice. "Excellent question. When an artist creates a work, a painting, a statue, or you see an architect's rendering of a new building, or you see a young child's scribblings proudly displayed on the refrigerator door, we name the one who created that image. 'This is Bobby's masterpiece,' a mother would declare." A couple of hands went up with that comment. "As the story goes, Michelangelo was asked, 'How did you create this amazing likeness of David out of a block of Granite?' He replied, 'I saw the image I wanted and simply removed the pieces I did not need.' Michelangelo envisioned his image of David. Then, he created the statue in his image. It is commonly known as Michelangelo's David.

"There is another question you must ask: if God created us in his physical likeness, why do we all not look exactly the same? Of all the billions of people throughout history, no two people are the same; even identical twins have some slight variations. I believe he gave us all his likeness in the spirit of love. It is a matter of how we use that gift." Justin leaned back in his chair, fully contemplating what he had heard.

Red moved on to the next point. **Third**, hallowed be Your name… Hallowed means blessed, made holy, righteous. God the Father should be honored for all that He has done. The angels praised Him, as described in the Psalms, during the creation of the universe. The angels honor and sing praises to Him every day because they are constantly amazed, not only at what He created, but also at what He continues to create. They are in awe when they see His plan unfold.

"Those that were caught up in the Rapture, the train to Heaven you and I missed, are praising and thanking Him for the grace He has shown and the promises He has kept. If you decide to be with Him, you will understand why."

Ruby did not bother to raise her hand. "Every day, constantly? That seems a bit extreme."

Red thought through that before he spoke. "If someone gives you a birthday gift, the natural response is a polite 'thank you.' The response is more for the thought than for the present. If someone gives you high praise for something you have done, the 'thank you' is more sincere because it touches your emotions and is personal.

"Now imagine you and your child walking to the park. You get distracted for just a moment. Looking back, you realize your child has wandered into the street. You see an oncoming car. You panic because you are too far away. A bystander sees what is happening before you see it. He lunges in front of the vehicle, dives, and grabs your child. Clutching your child, he rolls to safety.

"Would you thank that person the same way you did when receiving a birthday present or a compliment? Or would you lavish that person with excessive gratitude for saving your child from certain death? Now, when you realize that God, through the Holy Spirit, jumps in front of that sinful vehicle daily to save you, your family, your friends, and your colleagues, the gratitude and praise will be never-ending. In another lesson, you will learn that all of the saints, those who died knowing Jesus, are in Heaven singing songs of praise and thanks every day to honor God for what He has done and for what He is doing."

Ruby was used to winning arguments. If she got behind in any debate, she would go on offense with waves of logic, her logic. Defense was not her style. Ray watched her expression and thought Ruby may have just called a truce with Pastor O'Donnell. Red continued on his mission.

"**Fourth**, Your kingdom come… A Kingdom implies that there is a King. The Father in this prayer is that King. Remember that Jesus is teaching this prayer as a man on Earth with the Spirit of God. He directs the glory to God the Father. Jesus, at birth, was recognized as the King of the Jews, as referenced in Matthew 2:2: He will reign over the new Earth and a new kingdom.

"Revelation 21 describes the new Earth. Those inhabiting the Earth will have positive and heavenly experiences at the right time. Heaven on Earth is only a few years away and will last 1,000 years. Then it gets better."

"What happens during the 1,000 years?" The question came from three people simultaneously. Their voices harmonized like a vocal trio. There was a quiet laughter from the group.

Red would have liked to have kept things light, but reality set in. "First is the bad news. It is called the Tribulation. Since all who believed in Jesus, honestly believed, were snatched up to Heaven in an event called the Rapture, evil and demon-possessed people believe they are taking control. In a relatively short period of time, they will discover that God has been in control the entire time.

"In Satan's war against Jesus, the Earth will be destroyed. Billions of people will die without knowing that they could have had a place in Heaven. God will remind everyone that He is in charge through a series of 'natural' disasters." The Pastor used the two-finger quote sign with the word 'natural'. "The hard-core holdouts, especially the Jews, will realize these supernatural events could only come from God. At the end of the Tribulation, Earth will be unrecognizable. Spoiler alert: Jesus wins the war against Satan.

"The good news. Millions will see these events as an opportunity to turn to Jesus. Those who have decided to ask Jesus for forgiveness and accept Him as Lord and Savior will have a place in Heaven. Only a select faithful will make it to the millennium, to the new, upgraded version of Earth that Jesus will miraculously restore. During the thousand years, the millennial period, Jesus will reign. No evil will be allowed for a thousand years. The world will live in peace."

Ruby asked again, "And after the thousand years?"

"The final judgment will come. Satan, Antichrist, the false prophet, and all evil spirits will be cast into the lake of fire for eternity. God has not told us much more, but I guess we will learn more during the millennium years." Red knew that was the shortest answer he could give for now. He could see some wanted to ask questions but probably did not know what to ask.

"**Fifth**," Red returned to the handout. "Your will be done on Earth as it is in Heaven… God's will is joyfully done in Heaven and will be on Earth. We will see that directly in the millennium. Trust that God is in control of all things. When you read about Job, Daniel, Ruth, Esther, and others who experienced hardships that led to greatness, read about those events as you would any true-life story. These are not fictional tales. God's will is consistent and is for the ultimate good.

"When you pray, you can ask for anything. The answer given will coincide with God's will. I have prayed for the money to make repairs, replace the necessities stolen from the church, and hire people to help keep this church open. God answered in his own way. Our computers were stolen, and our communication system wiring was significantly damaged. The projector hanging from the ceiling is useless for now.

"Instead of God sending me the money to hire a tech firm to make the repairs, God sent the gentleman in the control room making the repairs right now. He is donating his time and has donated computers that replace two we have lost." Red had Ray's attention. But then Ray's alter ego told him that the odds were low that he would be the answer to a prayer.

"This leads us to the next point. **Sixth**, give us this day our daily bread… You are asking God to provide us, all believers, with what we **need** each day so that we can be the best we can be while giving God the glory for our opportunities. Bread was a staple food in every household. In the Bible, bread is also a symbol of provisions needed for mental, emotional, relationship, and practical needs. Your hunger and thirst for these internal personal needs will be satisfied.

"There are times when prayers are directed at *wants* versus *needs*. A need is something that is required. A want is something that is desired. A person may want to have a million dollars in the bank. That person may need the knowledge, relationship aptitude, financial know-how, and organizational skills to achieve the goal. More importantly, that person may need to understand and apply the grace principle as taught by Jesus.

"God has blessed many believers with wealth. For His purpose, God has also allowed evil people to be rich. God does not have a problem with wealthy people. God does have a problem with those who misuse and abuse the gifts that He has given them. As it says in Job 1:21: *The Lord gives, and He can take away.*

"**Seventh**, the sentence continues with 'and forgive us our debts as we forgive our debtors'… Give us this day our daily bread and forgive us our debts. Debts can be translated as sins. In some Bibles, the word 'trespasses' is used. To trespass is to go places you should not go.

"The prayer continues as we *forgive our debtors*. Those are people who sin against us. At first glance, it would appear that this sentence contains two distinct elements – daily bread and forgiveness. Indeed, these are separate issues and could easily have been two separate sentences. Jesus, however, decided to connect these two. The keyword is 'and.'

"Forgiveness needs to be addressed before making

the connection. God has a file on everyone who has ever lived. That file means that God knows everyone's heart, soul, and mind. He knows every bad and good word, every thought, and every action of each individual. He understands everything.

"Holding on to anger, hate, or both are negative emotions that do you no good. Jesus is teaching in this prayer that you need to let those negative emotions go. Give to Him that urge to exact revenge. Fighting evil with evil is a no-win scenario. Your sword and shield are in the scripture, the words of God. Christians need to use those words to fight evil at every turn."

Arnie jumped in. "Sorry Pastor, but if some gang banger breaks into my house, quoting scripture to him is not going to be my first move. My sword will say Smith and Wesson on it."

Red's first reaction was empathy. "We may be talking about two different things. Christians have every right to defend themselves and their family. When Jesus first sent His disciples out in pairs to teach the gospel, He told them to take no bags, food, or water. He told them not to worry because current and new believers would take care of them. And they were safe.

"But just before He was arrested, He told His disciples to prepare to go out again. This time, He told them to take a purse and a bag. He also told them to take a sword. You can read about this in Luke 22:35-36. Jesus knew the disciples would be going into treacherous territory. But the sword was for defense, not offense. Offense was in the word of God and the teachings of Jesus.

"Look around. You can see we were robbed. I know the thieves. I have forgiven them because I know in my heart that God will use this for good. How many of you are here because you saw the new name painted on the boards securing the broken windows? Or maybe it's because you were curious, and you approached to see information about this service?" All but one hand went up.

"In Revelation 6:9-11, the martyred saints, all those in Heaven killed because they stood by Jesus, asked when their deaths would be avenged. Jesus told them to be patient. The time to pass down the sentence on those who have done evil things will happen soon. Jesus let them know He was in control and justice would be done. This is not the message I had planned, but I believe it is the message God wants you to hear. The sign did not bring you in; the love of Jesus for you brought you in."

Red returned to the handout. *"And forgive us our debts as we forgive our debtors.* God is a just God. His punishment will be in the same proportion as the evil of the crimes. The parable in Luke 16:13-29 tells an important story on many fronts." Red again returned to his Bible. *"There was a rich man dressed in purple and fine linen who lived in luxury daily. At his gate was a beggar named Lazarus, covered with sores and longing to eat what fell from the rich man's table. Even the dogs came and licked his sores.*

"The time came when the beggar died, and the angels carried him to Abraham's side." Red looked up. "Abraham is in Heaven. That is a lesson for another time." He continued reading. *"The rich man also died and was buried. In Hades, where he was in torment, the rich man looked up and saw Abraham far away with Lazarus by his side. So, he called, 'Father Abraham, have pity on me and send Lazarus to dip the tip of his finger in water and cool my tongue because I am in agony in this fire.*

"But Abraham replied, 'Son, remember that in your lifetime you received your good things, while Lazarus received bad things, but now he is comforted here, and you are in agony. And besides all this, a great chasm has been set in place between us and you so that those who want to go from here to you cannot, nor can anyone cross over from there to us. Red closed his Bible.

"The beggar, Lazarus, was hungry and in agony, but the rich man would not even give him the leftover scraps. The rich man was thirsty and in agony because of all the heat in Hades. While alive, Lazarus was unable to satisfy his hunger with food scraps from the rich man's table. The rich man was not allowed to relieve his agony from thirst in Hades during his eternal death. God's justice is fair and equitable.

"This parable delivers another message about individuals in Heaven and Hell. Each will be able to see and speak to the other but will not be able to cross the dividing chasm. The John Denver song, 'Take Me Home, Country Roads', describes a section of the Appalachian Mountains: Almost Heaven, West Virginia, Blue Ridge Mountains, Shenandoah River…

"Some areas have very steep and narrow valleys in the beautiful mountains. The mountains, in essence, have hollowed out. A slang term for the gap is a holler, a hollowed-out place. Some mountains are close enough that a person on one side of the valley can see a neighbor on the other. Before electricity, folklore held that neighbors could yell or holler across wide gaps to communicate. The mountain walls would trap the sound.

"Imagine that one side of the mountain is still smoldering from a forest fire. The rich man is on that side, the other side remains "almost Heaven," and Lazarus is on that side. The people in hell will live every day seeing Heaven and what their decisions caused them to miss. Passing from one side to the other is not an option."

"The connection: And forgive us our debts as we forgive our debtors. Just as God will punish evil people according to their deeds, He will forgive you the same way you forgive others. God told you He would sentence the evildoers accordingly. By forgiving, you release negatives that may be holding you back. Forgiveness allows you to focus on the future and do the work God intended for you.

"You may also need to forgive yourself. That is easier to do when you know Jesus will forgive you. If it is good enough for Jesus, it should be good enough for you. By forgiving, you will be rewarded in Heaven." With no more questions, Red returned to the handout.

"**Eighth**: And lead us not into temptation but deliver us from evil… So basically, you are asking God to help you avoid physical temptations, immoral thoughts, and desires of the heart that would cause you to sell your soul. *But* if I have fallen into Satan's trap, please pull me from his grasp.

"The other point is to acknowledge that there is evil in the world. At times, that evil will be overwhelming. We will be tempted to eat from the tree of the forbidden fruit as Adam and Eve did in Eden. Another lesson for another day. In this prayer, you recognize and admit that you need help to resist evil temptations.

"Before the Rapture, angels and the Holy Spirit were able to protect believers from evil. Now that the Rapture has taken place, the job of the angels and Holy Spirit has changed. The angels will help you find your way to Heaven once you have decided to commit to Jesus. The angels know how great Heaven is, and they want to help you get there."

Red saw several hands go up. "If your question is about angels or the Holy Spirit, put your hand down." Everyone did. "Next week at this time we can have a lesson about angels. We can talk about how the Holy Spirit works in tandem with Jesus and God the Father. It is called the Trinity. I will post it on the board by the entrance. Let's finish prayer today.

"**Ninth**, for thine is the kingdom, and the power, and the glory forever. This line summarizes the prayer. The last word, forever, is eternity. If you have not chosen to accept Jesus as Lord and Savior, you may be missing the train to eternal joy. You should get your ticket sooner rather than later.

"You can use this prayer every day. If you do not remember the words, go with the intent. One, recognize that God is our Father. Two, He is in Heaven. Three, He must be honored for every aspect of creation, and we must trust His plan for each of us.

"Four, His kingdom on Earth is only a few years away. His will in Heaven is peace and joy. You are asking for that will to be transferred to Earth. Five, every day, we need wisdom. Six, every day, we need forgiveness for our sins. Realize the Father is a good and just God. He will forgive us in the same way we forgive others.

"Seven, sin is everywhere, especially now. Satan and his demons are liars and deceivers who will try to trap us into joining his sinful world. Eight, we need God's help to avoid the temptations. If we have fallen, we need God to pull us from the grasp of Satan. Remember, it is not what you say but why you pray."

CHAPTER FIFTEEN

Pastor O'Donnell referred everyone to the last page of the handout he had distributed. He emphasized the title on that last page - The Sinner's Prayer. "This prayer is a structured but more personal request for forgiveness and salvation. The sinner's prayer is a plea for grace instead of judgment. It is a request for mercy instead of wrath. You can pray this prayer with me right now if you want. If you are unsure you are ready to accept Jesus, you can just follow along.

"God, I know that I sin. I know that I deserve the consequences of my sin. However, I am trusting in Jesus Christ as my Savior. I believe that His death and resurrection provided for my forgiveness. I trust in Jesus and Jesus alone as my personal Lord and Savior. Thank you, Lord, for saving me and forgiving me! Amen." The group watched the Pastor standing quietly with his eyes closed. They sat silent, allowing the Pastor to finish his prayer.

With renewed energy, Red added, "The **first** aspect of a sinner's prayer is understanding we all sin. *There is none righteous, no, not one.* Those are not my words. They can be found in the Book of Romans. We all need God's mercy and forgiveness.

"The **second** consideration is knowing God's remedy. Romans 10:9-10 says: *If you declare with your mouth, Jesus is Lord and believe in your heart that God raised him from the dead, you will be saved. For with the heart, one believes and is justified, and with the mouth, one confesses and is saved.*

"**Third**, we can be saved by grace alone, through faith alone, in Jesus Christ alone. Ephesians 2:5 tells us *it is by grace you have been saved through faith*. We cannot buy a ticket to Heaven with money, rituals, or even charitable acts. God's grace is His gift to you.

"**Your personal prayer** directed to Jesus can be simple and concise." Red noticed the couple from the Catholic church exhibiting some defensive body language. "There are no magical words. When you are ready, say a prayer from your heart and soul. He **will** hear your words and know what is in your heart." The gentleman who noted he was Catholic before the lesson began, nodded in agreement with Red's remarks. Red made a mental note to explore that reaction further in a private session.

"As a note, when you say, Amen, you are saying 'so be it' or 'may it be so.' When you pray, you are committing to your request. Some people end a prayer: 'In Jesus' name I pray, amen.' Others may say, 'I pray in the name of the Father, the Son, and the Holy Spirit.' Those three names refer to the Trinity."

Button had tried to help when Eddie asked who people pray to. At the time she was confident her answer, God, Jesus" was right. Now she was not sure. "So, who hears my prayer? Which one of the three should I pray to?"

Red did not want to get into a full discussion on the Trinity, but a short answer might help. Most at tonight's session were new to Christianity. He could see that some were feeling a little overwhelmed. He tried to make his answer clear, but brief. "God the Father is the creator of everything. If you see a majestic mountain or a beautiful lake surrounded by a massive forest, or you watch the sun sink into the Pacific Ocean, feel free to thank Him directly for His creation.

"Think of the Holy Spirit as the invisible force that fills you with insight and guides you towards God's will. The Holy Spirit can guide you away from evil. Feel free to ask the Holy Spirit for wisdom and protection.

"Jesus was here once before. He is returning to justly judge the world and each individual. He is the one returning to set up His kingdom on Earth. Although you can pray to any of the three and you will be heard, Jesus is your best starting point. Also know, when you pray to one, all three will hear." Button's smile displayed relief. Red sensed that her question was answered.

Ray had noticed the lady in the pink blouse, one size too small. He labeled her Pinky. The size issue also applied to her tight, black skirt, which she constantly needed to adjust. The makeup around her eyes and the lipstick seemed to be overkill. Ray thought she was attractive enough; she didn't need the excess. Her arms were crossed for most of the lesson, and she slouched in her chair, not exaggerating, but enough for Ray to know she had misgivings about being there.

She didn't bother to raise her hand. Pinky asked, "If someone you know realizes she is sinning, but she needs to in order to survive, can that person ever be forgiven?" Red paused to gather his thoughts. Of course, that someone was her. Red knew this was personal.

"The short answer is absolutely. In the Bible, the Gospel of John, there is an account of a woman caught in an adulterous relationship. The scribes and Pharisees, strict followers of the laws of Moses, brought her to Jesus. She begged for His help. Under the law, the woman should have been stoned. Technically, the man should have been stoned to death as well, but he was not there. Jesus told them to follow the strict interpretation of the law and stone the woman. Then He said to the group of men, "The one of you without sin should cast the first stone." The men left. The woman was sitting beside Jesus. He told her that He was not one of the accusers. Then He added, "Go, and sin no more."

"If your friend does slip, if she does fall into Satan's trap again, have her ask for forgiveness once more. Jesus loves her and understands no one will ever be perfect. When asking for forgiveness, specifically acknowledge the sins. But when you, or anyone, asks to be forgiven for a particular sin, you can no longer repeat that sin. Otherwise, your actions will show that you were not sincere in the request. Ask for wisdom and strength. Ask for help. Help could come from a friend, a stranger or even an angel. Remember, God knows your intentions. Being insincere or trying to take advantage of God's love is a tactical error."

Pastor O'Donnell twisted in his chair to face Pinky. "Stay after the meeting. I feel Jesus would like to forgive your friend if He hasn't already. I think He would also like your help." Pinky wiped the tears from her eyes on the sleeve of her blouse before they started pouring down her cheek. She said nothing but nodded in acceptance of the invitation.

Then, the Pastor's last sentence hit her. "My help? I am not..."

Red interrupted. "David was a shepherd who became a king. Esther lived an ordinary life until God needed her to be a queen. Both saved the Jewish people from genocide. Neither of them, nor the others God chose to be in the right place at the right time, had a clue how God would use their help."

The Pastor returned to the group. "Most of you here have a limited knowledge of the Bible and biblical teachings. God brought you here tonight for a reason. What is that reason? I don't know. But God does. You might not know why, so you must ask for wisdom through prayer.

"What I am about to tell you can be an extremely complex topic theologically, but faith makes it a straightforward concept. God is omnipresent. Being everywhere at once means He is not restricted by anything, including time. Being omnipresent also means that He has always been in the past. He is always in the present. And, He will always be in the future. From the beginning of your life, He knew what He wanted from you. He knows what He wants from you today, and He knows what He will want you to do in the future.

"Everybody with me so far?" There were some blank stares, but everyone was engaged. "He has already given us the power to do our part to make this world a better place. You can have the power of the Holy Spirit in you today. You can find and activate your authority to do God's work through prayer. You might receive an answer after one prayer, but many verses indicate it could take multiple prayers: Elijah prayed seven times, Daniel twenty-one times, and others for extended periods. We also pray for health, family, a new job, or a career. Each prayer is stored in Heaven.

"Remember that God knows your heart. He also knows your destiny. Sometimes your prayer is answered in a different way than you expect. The intent behind your prayer may be manifested in something that you never even imagined." Red paused in reflection. All eyes were intently focused on him.

"When I prayed about going into the ministry, I told Jesus that I wanted to spread the gospel. I prayed for a position in a large church, preaching to hundreds of people. Jesus knew I was not a faithful servant and did not believe what I was telling others. I was going to be the authority. My request glorified me, not God. The previous church here worked in the same authoritarian way. I thought that this would be my path to bigger venues, fame, and fortune.

"I lost my way. The previous minister, I use that title for him lightly, taught me techniques that used guilt to trap people into giving the church money and resources. Donors were convinced that their acts of generosity would save them. The congregation was not taught the Bible or how to have a personal relationship with Jesus. They were taught to depend on the church leaders, not Jesus, for their salvation. That leadership, by the way, also missed the Rapture.

"I fell into Satan's trap of money and power. That is why I was not taken when the Rapture happened. All the people who disappeared had more faith and dedication to Jesus and the words of God than I did. But God is a good and loving God. I asked Jesus to forgive my sins. I asked Him to forgive me for the missed opportunities to help other people discover Jesus. I asked for another chance. This church is far better than the massive place of worship I wanted. This is the church God has given me. I pray for strength, every day, for Him to use me to bring people like you to know the glory of God."

A vacuum of silence encompassed the room as each

person absorbed Red's story. Red's deep inhale and exhale refilled the room as a breath of fresh air. In a somber voice, the Pastor gave words of advice. "As I said a few minutes ago, I want to ask you several questions. Before I do, I must let you know that your life will change if you accept my offer. You will experience both joy and trials beyond any wild imagination.

"The prayer in your handout, the Sinners Prayer, I will ask you to meet with me by the large wooden cross. I will ask that you accept Jesus as your Lord and Savior. I will ask you to stay loyal to Jesus no matter what tribulation you may have. And, if you say yes to all of those requests, I can guarantee, with no hesitation in my mind, that you will have a place in Heaven for eternity."

Ruby tentatively raised her hand. "What if I say no?"

"Then I would ask you to come to our next service. Don't give in to Satan just yet. God has always given free will to His children. I will pray for you. But I will ask you to read the materials and to join us again."

Ruby's expression told Red what was coming. "I didn't expect that answer. I thought you were going to tell me I would be going to hell. That's what other so-called Christians have said to me."

"Where you end up after death is not up to me or any mortal. I can tell you what the Bible says. John 3:16 says that if you believe in Jesus, you will have a place in Heaven. John 3:18 says that if you don't, then you are destined for an eternity of painful darkness. You can read it for yourself.

"I trust that you want to believe. When you pray, ask for Jesus to forgive whatever you know is holding you back. Ask for strength to resist any evil that might keep you from a devoted relationship with Jesus. Pray for wisdom to recognize God's direction for you. Be patient. The Holy Spirit will guide you."

The Pastor paused long enough for Ruby to respond with a comment or question. Even though her eyes were on him, Red could tell she was looking into her own soul. Pastor O'Donnell had advised each person to personalize their prayer at the end. To the Pastor's surprise, all but three, including Ruby, read the prayer. There was a time of quiet as the congregation finished their prayer and reflected on what had just happened. Red wrapped up the session.

A few people left, but most stayed to ask questions, pick up materials from the table at the back of the room, and generally mingle. Ray emerged from behind the electronic control center. His tool bag was closed, and excess cable was attached to the bag with a Velcro strap. "Sorry to interrupt. You are all set. Any problems, please call. I left my contact information by the control board." He started for the door but looked back at Red. "This evening was not what I expected. Excellent job."

Red could tell that Ray was engaged in the lesson for that day. He smiled and semi-busted Ray. "Took longer than you thought, I guess." Then he let Ray off the hook. "I appreciate your help." A sudden afterthought struck Red, but one that felt important. "I would like to meet with you again. I need your uninhibited directness."

Ray flashed a hesitant grin. "Any time after next Wednesday. You have my number."

Ray turned toward the entrance but stopped. He did not understand why, but he needed to know. Ray guessed that Pinky was not the woman she appeared to be. "Pastor, again I am sorry to interrupt." Red nodded to say okay.

Ray faced Pinky. "My name is Ray. And you are?" Miranda was the answer. "Miranda, the question you asked earlier was fascinating. I am guessing you will relay the answer to your friend. Sounds like she is in a tough situation." Ray also wanted to protect Miranda's dignity. Miranda's answer was on full display with her body language, but her silence was exactly what Ray expected. "Can I ask what your friend did for a living before she fell on hard times?"

Miranda stayed incognito. "She managed customer service for a beauty care company." Ray knew Miranda was intelligent because she did not miss a beat with the charade. "From what I understand, about six months ago, she aggressively defended three top-rated customer service reps who were accused of embezzlement. Those three met in the break room at lunchtime and studied Bible verses. A complaint was filed with HR, saying the group was pushing religion on everyone during work hours. They could not be fired for that, so…well, you get the idea.

"My friend was fired for being part of their scheme." The word 'I' almost came out. "All benefits were taken away, and her 401(k) money was illegally frozen pending a scam embezzlement investigation on all four. The whole thing was a total lie with manufactured evidence.

"She was already living paycheck to paycheck because she had prudently maxed her contributions to the retirement fund. Now, she has no money or backup savings. Her landlord offered to pay her rent for services rendered. Starvation makes people do… whatever is needed."

Ray felt the shame and defeat in her voice. He took the handout she was holding and made some notes. "Tell your friend to call the HR Director at Mimtrin Technology, Sophie Humphries. Make sure to mention my name. I wrote it next to the number. Our company has had several openings since everyone disappeared. Maybe you would also like to see what openings are available. No guarantees, but I will be glad to help." Ray waved at Red as he turned toward the door.

As Ray was leaving the building, he controlled his happy-dance urges. He knew that Red had a wealth of knowledge. Ray mumbled to himself, "I need to invite Enrique… Scratch that. I need to invite *Elias* to their next meeting."

He ambled over to his car. With the key fob, he unlocked the car, popped the trunk lid, loaded his tools, and opened the door. Before getting in, reality struck, stimulating a full-blown internal debate. "What were you thinking! You just gave a complete stranger Sophie's name. Miranda. I don't even know if that is her real name? She could be a drug mule. She could be… I don't even want to think about the possibilities. I hope she doesn't wear that outfit she had on tonight to an interview. Maybe she won't follow up. How am I going to dance out of this one if she does?"

Ray backed out. With both hands on the steering wheel, he gazed straight ahead. All he could see was a hologram of Pinky. He was shaken out of his trance by movement at the side of the building. That quickly brought him back to life. Two men were picking up the pace heading his way. The doors automatically locked when he drove forward at a pace far greater than the 20 MPH sign he just passed.

Ray stayed on the main roads instead of taking a creative path that might save as much as 10 minutes versus the map goddess. After seeing the two characters in the parking lot, safety took precedence over the urge to play games. That plan was working until, waiting for the light to change, he heard multiple gunshots ring out to his left. He turned his head toward the sound of screaming and more shots.

He looked right, then quickly looked left again. No

traffic coming either way. At this point, the red light was a major inconvenience that he ignored. Thoughts of the Tribulation he had learned about from various sources popped into his mind. "And this is just the beginning. If the Bible and Elias are right, today is only a brushfire that will become a wildfire. Evil will burn down the entire world."

Ray entered the safety of his humble abode, placed his computer bag on the dining room table, and finally plopped down, sinking into his recliner. He was ready for tomorrow. He knew, however, that being prepared with a well-thought-out plan was, at best, wishful thinking. Too many unknowns. Too many changes.

Ray's task list was spinning out of control. He needed to focus on what happens next. Reflecting on the constant changes that intermittently disrupted his plans, Ray was prompted to rethink his strategies. "Temple III. I definitely need to continue my research. And, just in case there is something to the information in the Bible, I need to know what is coming next."

Ray accepted that researching the Bible would now be part of his everyday life. Tweaking strategies to adjust for prophecy was not his preferred planning technique, but biblical predictions could no longer be dismissed. The spiritual aspects were not his primary goal. Ray was more concerned with logistics as a necessary safety net in the planning process.

The Enduring Philadelphia Church, under the leadership of Pastor O'Donnell, seemed to be building momentum. Although Ray was glad the church was recovering, he selfishly knew he would need another mentor, and Pastor O'Donnell might be the one to fill that need. Ray liked that Red was a determined survivor and patient strategist. The graffiti came to mind. He could see that Red was beginning to win the graffiti war with the taggers. Ray doubted deference to the church was the graffiti artist's motivation for gradually backing off, but he imagined they respected Red's tenacity and creativity.

Ray was not a fan of assumptions, but he was beginning to get a feel of how Red operated. By anticipating how Red might respond to his questions, Ray felt comfortable enough to ask anything or challenge any advice he received. Ray also knows that Red is a teacher. That is good news and bad. The clock is ticking. Ray does not need to know how the clock works; he just needs to know the time.

The sound of an argument in the hall disrupted Ray's train of thought. The couple from the unit two doors away were at it again. Something about leaving a bag of groceries in the car. The couple celebrated their thirtieth anniversary last month. Ray did not understand why those two were together for thirty minutes, let alone thirty years.

The hallway incident prompted Ray to reflect on the inexplicable circumstances surrounding Enrique, housed across the hall, at least for now. When Enrique morphed into Elias, many of his self-preservation problems were solved with a new name and citizenship. New challenges were on the immediate horizon. His brother's job at the publisher of Christian materials was going to need a short learning curve.

Ray knows Elias asked the Holy Spirit to guide him on how best to use this new life. He is also aware that Elias has made educating Ray on the ins and outs of the Bible a top priority. As a close second, helping Ray with the technology to defeat the saboteurs and expose those behind the espionage.

Thinking about their work and plan refocused Ray. "Take out the bad guys. That needs to be number one on the list. But who exactly are the bad guys? Maria and Tina are messengers, not decision-makers. Who is Jefe? Is Jefe in charge? If not, who?"

He returned to the standard fallback position. "Follow the money. But what money? Temple III is a nice payday, but the contract is more about prestige. I am missing something – something big."

As though someone whispered Leticia's name in his ear, her situation crept into his internal conversation. "On the surface, it seems like Leticia is collaborating with Mimtrin's nemesis. Mo wants me to back off. I am sure he has his reasons, but I do not like the loose ends. Talking to CPSM seems to be the only reason she traveled to Denver. But talking about what? A job? Espionage?

"She has access to everything at Mimtrin, particularly Mimstruct software. But why would she want to sabotage Mimstruct Pro? And if Leticia is behind this, why would Maria need to spy on her own boss?" The news that Leticia will be moving into the final stage of being brought out of the induced coma was a positive sign. Answers will come.

Ray's phone rang. An unknown number in the 707-area code flashed on his screen. He thought no telemarketers could possibly have been taken in the Rapture. He let the phone go to voicemail. If no message is left, his assumption of telemarketing would be confirmed. The number 1 popped up next to the voicemail icon. The message was barely audible. The sound was a muffled whisper. On the third try, Ray realized it was Leticia. Of the twenty-second message, the only word he could be sure of was "Help."

He hit redial. The fast, busy signal made him let out a

frustrated sigh. He called the hospital and asked for Leticia. A lady answered, "Intensive Care." Ray asked to speak to Leticia. "I am sorry, sir, she is sleeping. Even if I were to wake her, I doubt if she would be able to have a cohesive conversation." Since Ray was neither a medical practitioner nor a relative, the lady at the desk refused to provide any information about Leticia's status.

Even though warning bells were ringing in Ray's head, there was nothing more that could be done tonight. Leticia just became tomorrow's priority.

He thought a glass of port would be a good way to end the day. The recliner seemed reluctant to let him go. He surrendered. "Chair. Full recline." The whir of the motor began immediately. "System. Turn off the lights." As the lights faded to darkness, Ray's mind and body drifted to a deep sleep.

Ray needed to examine the situation from a different perspective. Instead of looking for culprits, he decided to become one. Getting inside the head of different people might help find a motive. He took on the persona of Warren Thorton first. "I already have plenty of money. I am already a powerful man. More of each would be nice, but would I risk getting caught and losing everything for such a small percentage increase. No I wouldn't. How much would I need to take the chance?"

Ray went through the exercise with Bryan Thorton and Leticia Jefferson. The risk-reward ratio made no sense for either one. He shifted gears again. "What if I had nothing to lose, but everything to gain? What if it would not matter if I got caught? What if I was being protected by someone in power? What if I was the target of extortion or blackmail? That would be a motive to act."

Ray added Jefe to the list. Jefe is a ghost, but Ray decided to discover his or her motivation. Tying Jefe to the Temple III project is a stretch, but there may be other explanations that come to light. This whole thing could be an exercise in futility, but he had to start somewhere. The Temple III project is more than it appears. The feeling that he is missing something significant keeps nagging at him.

Ray closed his eyes. Fingernails glided over his scalp as his fingers parted his hair. With a resolute tone, Ray declared, "I will figure this out!"

MAIN CHARACTERS

Mimtrin Technologies, LA

Ray Ferrari – Analyst Leader, report to Chen Huang

Ray Ferrari – Promoted to Temple III Project Manager reporting to Chas Jenkins

Chas Jenkins – CIO

Moshe Abrams (MO) – CEO

Paul Smiley – President

Maria Gomez – Leticia's Administrative Assistant

Tina Aguilar – Chas's Administrative Assistant

Leticia Jefferson – Analyst & Programming Director – Reports to Debbie

Chen Huang – Manager, report to Debbie

Debbie Hanson – Vice President, reported to Chas Jenkins – Taken in the Rapture

Jolie Lange – Head of Security

Sophie Humphries - Human Resources Manager

Paula Petrie – Help Desk Manager

Dominic Sanders – Director of Operations

Ariel Weizman – Director of AI development

Duggie and Karen – programmers who report to Ray Ferrari

SyberSek

Calev Macron – Security company owner
Deborah Engledorf (Tera) – Security Analyst
Cody – Security Analyst

Enduring Philadelphia Church LA

Pastor Patrick O'Donnell (Red)
Miranda Patterson (Pinky) – church attendee

Martinelli, Sakowitz and Martinelli Law Firm

Bernard "Bernie" Martinelli – Partner
Essie Bevelhimer – Jury Consultant
Samson Englebright – Corporate Lawyer

CPS Metrix Technology – CPSM

Warren Thorton – Proxy owner
Ryan Thorton – Owns Aliton Consulting, Son of Warren

Temple III Committee Representatives

Alwyn Goldberg – Orthodox Jew – Strict Law follower
Benjamin Abelman – Conservative Jew – Oral Tradition blended with the law
Ethan Cantor – Reform Jew – Stresses Ethics

Other Characters

Enrique Martin – short for Martinez – Maintenance worker
Elias Martinez – Brother
Arturo Guitierez – Mexican Army Captain
Colonel Torrez – Commanding Officer
Amir Acee – UN Negotiator

ACKNOWLEDGEMENTS

I thank God the Father for His steadfast love for all. I am grateful to Jesus for the opportunity to author this book and for providing me with the needed daily bread.

I thank the Holy Spirit for guidance. Many times after writing in the evening, I awoke early to revise or better align the text with biblical content. I was inspired to consult previously overlooked Bible passages, websites, videos, and articles for greater accuracy.

I acknowledge the Angels watching over me. Encounters with strangers who assisted my research seemed beyond coincidence. Were they Angels?

I thank my wife for her patience and support throughout this project. Her thoughtful criticism, which often aligned with the guidance of the Holy Spirit, led to valuable edits and rewrites. Her love has been and always will be invaluable.

I am grateful to friends, especially John Kroemer, for reading and critiquing all three books. I am also thankful to my family for their constant encouragement.

Thanks to Ken Raney of Raney Day Creative, LLC, for designing the book cover and summarizing the story in an amazing graphic.

Colin Smith of Colin Smith Creative is an excellent web designer. His expertise and patient guidance helped us understand every aspect of thomaslmadden.com.

Thanks also to Maggie Probst, who went above and beyond standard editing. Her biblical knowledge and recommendations greatly enhanced the story and readability.

ABOUT THE AUTHOR

Thomas L Madden brings executive-level business experience to life. Formally, as Vice President at a consumer goods company, he led Human Resources, Information Technology, Customer Service, and Project Management. He channels this expertise into books filled with authentic characters and compelling situations.

Thomas holds a Master's degree in Psychology from Pepperdine University, where his fascination with Accelerated Learning techniques led him to conduct seminars for schools and corporate training departments worldwide. The learning and memory methods significantly enhanced the learner's experience. In his stories, he weaves these methods into the dialogue whenever teachable moments arise. This transforms complex ideas into relatable exchanges for his characters, resulting in plots that feel authentic and engaging.

He was compelled to write the series, *Where Did Everybody Go?*, based on discussions with friends and family.

Regular churchgoers and many unaffiliated with a church seemed unaware of basic Bible fundamentals. Even the mention of the Book of Revelation caused some to glaze over. Thomas hopes these books will provide answers to the question, "Where Did Everybody Go?"

Visit his website at thomaslmadden.com to learn more about the characters, enjoy flash fiction stories, and read his blog.